MW01043495

DECADENCE 2

DECADENCE 2
Edited By Monica J. O'Rourke

Flesh & Blood Press
New Jersey

DECADENCE 2

Published by:

Flesh & Blood Press

121 Joseph Street

Bayville, NJ 08721

Copyright © 2002 by **Flesh & Blood Press**

Cover art copyright © 2002 by **Mike Bohatch**

Cover design copyright © 2002 by **Feo Amante**

ISBN: 1-894815-19-X

Credits

"Transcendence", copyright ©1997 by Edward Lee & John Pelan. Previously appeared in *The Brutarian* and on Horrornet.com; "Horrorscope", copyright ©2001 by Nancy Kilpatrick. Previously appeared in *Cold Comfort*, Dark Tales Publications; "Dead Girl on the Side of the Road", copyright ©2000 by John Everson. Previously appeared in *Cage of Bones &Other Deadly Obsessions* from Delirium Books; "Cold Plastic", copyright ©1996 by Mark McLaughlin. Previously appeared in *The Blue Lady No. 4*; "Black Velvet", copyright ©2002 by Trey R. Barker. Previously appeared in *Frontiers of Terror* by Marietta Publishing; "sweet vagina", copyright ©2001 by Simon Logan. Previously appeared in *Peep Show* Magazine; All other stories appear here for the first time.

No portion of this book may be reproduced by any means, mechanical, electronic, or otherwise, without first obtaining the permission of the copyright holder.

Contents:

Transcendence
by
Edward Lee & John Pelan

*But the third Sister who is also the youngest—! Hush! whisper
whilst we speak of her! Her kingdom is not large, or else no
flesh should live, but within that kingdom all power is hers . . .*
 —Thomas De Quincey

—room flickered out of existence, at once replaced by some . . . *other* . . .
place. A churning scarlet sky and a liver-colored moon. Beyond he spied
the silver lake—steaming, bubbling—and its endless shore of fine black
sand. Yet behind him, something beckoned but—*what?*

Behind him: a vale. But unlike any vale, dell—any terrain—of his
world. He turned, breathless, ecstatic, and walked ahead.

I'm here, came the tear-eyed thought. *I . . . made it . . .*

"Yes, traveler. You did."

The voice pinned his eyes open, the fugue murmured in his head. It was
the power of his providence, he knew, and his privilege, that allowed him
this revelation, this glimpse of what no man alive—and few dead—had
ever seen.

This glimpse of *Her.*

The woman stood beseechingly. Long legs, joined by an abundant plot
of thatch, rose to form the perfect silhouette. High, heavy breasts—four of
them—jutted in their macabre femininity, with nipples so distended it
was clear they'd been recently, voraciously sucked. The great mane of hair
shone dark as midnight, framing the shadows which claimed Her face.
Her hands opened then, as if to invite embrace, with fingers exceedingly
long, and nails protracted to foot-long pins.

Transcendence

*

Her, Grey thought. His sentience reformed, then emerged like a corpse rising from a lime pit. And the image—of *Her*—remained behind his eyes as his heart began to beat again.

Psychotic contraindication? he considered.

Hallucinosis? No, he'd had his bouts with that before. This was different. The dream—the vision—had too many edges, each sharp as the edge of the antique straight razor Xyra had produced from her satchel. *A Hoffrie # 10,* he knew at a glance. Circa 1788, one of five made privately for D.F. de Sade by the famed Erlangen metal works. "I stole it from a collector," she'd told Grey.

"Some fat slob I fucked in Prague. He had this heroin from Pakistan that was so hot, they'd sell it as Body Bag or Redrum in L.A. I cut his shot with diazepam; it put him in la-la land before he could even get the spike out. Then I ripped off as many of his toys as I could fit in my bag."

The calm with which she spoke of her crimes impressed Grey, along with much else. Would she do the same with him? Had she slipped any incipients into the dollops of red hashish he'd gotten from his purveyors in Europe? He sorely doubted it. She was as much of his mold as he hers, just different generations. But—

The Interstice, his thoughts returned.

Yes, the vision. He and Xyra. Just now as the newly stropped blade sparkled in lamplight. *The Final Intercession: the Prelude to the Bearing of Witness.* They'd smoked the hashish while taking turns etching the blade over the stencils—long shallow cuts welling up red beneath the rice paper. Perhaps they should've transferred the ink directly to their skin— it was a consideration for the future. If the glyph plates were forgeries, they were a job of exemplary skill. But just as their coupling brought them close to death, Grey delved into his lover yet again, felt locked in a sudden stasis. An amalgamation of scents and fetors sifted up his sinuses: spoiled fruit, raw animal flesh, honeysuckle and wisteria. It was then that the room flickered out and, next, he stood naked in the forbidden vale: the red sky, the silver lake like molten lead, the endless black sand and then, behind him, the steaming, chattering forests and—

Her.

Not Xyra, no. It was the goddess . . .

*

7

When Grey blinked, one of the oil lamps had burned out. Back with Xyra in bed, the sheets familiarly damp beneath them. Grey struggled for a breath as her white thigh slid up, nestling against the spent scrotum. "You passed out," she said.

"How long?" he queried, eyeing the lamp.

"Maybe an hour." Her small hand found his groin, cosseting it.

Did I . . . pass over? he dared ask himself. The vision gently blared behind his eyes, like blurred vision. *Was it the Interstice I was looking through?*

Light from the other lamp silhouetted the fine, petite curve of Xyra's breast when she leaned up. She'd removed the clamps, no doubt after days, which left the quartered nipples swollen to flowered plugs. "I thought you were dead—"

Dead, Grey baldly thought. The word tasted sweet as cane syrup in his head. *Death . . .*

"—but you came again when I blew you," she said. "Your come was really thin, like water." Eyes lined deep with black mascara indicated the Spanish cuspidor, to allay the technical fears. No, they mustn't swallow anything, either of them, for that would spoil their fast and everything else. Moisture left a delicate trail when she errantly slid her pubis—freshly shaven from the razor—along his leg. Just as errantly, his hand glided to her belly, feeling the crusted outlines of the glyphs which now had dried to a tracery of scabs. *Afterglow,* came the tawdry word. No love in this, nor even romance. This was an alchemy of arcane mechanics, a recipe of details, aura, and flesh. Psychical valence. They'd made painstaking preparations: the eight-day fast, the sequenced meditations, the consumption of only rainwater. The exquisite sensation of writhing over one another as their blood wept from the newly sliced outlines did indeed seem an ethereal experience. It was *so* close, Grey could almost feel himself being drawn somewhere else in a moist, enveloping cloud of pain, pleasure, semen, and blood. But if a full and total Consignment of the Flesh actually did come to be achieved, would they both pass The Interstice? Only he? Only she? The thin tome wasn't clear on that point, only referring to The Passage of the Transcendent, and then, optimally, The Bearing of Witness.

For hours and then days, the lamps filled each with precisely forty "drabits" of whale oil, they embraced each other and cut each other, engaged in every act of sexual congress conceivable and then some not conceivable, loving one another and then hating, pleasuring and brutalizing, flooding their senses in The Earthly Praise of She.

The second lamp, then, guttered out.

Transcendence

"Shit!" Xyra exclaimed.

Grey's hand stroked her back. Now that the moment was passed, his affections—his human ones—could drop their guard. Her warm, damp skin felt so soft beneath the fine grit of dried blood. He embraced her then, kissed her tears to taste her sorrow in the consolation he knew she must be steeped in. She wept in a silence as warm as her skin.

"Don't despair," he whispered. "We'll simply have to try again."

*

The abstraction, of course, was timeless. In fact it was Xyra who suggested that their transcendence had been arrested simply because they hadn't made the razor cuts *deep* enough.

But Grey didn't dare tell her that he *had* transcended, if only in part. He was nearly certain, that or he was mad. The image of what he'd seen— the irreducible moment of the vision—could hardly be mistaken for a night-terror. Lust, carnality—that's what he had seen. Venery more heated, more depraved than anything ever reckoned by the human species—all made flesh in that incalculable *terra dementata*—

Lust incarnate—

The embodiment of sheer lasciviousness—

Her.

Fragments of glimpses aimed past the Mistress' fine shoulder revealed slivers of Her domain: nude figures splayed out like hors d'oeuvres of living flesh. Inflamed privates hotly licked, tasted, sucked. Runneled erections—not of Grey's world—plunged into any available orifice amid a sound like footsteps through mud. Moans merged in a sacred litany, horror and jubilation singing as one. Kisses and bites indistinguishable. Exuberant sperm flying with exuberant blood. And more, delectably more: catheterizations, exsanguinations, the siphoning of spinal fluids to be greedily gulped down in crude tin goblets. Buttocks were parted, then plundered, then broken. Squab hands wrung blood from ears and nostrils, or simply pried apart whole heads. Sheets and sheets of something seemed to hang from low tree limbs; Grey could only cogitate that they were sheets of human skin.

Atrocities here, but *there*?

Pleasures untold . . .

Yes, Grey *must* have gotten there, though he darn't tell Xyra; she'd feel inadequate, she'd feel it was her fault they hadn't transcended together. He resisted consoling her now. She sat listless in the Katsura kimono he'd thought nothing of paying $5000 for. Her complete lack of awe at his

9

Decadence 2

wealth was only the first proof of her verity. Many more such proofs followed in the weeks after their meeting, which convinced him of not only her necessary preternatural purity but also of her peerless candidacy for joining him on these treks of the erudite damned. Her appearance fooled him: post-punk garb, all black; clove cigarettes in blue paper, body piercings and Everclear buttons, a page boy cut of snow-white hair fringed with bright crimson. No, these were just veneers of taste which had nothing whatever to do with the spirit. If anything, Xyra knew as much of the cabalistic codices as he, from the Callings of Osirisi to the Psalters of the Cenotes, the sacrificial rites of Moloch, Baalzephon, and the Chinnamasta, the Order of the Illuminati and the Invocations of Fong-Chur. In more than six decades, Grey had never come upon a woman so well-versed.

Nor so sexually provocative.

The seekers of truth, transcendence and human providence in Seattle, Washington proved regrettably few. Here truth was mused of as the icon of Kurt Cobain, and the droves of spiritless youth transplanting themselves here to give their icon homage via the specious chicness of I.V. heroin use, grunge rock, and homelessness. *Damned of their own,* Grey realized. *Such a useless expenditure of spirit.* True, drugs played paramount in the occult pursuits, but only as preambles and only when pure. Heroin, opium, psychedelics—Grey had used enough to create an unparalleled clinical addiction—and so had Xyra—yet they'd never lost the vision of their use. Mere accessories for a higher, holy purpose. The weak-minded and derelict—the truly lost—had earned their interminable curse. But the *control* of such delicacies remained open only for the truest seekers. These substances were nothing but tools to be used with an undiluted mindfulness, for providence.

Close to seventy now, the decades had scarcely exhaled on the body and mind of Brentford Etter Grey. Lean, tanned, clear of eye and clear of mind, he'd pass for fifty in a day, even forty if he chose to dye the dust-gray edges out of his shoulder-length hair. Perhaps chasing immortal visions had left a tincture in his blood, or some spit from the gods. Xyra, too, carried the same agelessness, thirty now but embodied like a school girl a year or two into pubescence. And looking at her now, the shiny Katsura draping but her arms and shoulders, Grey was stricken not only with appreciation but gratitude to have happened upon this angel of wise darkness. She sat and silently smoked her clove cigarette, her breasts delineated to small, hard fruit from the fast. Inordinately large nipple-ends, long and stout as the end of a pinkie, she'd previously quartered with a razor in the fashion of dum-dum bullets. Once they'd healed, the

10

effect was gorgeous: buds of starred flesh. Her legs rose coltish in their leanness, her skin white as the rice paper she'd made from scratch to fashion the stencils. The inclined abdomen, totally bereft of fat, showed off the outlines of the glyphs he'd etched in a tender and quite beautiful hue of a blushing orchid rose now that the scabs had cleared. It was the truest art they'd carved into themselves during the Intercessions. The art of the Glyphs.

Eventually she rose and dragged the linens off the bed. He could sense her distemper but still refused to speak of it. The now dry spillage on the bottom sheet reminded him of the snow-angels he'd made as a child, only these angels were scarlet.

And not so innocent.

I thought you were dead, he remembered her saying, and again he thought: *Death . . .*

But the tome made no mention of Death Rites, nor anything so uninventive as sacrifice. *She* was an incongruous goddess, and an surreptitious one, so surreptitious that none of the pre-Bruscan archives nor the extensive Roman registries even mentioned *Her* name. Only *She.* Much came, Grey knew, with the accuracy—or *in*accuracy—of the translation, but these paraphrases were culled from the genuine Frisian tablets excavated by Deniere in 1837, from Brython urn fields near Gatwick, and personally transposed into English by the reputable Dr. John Dee. *The Intercessions of Transcendence,* was the good doctor's best guess at the actual epithet of what would later be published by the intaglists at the McKellan Press in Edinburgh in 1850. Five hundred copies were printed, which hardly made the sixteen-page volume rare by the standards of a collector of Grey's wealth. But when the actual glyph tablets were found some thirty years later, the McKellan's had printed only four copies of the necessary plates before the famous fires had burned down half the city. All four copies—entitled merely *The Glyphs*—were luckily spirited out. And then lost, of course, to time, forgery, and greed.

Grey, after his own schooling at Exham, Harvard, and the Academy of Nurnburg, would then spend the next four and a half decades searching for a genuine copy, and would pay any price.

More providence, then. Or perhaps something even more divine.

*

He'd met Xyra while perusing one of the hundreds of used-book dealerships that seemed to occupy so much of his life, the endless search for volumes worthy of his collection. Usually these trips were pure waste, yielding nothing more interesting than a watered-down treatise on Satanism by someone who may (or may not) have actually read Crowley. Grey couldn't count how many "genuine" copies of *The Necronomicon* he'd been shown, all complete with "a genuine certificate of authenticity, sir." God. But this particular establishment—drably, Bill's Books and Antiquities— proved its salt at Grey's first glance into the glass-cased Metaphysics section. Two copies of Beddoes' *Death-Jest Book*, First Printings and both with slipcases in VG condition, the impossible to find pamphlet *The Synod of the Aorists* from the original presses in Bamberg, and the even rarer *Megapolisomancy* by deCastries, a book thought not to even actually exist until Leiber happened upon a copy while living in Corona Heights in 1957. Grey, of course, owned all of these himself, but the mere fact of their being here made him wonder what other dim gems might lurk amongst the shelves. He was peering into the case at the deCastries, without a thought considering its $1,700 price tag (it appeared in slightly better condition than the copy he'd found last year in New Orleans) when he sensed the lithe shadow behind him. "I'll bet you already have that," came a voice that seemed leather-tough but uniquely feminine. "I can tell by your aura."

Grey frowned as he turned. Then narrowly stared.

Not a typical Goth Girl playing vampire, no. This *figurine* radiated something—her own aura perhaps—well past the poseur garb, eyebrow studs, and Joy Division pins. Grey assayed her raptly: luminescent absinthe eyes, the severe lipline, teeth white as the shell-lining of a butter clam. The red-fringed ivory-white page boy caressed a countenance that he could only describe to himself as paramental—the visage of a subcarnate, or a lower deity; he struggled not to appear taken aback. "Yes, I do own a copy." He cleared his throat. "I commend your establishment, though. Most such places boast little more than dust-jacketless first editions of more Crowley-clones, only to camouflage the forgeries of the *real* books."

Her hip cocked, long white legs lambent beneath black fishnets. "Oh, there's a sucker born every minute. Do you know how many times I've sold the 'genuine' *Necronomicon?*"

Grey couldn't help the chuckle. "With 'a certificate of authenticity,' I trust."

"My boss makes the certificates on his Page Maker."

Grey let his eyes fall. In his sight, then, he could see her truth somehow . . . and her lust flowing beneath her edges. *Just like my own,* he supposed. In a dream he saw them fucking on the floor, like animals, Grey's seed filling her up and leaking out, then more in her pert mouth, fat, viscous white lines on her tongue, savored then swallowed. Again, though, he caught himself. Such blatancy would seem wasted on her; he had whores for that, women who would do anything for crack money. No spirit, no truth. "But I'm impressed," he eventually returned. " The Beddoes, the deCastries. Not exactly the wares of the local Barnes & Noble."

Unconsciously, her white hand—like a fragile porcelain dove—opened on her thigh. "We've got *The Intercessions,* the real Edinburgh printing. So far the highest bid is fourteen grand, but . . . you already have that too."

Grey's gaze thinned, finally looking past her primal desirability and into whatever it was that shone behind her eyes. "You're quite brazen, miss. Tell me what you have that I *don't.*"

"*The Glyphs.*"

"Bullshit," Grey departed from his usual refrain from profanity. "You're as beautiful as you are a liar."

"And plates from the original linoleum blocks, not copies . . . You think you're hot stuff in your Italian suit. That's Claro Silk, isn't it? I can tell by the shine. Walk in here an act like a 'collector.' You just want to fuck me, like every other swinging dick who comes through the door. But—" A tiny smile, like a cat's. "That's okay. You're just like me—"

"I think not," Grey recoiled.

"—so I won't hold that against you. Now, are you gonna stand there like some smug, family-inheritance dilettante, or do you want to see it?"

"Your acumen is atrocious. I've a mind to talk to the manager, and *pay* him to fire you. But . . . Yes, young lady, I'd very much like to see it if you'll be so cordial."

"Cordial? I wish I had a cock so I could make you suck it. Then I'd stick it up your ass and wipe the shit off on that $1000 Burberry."

Grey was mortified . . .

"Come on, killer. It's in the vault."

She opened the coded lock in the back of the store room. Grey noted a respectable Arrowhead alarm system with sensored triggers, tape-switches, and motion-detector heads. If this was a sham, it was a good one. His doubts dwindled further when she gave him a pair of acetate gloves and a surgical mask, then donned the same herself. Not much lay on the vault's shelves, just a few glass cases and several boxed editions.

"We got it from Antwerp last spring, an estate sale. The auction's next week, open bid. So far the highest offer is $70,000." A tiny key opened the lock on the case—its contents stank horribly, not the musty smell of old books, but more like something long dead. All Grey could do then was stare—

—as the volume stared back, gold flake on an oddly white cover spelling, simply: *The Glyphs.*

"I don't have to tell you to be very careful," she warned.

Grey daintily opened the cover, scrutinizing. The copyright was correct: McKellan Presses, 1881, Edinburgh. And after that and a title page, only two more pages remained, linoleum prints of what were allegedly exact copies of the original glyphs from the Gatwick tablets.

"I'm . . . stunned, but still, it could be a very expert—"

"Forgery," Xyra finished.

"So I'll need to check the—"

"The watermark." She handed him a Leica jeweler's glass. "Slightly off-left and off-center over the copyright."

Grey's eye squeezed the glass; the blood seemed to drain out of his head when he saw the impossible-to-reproduce trademark.

"I need—I need to—speak with the manager."

"Fuck the manager," the girl replied. "He's downtown having crab balls at the Flying Fish. And the book isn't for sale."

Outrage! "But you just said—"

"I don't give a shit *what* I said. You know what this is, and so do I. It's not a *toy.* It's not something to sit in some asshole's stuck-up *collection* so he can show off to his friends while they drink wine with their fucking pinkies in the air. This is the portal, you *know* that. This is the passageway to—"

"Transcendence," Grey whispered as though crushed glass filled his throat. What he'd been searching for—for forty years—he now held in his gloved hands. If need be, he knew, he'd kill for it. If need be, he'd reach into his pocket, withdraw his Al Mar, and shear her lily-white neck to the vertebrae.

"Transcendence, that's right," and only for a moment did she look directly into Grey's eyes. "Yes, yes," the words slipped. "You're the one, and so am I." Then: "Come on."

Grey stalled. "What—what do you mean?"

She closed the case, pulled off the gloves and mask. She tucked the case under her arm. "What do I *mean?* Three guesses, Sherlock. The first two don't count. Get it? Now let's get out of here before my boss gets back from lunch."

Speechless, Grey followed her hair-scent out the back door. "My boss is gonna croak," she giggled. "It was a shit job anyway."

Then they got into Grey's Daimler and drove away.

*

Transcendence

And fell in love, not nearly so much as with each other, but with the true lust of what they both longed for, and what they knew they'd been put on earth to achieve together.

Grey's downtown loft was now a temple. Since their first venture, they started over again completely. For weeks they'd reread *The Intercessions*, parsing each phrase, dismantling every syllabic gesture, poring over every possible inflection and tense-variation. They considered any and all interpretation. Nothing could be inexact, not the sheerest oddment nor appositive. Xyra made the rice paper for the stencils while Grey himself concocted the ink from sesame oil and pestled buds of Queen Anne's Lace. Meanwhile, they began the next fast at the first astronomical minute of the new moon—the Druid moon—and then began the Cleansing.

First the initial Bleedings, then the Baths (in Calistoga ash), then the Irrigations. Gastric lavage and enemas with lavender water, daily flushing the more unsavory snippets of *humanness* from their systems. For the goddess was so much more than human—and excitingly so much less, was She not? Grey still strongly suspected that he had indeed seen Her, and knew what that seeing meant. The kissing of two worlds. The prolapsation of agony into rapture.

—pain as deliverance of pleasure, lust made flesh, made so diabolical, atrocious, and corrupt, so purely *evil*, that their nameless seductress had been banished to someplace infinitely lower than hell eons before the fall of the Morning Star from God's left hand.

No, Grey could not reveal his secret. Why had he seen Her while Xyra had not? Via the lexicon it wasn't even clear that two trandscendents could pass the Interstice. Perhaps only one was meant to pass, but if so . . .

Why me and not her?

Grey could not calculate the answer in spite of its being right in front of his face.

*

As the Epiphany approached, their starved physiques grew ever leaner—beauty in emaciation, stick-people—death camp paramours. Slat-ribbed now, hollowed-eyed, maps of veins denuded beneath skin which stuck to their sinews like damp tissue wrapping. Grey began to lose his hair but this he viewed as a positive. On several occasions, Xyra blacked out from lack of nourishment, then staggered to the black-marble bathroom to vomit low-grade bile. "It's a positive," Grey assured her. "It's just

15

more proof of our providence, is it not? More proof—to *Her*—that we are worthy to be Her acolytes, to be Her—

"Her Transcendents," she coughed, gagged, and grated. The lines of bile swayed over the toilet even as she nodded her agreement.

Hollow-eyed, yes, but bright-eyed too, their bodies now purged of toxins and wastes, defectibilities burned off by the light-headed furnace of glucosis deficit and ketolysis. Indeed, theirs was an emaciation not only beautiful but *pure.*

The midbook intercessions, allowed on the fifth day, granted preparations of a more creative nature. Grey, with the razor, cleaved into quadrants his own nipple-ends just as she had. The pain was like bright white light, licking every nerve, and hardening ever still the erection that had throbbed for nearly a week without abatement. But Xyra sported a more deliberate aesthete, performing crude surgery on herself with homemade catgut and genuine Conoye bone needles. She shuddered for hours, sweating out the pain as she nimbly stitched the lips of her majora an inch below the creases of her groin. The result was sheer functional beauty: when she parted her legs, her sex yawned open as if in plea, a ravenous mouth agape. Grey nearly swooned at the image.

Embellishments, too, were allowed now, at the discretion of the participants. Precursors to the Epiphany serving to slake the senses all the more. Distilled poppy tar from Burma, opium bulbs from Afghanistan, and China White tested by Grey's contractors to a purity of ninety nine percent.

Bliss so potent, even God Himself would be jealous.

*

On their bellies, then, they laid the stencils. Near scalding linseed oil transferred the ink to their skin. The razor flashed, newly whetted—then they began to cut each other. Just nips at first, slicing into the lush lines of the Glyphs. Agonizing pleasure, excruciating joy. They cut deeper, deeper still, reverting the ink outlines to gorgeous open wounds. Their bodies were now each a master's canvas, their blood the paint, and their lust each a searing brushstroke of the art they strove to create. And next—

"Now," Xyra pleaded, the word issuing like steam. Blanched by malnutrition, eyes closed to slits narrow as the razor's edge, she lay on the drenched bed and opened her legs, wide, then wider, the catgut stitches stretching the inflamed labial folds—wider, wider—stretching, stretching—until the act pulled her sex into a pink scream. Grey fell on her, his wounds singing. She bit his lip, drawing blood, and Grey bit off one of the tiny pedals of a cleaved nipple.

"Now," she whimpered.

His cock sunk deep—as a dagger might, to the hilt—as much into her sex as into her soul.

*

"Our journeyman has returned. Such . . . *venturousness!*"

It was not Xyra who spake the words. The black sand burned his feet, the mercurial lake babbling, disgorging bubbles of oily smoke behind him. But *before* him—

I'm here, Grey realized. *In totality this time.*

The goddess stood in wait, idly fingering the furred cleft between her legs from which peeked a clitoris the hue of adder berries and the size of a walnut. At either side, amongst the vale's strange brambles, stood squat attendants, gray as death, with knife slash mouths and chisel-slits for eyes—stout clay-like *things* at her beck and call. Unafraid, Grey stepped forward, then lay down at her pristine feet, let the slavering slug-colored golems splay him out.

Her shadow-veiled face gazed down, and he sensed more than saw the tinseled grin. "Are you ready?" the goddess asked in a voice like rushing water.

"Yes," Grey replied.

"Are you sure?"

"Yes."

A titter, then a longing sigh. "Indeed. Then let my ushers begin."

It was then that her attendants—these slag-faced *ushers*—commenced with the preludials. As surely as Grey's physical body had transcended, so had his pain—to sheer, coruscating pleasure. Bone slivers were promptly sunk into his eyes, directly into their optic canals. His nipples were pulled, then snipped off. Grey's form flexed upward, the pain burning to luscious pinpoints. "My surgeons need to work on you for a bit," he heard the dark voice plushly resonate. Ancient blades adroitly sloughed off long strips off skin—Grey thought of peeling wallpaper—while a great reeking mouth bit off all the flesh from his face, chewing, then swallowing. A third deft surgeon intricately removed all ·the skin from Grey's penile shaft, then clipped off his scrotum, leaving the raw testes to depend from ve-sicular strings. Yet each atrocity only left him pining for more in the ag-ony that purveyed pleasures as no human man had ever conceived. Grey's tongue wagged ludicrously in his mouth as a fine-toothed saw removed the top of his skull. Scalpels, then, peeled away the tulle-like dural membrane, exposing the raw brain which was then feather-brushed with arcane oils and narcotic elixirs, bidding more and more bliss until he was exuberantly drowning in it. Drool poured into his mouth, then his tongue was sucked out, bitten down upon, and gnashed away. His limbs were summarily sawn off and tossed aside, until all that remained was the quivering trunk now completely bereft of skin, a fleshless face at one end, flensed genitals at the other—

—and wave after wave of pleasure solely defined by pain.

Long pins were inserted into his sinuses, then pushed until they emerged from his untopped gray matter. More pins similarly punctured his eardrums, and still more skewered the hot meat of his heart, his liver, his kidneys.

And the goddess knelt, elegant needle-tipped fingers tickling the scarlet sheen of sinew and venosity where his skin used to be. Sightless now, deaf and dumb, all he could do was quiver and wait, quiver and wait for more and more and more. The needled fingertips sunk into his testicles like toothpicks into plums, as the goddess' mouth engulfed the denuded cock, suckling, as an infant at its mother's teat. Meanwhile, the ushers used his brain as a pin cushion, gingerly sinking long curettes and dental picks into the tender, hypersensitive lobes.

When She ceased her fellatio, a white-hot wire, a yard long at least, was proficiently slipped into his urethra, fed down and down until it disappeared.

Narrow awls etched latticeworks on his brain, and more curettes and picks teased through the wet convolutions. But Grey could still think and still feel—*everything.*

Never stop, he thought. *Never, never. . .*

A sigh flowed from the goddess' throat as She straddled the inflamed torso, then sheathed the skinless cock with Her slick, unearthly cunt. The four laden breasts swayed over his stripped face as She fucked him, while the ushers' nimble fingers pinched sugar-sweet milk out of each swelled nipple.

"Here is what you want," came Her rich whisper. "Here is your transcendence."

The luciferic cunt tended his cock like the mouth of an expert fellatrice. Each motion back and forth lead him into death and then back again as the immortal moment ascended to its pinnacle, then—

Exploded forth.

A denizen hand reached back, crushed Grey's balls to puree at the precise moment of his orgasm. He came and came for what seemed hours or

18

days, emptying an inexhaustible reservoir of sperm deep into the loins of the netherworld.

He came and came—
Never stop, never stop—
—and came and came—
—*forever and ever . . .*

*

Amen.

*

Grey's halted heart tremored, beat once, then twice, then slowly resumed its rhythm of life. When his eyes opened, it was lamplight that filled them, not the maleficent sky nor the rot-colored moon.

He lay shivering in bed, *his* bed, in *his* Madison Park loft. And he lay whole, intact, uninjured save for the glyph etchings now dried to grit on his abdomen.

I was there. With Her . . .

Of that there could be no doubt. He gagged, his chest hitching, then a violent cough expelled not blood or phlegm but remnant oversweet milk. Semen, in an impossible volume, had dried to a veneer of white incrustation covering the entirety of his groin. His cock lay utterly spent, a dead bird in a sullied nest.

Xyra! I have to tell her this time! I transcended! I made love . . . with Her!

But there would be no such telling, ever. While Grey lay whole now, his mortal lover did not. She'd been reduced, in fact, to the same limbless, faceless, skinless hulk that Grey himself had been reverted to on the other side. All of her remains, and all of her *pieces,* lay about the hardwood floor like garments flung aside in haste.

And as to who exactly had done this to her—Grey needn't speculate.

When he reached out to touch her, the straight razor fell to the sodden sheets; the hodgepodge of tools, too, lay all about him: the saw, the flensing knives, the wires and snippers. Curettes and needles turned her exposed brain into a macabre porcupine. Blood dried on his forearms to the elbows, like scarlet tempera paint, and when Grey reglimpsed her unfleshed face, only then did he realize how full his stomach felt . . .

But it had been worth it, he knew that without even needing to think, and he also knew that Xyra, her quest being as impassioned, would agree.

19

I have experienced the unexperiencable. Pleasures defined by another order of sensation altogether. I . . . have transcended.

Grey blinked, remembered.

Never stop, never stop . . .

*

"Hold still!"

*

"Like that, yes. The same way— Be careful! The ink will smear!"

*

"*Damn* you! Don't die! Not yet!"

*

The face formed through electric fuzz. "In all my years, I've never—and I mean *never*—seen anything like this," came the quite dour remark of the Special Agent in Charge of the F.B.I.'s Seattle Field Office. Shell-shock burnished his eyes like the deadpan gazes of veterans remembering the Tet Offensive. "This guy's doing things that—I'm sorry, I just can't—I can't talk about it." Grey changed the channel—

"—unlike any serial killer manhunt since the Green River Case, yet authorities have hinted of atrocities performed on the victims more per-verse, more sadistic than any case on file—"

"—a modus of extreme psychosexual violence involving dismember-ment, necrophilia, genital mutilation, cerebral dissection—"

"—a monster, a monster—"

Grey flicked the set off only moments after turning it on. They simply didn't understand—no one could, no one who hadn't seen with their own eyes and who hadn't felt with their own nerves . . .

Disconsolate, yes, but Grey would not be thwarted. From the end table, several newspaper headlines barked at him: MANIAC STRIKES AGAIN and CLUELESS POLICE MAINTAIN MANHUNT and EIGHTH MUTILATION MURDER STUNS CITY DISTRICT.

Make that the ninth, Grey commiserated, placing sheaves of skin into a handle-tie garbage bag. Hands and feet, arms and legs, gobbets of brains—it all went into the bag.

20

Transcendence

Prostitutes provided the meat for his first attempts but, alas, all failures. Ruminating now, this made sense. Corrupted bodies, corrupted spirits. Then a business woman from Microsoft, a critical care nurse, a Catholic nun and then an Episcopal Deaconess. He'd gotten close with the nun, close enough to catch the goddess' scent and to taste a single drop of *Her* sweet milk on his tongue.

Close. But not close enough.

The next new moon starred his calendar, not far off. Grey took a respite from the indecorous chores, and ate voraciously: *foi gras* with lemon grass on toast points, flatbread from an actual Toltec recipe, a favorite variation of *Miso* crafted by the careful squeezing of Iranian sturgeon roe, all washed down with a bottle of Montratchet 1856.

Perhaps someone was watching over him; disposing of his latest suitor took all of twenty minutes, in broad daylight no less. *Where is your soul?* he wondered. It was a forlorn thought. He dropped the laden bag into a dumpster behind the Mecca Cafe. *Is your soul with Her?*

Who knew?

Later, as night reclaimed the city, weeping strains of Vivaldi's fourth opus caressed the soothing dark. Grey sipped Louis XIII. No taste registered until after it was swallowed, like the honey of Xyra's sex just after a Calistoga bath. Poor Xyra. She would understand; she'd even be proud, for it was through her verity—unmatched thus far—that Grey had made his only fully successful Transcendence. One of the prostitutes had simply died halfway through the Third Intercession—starvation, he supposed. Another had strangled on her own vomitus while Grey was working on her. He wondered who to choose next. A dominatrix, perhaps, someone from the "adult" ISOs. A philosophy student? A theologian?

The pickings, indeed, were ripe, and endless as his ardor. A calm moon shone in the high window, stars coming out like luminous breath. *She* was out there, somewhere. Was *She* waiting for him? Or tending to other voyagers?

Who knew?

Tomorrow he would embark to find more Queen Anne's Lace and their lovely amaranthine buds. After that he would make the rice paper, as Xyra had shown him. Then he would begin to strop the blades.

Grey realized he may never achieve a full Transcendence again. *Such . . . wonders . . .* But at least he'd been blessed the once, granted the gift that only a handful, in all of history, had been allowed to unwrap. No, he may never get back to *Her* again, but he did know this—

Never stop, never stop—

He would never stop trying.

IN THE DARK WOODS
by
G. Allen Wilbanks

Jordan strolled unhurried through the thick tangle of trees that comprised the majority of the green belt sprawling north of his middleclass neighborhood. Eucalyptus, oak and pine trees covered acres of the planned nature reserve providing homes to numerous types of animal and insect life, and giving the local residents the illusion of wilderness despite the freeways, supermarket chains and fast food restaurants only minutes away on foot.

Having grown up exploring these woods, Jordan knew every inch of the grounds and practically every tree by name, so he did not worry about getting lost. Not that it was truly possible to get lost. Even someone brand new to the area could find his way out by simply walking in one direction until the trees gave way to the mowed lawns of the park surrounding three quarters of the forest, or to Jordan's hometown to the south. At most, the walk would take twenty minutes in any direction. But even so, for a boy searching for someplace private to play, the woods were perfect.

Jordan looked over his shoulder as he weaved through the trees. "You still there, boy?" he asked.

In his right hand, Jordan held most of a bologna sandwich he had saved from his lunch. Periodically he would tear a small morsel from the sandwich and drop it on the ground behind him as he walked. Not far behind, a stray dog followed his progress, greedily gulping down each bite of sandwich as the boy dropped it, wagging his tail in anticipation of the next tidbit. The dog was a mutt, with so many breeds mixed in that it was impossible to tell what the parents might have resembled. With its short hair, stocky body and short legs, it could have been some sort of terrier, but then again it could have been some kind of mutant bear for all Jordan knew. Or cared.

The dog had been hanging around Jordan's school for the past week, and although the animal acted friendly when approached, the matted hair and lack of a collar marked it as a stray. Or at least a runaway. Several of the boys felt sorry for the animal and started feeding it from their lunches. Some kids had even started packing dog treats and leftover bones. Although Jordan had different reasons than his classmates, he made sure he fed the dog every day as well. He very much wanted to gain the creature's loyalty. He did not want the dog to shy away right when he needed it to trust him the most.

Now his patience was about to pay off. He led the animal to a small clearing ringed with eucalyptus trees and tossed what remained of his sandwich on the ground. As the dog pounced on the final treat, Jordan knelt by a pile of dead leaves and unearthed the aluminum baseball bat he had carefully buried the night before. He smiled and ran a hand along its smooth, cold surface. This was not just any bat he had chosen to use. This was his favorite bat. Last year as a freshman, he hit fourteen home runs with the Metal Wonder, as he called it, and he was about to crush another one out of the park.

Casually draping the barrel of the bat across his shoulder, Jordan rose and sidled closer to the dog as it snuffled along the ground where the last of the sandwich had long since disappeared. Jordan inched his way along, trying not to frighten the animal, but he need not have worried. The dog had no intention of leaving the clearing while the slightest hope of food still remained.

"Hold still, boy. I'm going to try to make this quick. But it's going to be real painful. At least I hope it is."

Jordan raised the bat over his head with both hands while his target, tongue lolling and tail wagging, gazed up curiously at him. He swung down with all his strength, striking the dog's back just over its hips. The animal's pelvis and spine shattered with a surprising ease and lack of noise. Instead of the tremendous crunch Jordan had expected, the dog collapsed with only a dull thud that one might expect to get from beating a sack of flour. The dog itself was not so quiet, however. Piercing yelps and whines bounced off of the trees around the clearing and echoed through the woods. Jordan knew the noise could probably be heard a mile away, but he also knew anyone listening would have a difficult time pin-pointing exactly where the cries had come from among all the trees.

Shrugging off his initial disappointment, Jordan surveyed the damage. His blow had not killed the animal, but, as he hoped, it had completely disabled it. The dog clawed frantically at the soft ground with its front feet, trying to run away, but its crushed and paralyzed hips kept it from escaping. After several seconds of futile struggle, the animal appeared to give up. It dropped its head to the ground and lay still, gazing up at its tormentor with confusion shining in its glassy black eyes.

"Okay. That was interesting. But let's see if this works any better." Jordan hefted the bat once more into the air, this time aiming for the front legs where they sprawled to one side of the hapless beast's body. Unlike his first blow, this time contact brought a satisfying crack, like dried twigs breaking under foot. The dog howled and struggled again to escape but got no further than the first time. Jordan waited patiently, watching the tormented creature's thrashing as it floundered and flopped. Jordan could not help but think of a fish tossed on shore and left to struggle back towards the safety of water. Except this particular fish would never see the water again.

Jordan squatted next to the dog's head to get a closer look. The animal craned its neck toward his boot, but instead of trying to bite, as Jordan more than half expected, the dog sniffed him and licked his shoe as if it had found a savior and were thanking him for his kindness.

Jordan leapt to his feet. Revulsion twisted his features and anger touched him as he realized the animal was too stupid to know it was about to be killed, or that Jordan would be the instrument of its demise. What good was murdering an animal that couldn't understand its own death? Where was the fear? The panic? Where was the fun?

Jordan let his anger fill him and the baseball bat rose once more into the air. The heavy metal tube crashed down on the dog's head, collapsing bone and brain, and pouring red and gray tissues onto the ground. Letting rage fuel him, Jordan beat the animal mercilessly, pounding it relentlessly over and over, raining crushing blow after crushing blow down on the unmoving corpse long after death had already claimed it. He continued his gruesome work for several minutes before exhaustion forced him to stop. With the bat dangling in his right hand, he stood panting and sweating from exertion, examining the pile of bone, meat and hair that had so recently been a living creature. The anger and frustration had gone. Instead, a new feeling infused his body. Exhilaration. Jordan's hands began to tremble from adrenaline coursing through his system, and, to his surprise, he realized he had an erection.

Without thinking, he tossed the bat aside, unfastened his pants and began to masturbate. He stared intently at the mangled carrion at his feet as he stroked himself, examining the puddles of blood like some grotesque Rorschach blot. His breathing became ragged as an orgasm built, tightening his balls against his body. And as he came he closed his eyes, remembering how remarkable it felt to beat the life out of a helpless animal. Jordan shuddered violently as he climaxed, releasing his seed wildly into the air. He almost cried from the emotional and physical release of the act. The sheer intensity amazed him. Although he had jerked off countless times before, it had never felt so glorious. So . . . spiritual. The act of killing was—at least for him—the ultimate aphrodisiac. As he watched the streams of his semen mixing with the blood soaked fur of his victim, he wondered what it must feel like to kill a human being.

That night, asleep in his bed, Jordan had the most wonderful dream. He dreamed of a girl from his English Lit class, Cindi Marin. This at first surprised Jordan, because although she was attractive, he had never thought much about her. However, in his dream she knelt naked before him, gazing at him adoringly, almost worshipfully. Jordan realized he too was naked as Cindi began stroking and sucking his cock in ways he could only pray a girl might one day do for him in real life.

As she licked and sucked him toward climax, Jordan felt a deep need rising in him. The fingers of his right hand closed around something solid, and raising it to his eyes he realized he now held a revolver. The gun weighed heavily in his hand, cold and satisfying to the touch. He stroked the trigger with his index finger and placed the barrel against Cindi's head. She continued her ministrations without the slightest pause when the metal touched her skin, but her eyes locked onto the weapon in Jordan's hand and she began to moan softly.

She wanted it, he realized. She wanted him to pull the trigger.

Orgasm seized his body and locked his muscles tight. As his cock spasmed in Cindi's mouth, he fired the revolver. He watched the back of her head explode in slow motion. Bone, blood and brains sprayed outward as he came, making it appear his ejaculation had caused the horrific damage rather than a bullet. Red tainted gray matter oozed from the wound and flowed down Cindi's bare back and buttocks like so much gory mush. The gun disappeared from his hand, but it did not matter. An overwhelming feeling of power had engulfed him and he no longer needed the weapon.

Cindi pulled away and smiled up at him. Jordan could see light in her smile and behind her eyes, shining through from the gaping hole in the back of her skull; a busted grinning jack o'lantern. "You're the best, Jordie," she said, before collapsing to the ground.

Jordan awoke to a warm stickiness on his stomach and leg. Pulling the covers off he discovered he had just had his first wet dream. Quietly cleaning himself up and replacing his soiled sheets so as not to wake his parents, Jordan decided that one day he would know what it truly felt like to kill a human being.

*

In class the following day, and much of the next week, Jordan found it difficult to concentrate on his schoolwork. His thoughts frequently drifted back to the dead dog in the woods and his dreams from that night; especially during his English Lit class, where Cindi Marin sat two rows away from him to his right. He caught himself several times staring at her profile and absently fondling himself through his pants. He only hoped no one else had noticed his preoccupation. Especially Cindi.

After school, Jordan walked back through the trees to the eucalyptus clearing. Each day he masturbated on what remained of the decomposing dog, then he sat and planned how he might secretly bring a person to his killing spot in the dark woods. After more than a week of this routine, he finally decided on a victim.

Two blocks east of Jordan's neighborhood lived a young girl and her family. The girl was thirteen years old, but due to a scrambling of her genes in her mother's womb she only had the mental capacity of a six-year-old. The parents, horrified that they could produce so damaged a child, simply pretended she did not exist; at least as much as legally possible anyway. The girl was regularly turned out of the house by herself for hours at a time, and only allowed to return after dark or for occasional meals. Although the parents had never physically harmed her—their own sense of guilt would not permit them to go *that* far—their behavior made it clear that should some awful fate befall the child, she would not be unduly missed. Jordan saw her many times playing along the green belt park just outside of the woods, and he figured if he spent a little time gaining her trust as he had done with the dog, he could easily lure her into the trees.

The second part of the equation was even simpler to solve. Jordan's father owned a gun and kept it somewhere in his closet, up on a shelf. Jordan need only find exactly where his father kept it, make sure it was loaded, and slip it into his school backpack on the day he chose to kill the girl. Afterward, he would clean the weapon, reload it and put it back where he had found it, with his father being none the wiser.

With his mind made up, Jordan began to put his plans into motion. Each day he would walk to the green belt and search for the girl—Laurie, he discovered her name was—and when he found her he would smile and talk to her about flowers, birds, or whatever she found amusing at the time. He brought candy for her occasionally, and she practically squealed with delight each time he did. Apparently her parents did not permit her to have too many sweets, so Jordan's offerings were special treats. Before long, Laurie would run to Jordan's side eagerly when she saw him in the green belt, and he decided the time had come to kill her.

On a Tuesday afternoon, immediately after school, Jordan ran from his last class of the day out to the green belt. The heavy steel bulk of a fully loaded .357 Magnum revolver bounced against his spine as it jostled in his backpack nestled between his history textbook and the next day's reading assignment. He knew Laurie would be in the park that day. She always showed up on Tuesdays. Her mother threw her out of the house to go play at the green belt while her dad was at work and her mother's friend, "Dave," was over to visit. Laurie told Jordan that Dave and her mom did funny things while she was gone. She confided that once she had snuck back to the house and saw the two of them naked and wrestling on her mother's bed. Laurie did not completely understand what was happening, but she did know enough to realize that she should keep her mouth shut and never tell her mother or father what she had seen.

Jordan understood completely. The cunt was getting a little on the side while dad worked to pay for the bed she was fucking in. Well, good for her, he thought. And maybe one day Dave would pull out a gun and blow her fucking head off, too. Just as Jordan intended to do to Laurie.

When Jordan arrived at the park, sweating and out of breath from running the entire distance, he spotted Laurie immediately. She was sitting on a stretch of grass near the park swing set, picking dandelions from the lawn and placing them in a neat row in front of her. She wore a frilly pink dress and her hair had been pulled into pigtails tied with pink bows, making her look almost as young as she acted. The affect of the clothes and pigtails on her budding thirteen-year-old body was odd, but strangely alluring to Jordan. Laurie had pulled the skirt of her dress out and fanned it in a perfect circle around herself, making Jordan think of a great big, pink flower blooming out of the tended lawn. He smiled at the ideal setting she had selected to begin her personal tale of tragedy.

As Jordan approached, Laurie saw him coming and leapt to her feet. She ran the remaining distance between them and threw her arms around Jordan's chest in a grinning bear hug.

"I was hoping you would come, today," she squealed. "Did you bring any candy?"

Jordan glanced around the green belt and saw they were completely alone for the moment. He had to act now, or he might not get another chance.

"Yeah, I did," he answered. "But it's in my backpack. Why don't we take a little walk through the trees, then you can have some."

Without another word, Laurie grasped his hand in hers and started toward the tree line, pulling Jordan after her. She swept his arm back and forth as she skipped along and he was forced to almost jog to keep up with her. Trying not to appear too eager, he let her pull him along as he carefully guided the girl through the trees toward his favorite sheltered clearing among the eucalyptus.

Several minutes passed as they moved on through towering oaks and pine trees, but the girl did not question him as they traveled. She had complete trust in Jordan and merely let him take her where he wished. Besides, he had candy. As the two entered Jordan's killing grounds in the dark woods, he dropped all pretense of friendship. Sticking his leg out in front of Laurie's feet, he placed a hand on the back of her head and pushed her viciously. The girl tripped and tumbled face down into the dirt and rotting forest ground cover. She cried out as she fell, surprised more than she was hurt, and Jordan dropped down immediately on top of her, pinning her to the ground beneath him.

Jordan thought about killing her as she squirmed underneath him, but as her flailing leg brushed against the hardness in his jeans he decided she could be a lot more fun if he let her live just a while longer. Holding her head down with one hand, he slipped the other hand under Laurie's dress and into her panties. The girl began to cry as he groped her, squeezing her firm ass and sliding his fingers in between her legs.

"Go ahead and fight, Laurie," he laughed. "It makes it more interesting."

"Jordie? Where are you? Are you okay?" A female voice came to him from out of the nearby trees.

Jordan froze in panic at the sound of the new voice. He cast his gaze around the clearing, but saw no one, which meant he still had a few seconds to figure a way out of his situation. Leaning close to Laurie, he hissed desperately in her ear.

"Don't say a word. If you talk, I'll tell your daddy what you saw mommy doing with Dave."

Hastily straightening Laurie's dress and helping her to sit up, he called out to the unknown person still among the trees. "I'm over here. Who is it?"

Another few seconds passed before a girl wearing a gray sweatshirt and blue jeans stepped into the clearing. Jordan's jaw dropped at the familiar blond hair and blue eyes. It was Cindi.

"What—? What are you doing here?" he asked. The question came out harsher than he had intended.

"I followed you from school. I wanted to talk to you, but when you went into the woods I lost you. I was about to give up when I heard someone crying. Is everything okay?"

"Yeah," said Jordan, still trying to figure out why Cindi was here. "Uh, Laurie and I were going for a hike and she fell down. I think she's okay, though. Aren't you, Laurie?"

Laurie let Jordan help her to her feet and nodded in silent agreement. She looked from Jordan to Cindi with wide frightened eyes. She did not understand why her friend Jordan had attacked her, or even why he had suddenly stopped. And she was desperately afraid that he and the new girl might try to hurt her again if she said something wrong. So she stayed quiet and let Jordan talk.

"Why don't you go home, Laurie," said Jordan. "Do you know how to get home without getting lost? Cindi and I want to talk a little bit, so I'll see you later. Okay?"

Again, Laurie nodded. She started to brush the dirt and leaves from her dress, but suddenly decided against staying with Jordan and the new girl any longer. She bolted from the clearing into the surrounding trees.

"Kind of a strange kid," said Cindi, staring off into the brush where Laurie had disappeared.

Jordan buried his hands in his pockets to hide their shaking and stared at the ground at Cindi's feet. "Yeah, well, she's kind of retarded. Her parents pretty much ignore her, so I watch out for her sometimes. But, why did you follow me? What did you want to talk about?"

Cindi looked at Jordan and, to his surprise, began to blush. "I wanted to ask you a question. You see I always thought you were cute, and I've had a bit of a crush on you since last year when you played baseball for the school. I was just wondering if, maybe, you liked me a little bit, too."

Cindi stepped up close to Jordan. She was a few inches shorter than he, so she was forced to look up to meet his eyes. "I've noticed you staring at me in class lately, and I thought it might be because you like me. Do you?" Jordan felt an electric shock jolt through his body as Cindi placed her hand against his groin and gently squeezed the bulge she found there. "I think you do. It feels like you do."

"Yeah. I mean I do . . . like you. I even had a dream about you recently," Jordan said, struggling to regain his composure.

"I hope it was a good dream." Cindi continued stroking Jordan's erection until it felt ready to burst out of his pants.

"The best. That feels good, Cindi."

"I'm glad," she said, smiling up at him.

Jordan felt another shock when he saw her smile. For an instant, he would have sworn he saw light glowing behind her eyes and in her mouth. He recalled vividly the busted jack o' lantern face in his dream as she smiled up at him with the back of her head blown away.

"Is there something else I can do that would feel good, Jordie?"

Her aggressiveness and the light behind her smile—whether real or imagined—made him bold. "How would you feel about a blow job?" he asked.

In response, Cindi slipped down onto her knees in front of him and unfastened his pants. Slipping her hand into his underwear she released his straining cock from its painful confinement.

"Oh, God," he moaned as he felt her lips press against his swollen flesh. "That is so good. Oh, so perfect."

Jordan slipped the backpack off his shoulders, unzipped the main pouch, and reached inside.

Horrorscope
by
Nancy Kilpatrick

Last Friday, Jerry had polished off the breasts for lunch and roasted the rump for dinner. That left only the sweet liver; he'd saved the best for last. Sautéed with prunes in butter, he devoured it for breakfast Saturday. Saturn's day it didn't matter how much he ate. The dark planet, negative as opposed to positive, ruled his sun sign Scorpio, which ruled death, power and sex. He could consume anything. It would all end up transformed anyway.

Jerry sat in his favorite chair beside the tank of scorpions. While he sucked the marrow out of a thigh bone, he thumbed through the astrological alignment tables in the ephemeris. Fast-moving Mercury trined sultry Venus and angry Mars, same as when he was born. He could blow hot or cold. Love or hate. Female or male. And quickly. Of course, with Venus on the cusp between Aries and Taurus in his third house of relationships, he wouldn't be surprised if he met a lusty and unpredictable fire sign. That would be interesting. Especially a female. He hadn't savoured fem flesh for over a month.

At seven a.m. the paperkid braked his mountain bike on the sidewalk and pitched *The Observer* onto the porch. Jerry stood in the shade and turned to the horoscopes. He folded the paper back so it was manageable and ran his finger down the column of signs to Scorpio. "Excellent day to begin a diet. Don't be greedy. Restraint brings permanent changes."

Jerry made a kind of grumpy grunt and mumbled, "A cannibal on a diet! Restraint. Right!" Who the hell's this 'Lodestar' who writes this crap, he wondered, not for the first time. Obviously no astro pro. Misinfo gives the science a bad name. Why can't the dingbat line it up straight?

His sun and moon had been caught in Scorpio the day he was born, and boy, was he ever ruled by his dick. Even without the rest of his chart, any fool could tell that today's lineup meant it was a good time for arachnids to party.

He crushed the entire newspaper and chucked it into the trashcan beside the driveway. He'd suffered one too many lame forecasts from *The Observer*. He'd better have a chat with this Lodestar babe.

*

Downtown at number one Bay Street, The Observer Building, a bag of bones stopped him cold. The newsroom anorexically flashy receptionist with baby orbs and hungry lips folded her arms protectively across her ribs, tossed back her mane and said again, "Lodestar don't see her readers."

Jerry thought of turning on the charm but it would be wasted on this lean Leo. She wanted the spotlight all to herself. Instead he said, "I'll leave her a message."

"No prob."

Bright eyes passed a ballpoint and an inner office memo pad and Jerry wrote a terse, "Burger King at five fifteen. Bay and Willow. N.E. window. Red tie." He signed it "An arthropod admirer", wrote *Lodestar* on the outside before sealing it with tape from the receptionist's dispenser.

"See she gets this *tout de suite*," he said, handing it over. "That's French for 'have a nice day while you still can.'"

He shelled out for the new Sidney Omarr paperback and stationed himself in the restaurant near the plate glass.

The newspaper building had been emptying for a while but even though it was a Saturday, by five the crowds thickened. He sat in the darkest corner; he could see everybody outside but the book made it look like he was reading. Plenty of females passed, mostly air signs. Few noticed anything below the second floor. Only one searched the North East corner.

Surreptitiously he watched her root herself to the pavement, check out his tie then his face and, when recognition didn't dawn, move on. Jerry got up immediately and followed.

She crossed to the bus, and he was on her heels, which were high. Firm calves, a little thick. Sensible brown dress. Juicy ass that swayed a bit. Long red-fire hair bounced as she ambled down the steps. She was big and he felt dwarfed by her.

They disembarked at Front and she boarded the subway, the northbound train, and he was right behind. She sat facing forward and he stood well away. She pulled papers out of her calf-skin briefcase. Probably her column for tomorrow, he thought. No wonder she gets it wrong. Lazy cow—it's all out of her head.

Horrorscope

The train was packed. He felt claustrophobic and wished he could crawl under a seat, but being underground helped. At the last minute she jumped to her feet at Placid and ran out the door. He slid between the closing doors just as the chimes sounded before the rubber had a chance to slam together and crush him.

She was plump enough to be slow, which suited him, but it took too long to travel the six blocks to her high-rise. Through the glass in the front door he watched her take the elevator. An old lady with a face like a goat admitted him to the building. He was just in time to catch the light on the master panel stop on six, then descend.

On six there were eight doors. He paced the corridor. A door at the end of the hallway with a brass stylized bull's head knocker made him smile. She was a Taurus, not the fire sign he'd imagined, but a terran planet. Ruled by Venus, the love sign, and the direct opposite of his sun sign Scorpio. This would be interesting.

He smashed the knocker down against the bull's muzzle and was amazed when she opened the door without the chain.

Before he got a chance to sling any manure, she said, "Enter at your own risk," like she'd been expecting him.

The place was farm house, a wash of brown, beige and yellow, even barnboard half way down the walls. She showed him to a couch the color of a beef steer and sat next to him. "I saw you in Burger King." Her voice was thick and moany.

Without a doubt she had led him here; that put him on guard.

It was the first time he'd gotten a good look at her. Eyes big and brown and sadly liquid. Face square but pretty, in a country-fresh sort of way. Neck typically thickish for her sign, with the Taurus symbol hanging from it on a gold chain. Ample tits. But the red hair seemed artificial—distinctly un-Taurean. As if reading his mind, she said, "I'm on the cusp of Aries. Fire and Earth. A cross breed." Her smile was a tad melancholy. "You're a solid Scorpian," she said brightly.

He nodded, thinking, not bad. But if she's so insightful, how come she makes such lousy predictions. Instead he asked, "How'd you guess?"

"The stinger. Scorpioid men out in the daylight can't hide them. Besides, Taureans know our natural enemies," and she giggled, but it sounded forlorn.

Jerry felt uncomfortable, like she'd cracked his shell and was examining his vulnerable innards. Instinct told him to do her right here, but then how would he get the meat to his place.

"Drink?" she asked. "Water signs are always thirsty."

"Mineral water, if you have it." He watched her slip off her shoes and plod into the kitchen, rear end swaying. He felt a bit overwhelmed; she was in control, he was not. He had to turn this tide now.

When she came back she was chewing on something green. "Chive?" She offered him one. "Good for the digestion."

He reached for the glass but waved a pass at the solid food.

"How long you been reading my column?"

He sipped the water before answering. "Too long. You're always off, Lodestar."

She looked at him with those bovine eyes, still masticating. "That's my pen name. Call me Bess. I guess I'm lazy by nature. But I try, you know. You can't ask for more."

Can't I? Jerry thought. But she grinned and one of her ears twitched and that caught him off guard.

"Listen." She touched his knee with a hot and heavy hand. "Why don't you tell me what you see as wrong, and maybe I can make it better. Come on. We'll have some munchies while I start dinner. I'm a good cook."

He followed Bess into the country kitchen. One wall was covered in copper pots. A butcher's block sat in the corner. She hauled a huge skillet out of a cupboard, poured in oil and placed it covered on the old-fashioned stove. He sniffed the air and caught a sweet scent, like hay.

She looked sluggish as she pulled vegetables out of the crisper and began chopping up celery, snap beans, green onions and broccoli. She nibbled as she cut and then arranged a few pieces on a small plate that she placed in front of him. The bulk was tossed into the hot oil. "I'm basically a vegetarian," she said apologetically, sitting across from him. "Meat rarely. No dairy. You?"

"Carnivore all the way." He left the greens untouched.

"Well, there's a little meat in the house. So, tell me how to make the column better." She looked needy, like someone who can't be apart from the herd without suffering pangs of loneliness.

"What are you using for references?"

She reached over his head to a bookshelf, her large breasts mouth level, and he had an urge to bite. From amidst the cookbooks she pulled out a massive volume twice as thick as the Yellow Pages. He saw that it was a giant ephemeris; it made his paperback seem shabby and trite by comparison.

She plunked the book onto the table and he read the gold lettering on the spine. "It was mother's. She liked to cast charts and cook at the same time. She taught me." Bess caressed the smooth black leather with her fingertips.

34

Horrorscope

He opened at random. Along with the numerical charts he found detailed interpretations, the language scholarly and arcane. Modernized, it boiled down to some of what he'd read in the paper today. At the bottom of each page recipes had been penned in, the ink fading.

He closed the book to find her looking at him with those sadly trusting eyes. He thought about killing her here, eating some, taking part with him and leaving the rest.

"Ever tune into 'Signs'?" she asked.

"My favorite show."

She glanced at the black and white cow clock. "It's on now. Want to watch? Dinner can wait."

She switched off the gas and they went back into the living room. Bess pressed the remote; the TV flickered on. Bailey Ferguson, the program's Libran host, was just introducing a couple. She was a Taurean from Montana, he a Scorpian from Arizona, which got a lot of *uh ohs*! from the audience. Bess glanced at Jerry and snorted; he felt poison surge through his veins.

The Taurus/Scorpio couple played the Astro Wheel. No matter what the question, their answers were at odds. There's no way for these two, he thought. Bess, however, said, "I think they'll make it."

"Why?" he asked gruffly.

She gave him that patient and soulful look. "Opposites attract."

The strain of being with her made his stomach churn. He decided quick and neat was the best way to go. He was about to wring her neck when a commercial came on and she blurted, "Want to see my bedroom?"

"Why not?"

Bess led him down the hallway. She left the overhead light off but opened the blind to let in moonlight. She sat on the edge of the bed and patted the space beside her. When he joined her, she turned to him with languid eyes and said in a throaty voice, "So, let's see that stinger."

Jerry thought, what the hell? She wasn't bad looking. He'd give it to her then he'd give it to her. It wasn't unheard of for a scorpion to sting a sex partner after the act. Besides, the exercise would sharpen his appetite. She'd taste just that much better.

He stripped off his pants and underwear and stood before her. Bess undressed slowly, the way she did everything. Her nipples were unusually long, hard red fingers.

Suddenly, Jerry flew backwards. He slammed against the floor and air whooshed from his lungs. Before he could reestablish control, her weight was on him, her hands holding his ankles, her legs pinning his arms. She began grazing at his crotch. He wondered idly about the symbol for Cancer—sixty-nine—and if she had much of that sign in her chart.

When she'd gotten him hot and bothered, she hauled herself to her feet and looked down. Thinking about what part he'd ingest first got him even more excited. The thighs and back would be gamey—he'd definitely take those home. Her white breasts made him drool. And he hadn't had female sweetbread in, God, how long?

The moonlight was faint but he thought he saw her nostrils flair and smoke curl up around her nose. Jerry was on the verge of striking when a heel stomped onto his genitals. Pain splayed his body. Tears erupted from his eyes. When he was able to make a sound, a cry lurched up his spine through his tailbone and he screamed. He tried to shield himself but she stomped again and again, a mad bull trampling him underfoot. By the time she finished and left the room, he was barely conscious but recognized he would never be the same.

Bess returned carrying two things: a meat cleaver and the ephemeris. She looked at him as if he'd just crawled out from under a rock. Excruciating pain curled Jerry's body. He barely felt the sharp blade sever his testicles. Her rage had faded; the phlegmatic eyes returned.

Blood gushed up over his stomach and wet his chest and face. Through crimson tears he saw her open the book. She took her time but finally found the page she was looking for. "Gee, you're right. I got Scorpio and Taurus mixed up today. Listen to yours: "Don't hold back now. Go ahead and indulge. You've earned it." She looked at him forlornly, chewing her lower lip. Suddenly she brightened. "You've got a terrific recipe today for prairie oysters." She bent over and scooped up the dripping mass of red pulp from between his legs. "Don't worry, we'll make it together."

Dead Girl on the Side of the Road
by
John Everson

The girl was blue-faced and cool when I found her, lying there on the side of the road. She was maybe twelve years old and shaping up to be pretty in a few more years. Long auburn hair tangled in the grass where she lay; thin elfin features looked delicate as a porcelain doll's. And those same features were discolored as if the dye for her eyes had run throughout the mold to ruin the piece. Purple bled along the rim of her eyes, which, thank god, were closed.

I didn't know what to do. It was near dusk, I was traveling in a rental car on a gravel road in the middle of god-knows-where about an hour outside of Atlanta. My client, four beers happy and eager to please, had sent me down a shortcut to return to my hotel. If I'd gone the long way, I would've been there by now. I was about forty-five minutes into being solidly lost.

This was only supposed to be a one-day business trip. In and out, get what you need and be back home the next day. Love 'em and leave 'em.

And now, here I was at the crossroads of a gravel intersection in the middle of the country, a dead girl lying at my feet.

I didn't want to leave her here, but given the stories told about the "hospitality" of southern police towards Yankees, I also didn't want to be the one to report her body. They'd keep me in a cell for interrogation for the next three days and if they didn't like the color of my eyes or the tilt of my chin, maybe never let me out.

I put my hand behind her head, trying to turn her face towards me to get a better look and felt something cool and sticky there. Reflexively, in disgust, I pulled my hand back and her head dropped with a soft thud back to the grass. I saw the dark crimson gel of the girl's congealed blood slicked across my fingers.

*

I also saw her eyes pop open. They were green, and flecked with blood. Her lips parted then and I could see a swollen purple tongue within as she started moaning. I petted her forehead with my non-blood-smeared hand and tried to calm her.

"Shhhh," I whispered. "It'll be okay."

My voice cracked on the okay part. The girl was blue and purple, not to mention cool to the touch. In fact, clammy cold. I hadn't seen her take a breath. I really didn't think anything was going to be okay for her ever again.

"It hurts," she mumbled. I could barely understand her, it sounded more like "ith errs," but I could tell that her voice was high and innocent. And afraid. Now I was really stuck. There was a dying kid at my feet and I couldn't even consider driving away to leave the body for someone else to find. Someone local.

"Water?" she whispered, her eyes staring into mine with piercing need. I wondered if her brain was hemorrhaging. Or what bones were broken.

"Can you move at all?" I asked, and slowly, carefully, she wiggled her right hand, then her left. Her arms lifted then, and she gripped my shoulders.

"Hurts."

"I know, baby, I know. We've gotta get you some help."

"Water," she said again, and then pointed into the trees off the side of the road. "Creek."

I nodded and went to the car to find something that I could put water in. I didn't know what good it would do her, but I was selfishly glad for the opportunity to step away from her and think for a minute. There was an empty Coke can in the back from my drive out to the client's this morning, and I grabbed that and went back to her.

"I don't know how good the creek water might be," I cautioned, "but if it's clear enough, I'll put some in here for you."

She smiled and closed her eyes.

I ran into the brush with my can, wondering if she'd still be alive when I got back.

*

She was. She even held the can herself, drinking it so greedily that some of it washed down the sides of her cheeks to dampen the grass below. When it was gone, she said, "I kin move some."

She lifted her legs, one at a time, to demonstrate. Her voice was clearer now, soft as peaches and just as southern. The last fiery glow of the sun had completely vanished, so now I could only see by the lights of the idling

Dead Girl on the Side of the Road

Ford Escort on the shoulder of the road, but her face seemed to have better color to it; the blue had diminished. I noticed she was very tan.

"My name's Heather," she said.

"I'm John. Who did this to you?"

"Don't know. I was just walking by the road, on m' way home. Heard a car and then, you were here."

She said "you" like "yee-ew", a drawl that just melted my heart, and I stroked her cheeks with my hands, promising, "Well, we're gonna get you to a hospital, hon." But with my touch her eyes seemed to widen and then her arms stretched around my neck.

"Careful, careful," I said, thinking that her brain might be likely to siphon right out of whatever kind of hole she had in the back of her head, but instead she pulled herself up, fastened her lips to mine and kissed me.

Hard.

With tongue!

I broke her embrace with an explosion of air and a "hey!" and forced her back to the ground. "Whoa, honey," I said, and she laughed.

"Don't ya'll like me?" she pouted, and it occurred to me that her face no longer was discolored at all.

"Honey, I don't even know you. You're hurt, you're a kid, and I'm gonna get you some help."

"Don't ya'll like 'em young?" she asked, winking one eye at me, and suddenly I realized that she wasn't *that* young, she'd only looked it. Her breasts were now obviously aroused, her nipples poking through the grass-stained white T-shirt she wore, supported by a fullness that I hadn't noticed earlier. Her lips were thick and deep blush pink, the kind that scream "passion" even when they're dictating the contents of a spreadsheet. I saw that the curve of her hips beneath her cutoff denim shorts was not the angular utilitarian architecture of a pre-teen.

"I'm legal," she declared, "and I don't need help. But you kin make me feel better."

"You're hurt," I said, becoming increasingly confused by this whole situation.

She raised herself up on arms that I swear were a good six inches longer than they'd been when I first found her, and with a quick shrug, pulled the T-shirt over her head.

"I'm not hurt, just a little hot," she purred and thrust her chest in my face. I had to admit, the view was stirring.

"Cool me off?" she asked, and suddenly her hands were undoing my buttons, and we were wrestling for balance. I don't think I made a conscious decision to allow it, but I didn't fight too hard either, and suddenly there she was, straddling me in the grass, those soft Southern belle

39

breasts in my hungry mouth and the creamy globes of her ass cupped in my hands.

She fucked like an animal, all teeth and nails and grunting urgency, rolling me down the incline of the ditch 'til we were hidden in a thicket of weeds and sweaty as workmen on a Louisiana chaingang. At some point during the whole thing I realized that I must have completely lost my mind and tried to stop, but she silenced me with her mouth and I entered her for the third time, this time pinning her to the ground with my own need. It seemed to go on for hours, this sucking and grinding and taking and giving. And as I came for the third time, amazing myself with a stamina I'd never had before, she laughed.

It's amazing how fast a laugh can shrivel a man's privates, especially when they're busy doing what God designed them for. But when the laugh sounds more like the cackle of a devil than an angel, well, let's just say it deflated my ego, among other things.

"Who are you?" I finally asked, breathless and now suddenly a little scared, as her face sneered back at me down the naked ribs of her body, crouched like a dog's. She wiggled that shapely rear end in my face and drawled, "Just think of me as a friend of the devil."

She grinned, but there was no humor in her smile.

"Let's you and me go back up to the car. I've got something for ya'll, I left in my jeans."

"For me?" I asked, and watched as her haunches jiggled, a perfect *Penthouse* picture as she strode up the small berm to the road.

I followed her, and watched as she pulled a single sheet of folded paper from the pocket of her cutoff denim shorts. She held it out to me and I took it, unfolding it with a single shake.

"Give me your hand," she said, and without thinking, as I began to read the paper, I did. She immediately poked my index finger with a small piece of glass plucked from the roadside gravel and I yelled.

"Hey!" I pulled my hand back and sucked at the wound. "What the fuck?"

"Sign it with blood, please."

The paper was a contract awarding my soul to the devil in exchange for enjoying the pleasures of one Heather Collins. Her body was mine, unchanging, for twenty-five years to enjoy whenever I chose. At the end of that time, my soul was forfeit.

"You're Heather," I asked.

She nodded.

"You're very good," I said, "but you're not worth my soul. And anyway, I don't think my wife would approve."

Dead Girl on the Side of the Road

She shrugged, honey curls flouncing down the sides of her beach brown biceps.

"Your call. You've got five minutes to decide."

"And then?"

"And then it's midnight. And I'm just a dead girl on the side of the road."

I threw down the paper and gathered my clothes.

"Then I guess you're going to die again," I said, starting back towards the car. The moon was high overhead and so bright that I didn't need the headlights to see how beautiful the girl was that I was walking away from. She was certainly tempting.

"A dead girl with your sperm inside her," added that smooth Southern voice without expression.

My heart stopped dead.

Could they identify me that way? If they didn't know I'd been here?

I thought, police can only compare sperm DNA if they've got a suspect, right? I tried to convince myself of that, and hurried around to the driver's side of the car. They'd find a girl, they'd find she'd been raped and run over, but what would make them ever suspect a guy from 1,000 miles away?

Heather stood quietly next to her discarded clothes and watched me back the car away from her. As I turned the wheel to return to the road, I saw the blue LED on the dash read eleven fifty-eight.

I lined up with the road and threw the car into drive, stomping on the gas and kicking up gravel in a plume behind me.

And there Heather was, bareass naked and five feet in front of my car in the middle of the road, smiling with a sad look that said, "they never learn."

I punched the brakes but it was too late. Her face disappeared beneath my hood and I felt the car shudder as I skidded over her body.

I threw the car in park and dove from the seat to see what I had done.

The body of a naked twelve-year-old was bleeding all over the road behind me. She was pretty, in a beat-up way, auburn hair wet with blood from the cuts on her forehead. The stones behind her head were quickly darkening. I could see one pale pink nipple that would someday have developed into the spectacular center tease of a gorgeous breast; the other one was hidden beneath a smear of gravel-specked gore where my bumper had caught her.

I cradled her head again in my hands and cried.

"Why me? Why her?" I called out into the silent night. A breeze rippled the grass nearby, and I saw a flash of white, a bit of paper rolling end over

41

end into the ditch to my right. From the throat of the dead girl in front of me, a thick, gurgling voice whispered in frightening monotone:

"Don't you want me, baby? Don't you want me. O-o-o-ohhhh."

In the distance, I heard sirens approaching. I looked down the road and saw red and blue flashes swirling through a cloud of gravel dust a mile or so away.

Now her blood was on my rental car, and that was evidence that could easily be linked to me. And my sperm. Which the police would find inside a dead girl who had never even had a period, from the looks of it. I was either giving my soul to the devil or my body to some inmates. Either way, I was about to become the property of someone else.

"Time's up," the body croaked. "Take it or leave it."

I dropped her bloodied head to the gravel and ran to retrieve the contract that would give away my soul. I could almost hear the toll of a churchbell ringing in the midnight hour as I scooped up the deadly parchment from where it had lodged in a thatch of Queen Anne's Lace.

When I came back to the road, the sirens were almost upon us, and the corpse of the blue-faced young girl was still as stone. With a rock from the road, I reopened the wound on my finger, and began to slowly trace my name upon the contract in blood. I prayed that when I finished, Heather would once again transform into the beautiful Southern belle I'd been promised. But all I really cared about was that she stood up and seemed alive before the police got here. As I closed the loop on my last name, which closed the noose on my soul, the bruised lips of the dead girl split in a smile.

Oges
by
John Graham

"Could you pass me the clicker?" I said to the new bartender. She was a big, sloppy redhead wearing globs of purple mascara and a matching oversized T-shirt.

"The what?" she said. Her butchy haircut made her red hair stand up in places. Her pals probably called her something like Jo or Sam.

"The clicker," I said. "I can't watch any more of that." I nodded at the bodybuilder being interviewed on the TV above the ratty pool table. He was talking about his work in underdeveloped countries. I wasn't sure if he meant poor countries or skinny countries.

"Hmm," said Sam. "I kind of like it." She folded her arms over her purple T-shirt. She wasn't carrying a grubby rag like Bob always did, pretending to clean the grubby glasses that were a specialty of Oges Tavern. Sort of ruined the ambience.

I smiled at her, putting some heat in it. "What if I told you I'm allergic to men in thongs?"

She laughed. "Okay, you win, handsome." She reached under the bar for the clicker.

"Thanks," I said, and zapped the bodybuilder. I stopped clicking when I reached a Gilligan's Island rerun. Maryann and Ginger. Technicolor dream women. Why did Gilligan and his buddies want to *leave* the island?

"You like that show?"

I gazed at her, putting some smoke in it. "It's Ginger. I'm a sucker for redheads."

She laughed again but I could see I had slipped one through. Her cheeks were flushing, making her look like the world's largest schoolgirl.

"I have another question for you," I said. I smiled, trying to make more pink appear in her cheeks. She wasn't buying this time. The schoolgirl was hidden back in grade school memories. I'd have to put more heat into it to get a response. I had three thousand green beauties tucked away in the lining of my suit jacket. What did I need to get Sam all hot and bothered for?

43

She crossed her arms again, waiting.

"It's about the name of this place," I said. "Do you know how to pronounce it?" Bob had said it twice in the five months I'd been coming to Oges Tavern. One time it had sounded like *Hodges*. The other—and I think Bob had been a bit soused — like *Ogle*.

She gave me a purple shrug. "I dunno . . . Oggies?"

That's why I loved it here. The element of mystery.

"Do *you* know?" She cocked an auburn eyebrow at me.

"Yes, I do." I took a long sip of Glenfiddich, waiting to see what exactly it was I knew. "It was originally two words. During Prohibition, this place was an illegal speakeasy and didn't have a sign. The two words were a secret code for patrons to identify the place without getting nabbed."

She leaned on the bar. "Really?"

"Yup. The two words were 'Oh geez'. So one guy might say, 'Oh geez, I'm thirsty', and the other guy would know exactly what and where he meant."

"That's pretty wild," she said.

I nodded sagely. "Even today, some of us regulars still use the secret code. For example—" I waved at the ratty pool table, the mismatched tables and chairs. "*Oges*, I can't believe I'm in this dump again."

She loved it. "Oh geez," she repeated, still laughing. "Is that really true?"

"Would I lie to you?" And then, because I was rich again, because I didn't have a date with Mrs. Welton until next Friday, I broke the most cherished of the Oges Tavern rules—I spoke to another patron. He was drinking alone at the other end of the bar.

"What do you think?" I said. "How do you say the name of this place?"

He was large, with a glistening bald head. He'd made the unfortunate choice of packing his hamhock thighs into acid-washed jeans. The first name that jumped into my head seemed more than appropriate. Mung.

"Fuck off," said Mung, without looking at me. He emphasized his point by flexing one bulbous arm.

"Hey," said Sam to me, "don't bother the other customers."

"I know how to say it," said the old black guy sitting at the table next to the entrance. He had a basketball-sized afro. Like Linc from the Mod Squad. His papery lumberjack shirt hung down to his knobby knees. I smiled at Linc, more than a little surprised another patron had spoken.

"It's Ojays," said Linc. He nodded his chin at the dented jukebox on the other side of the entrance. He bopped his afro around, as if he could hear "Love Train" coming from the jukebox.

"Ojays Tavern." I snapped my fingers. "I like the sound of that."

44

Oges

"Damn straight," said Linc.

I turned to the last patron. She was hunched over the PacMan video game table near the hallway leading to the washrooms. A piece of cardboard with OUT OF ORD scrawled on it was taped to the side of the table.

"And what do you think?" I said. I kept my smile friendly. No point wasting any heat on her. She looked too housewifey to be a potential client. Her purse was way too big, almost a sack, to have any real money in it. Her mousy hair was braided into two stiff pigtails. A Doris, if there ever was one.

"Pardon?" she said, looking up. She had a fresh black eye.

"You talk too much, pretty boy," said Mung. He levered his acid-washed bulk off his stool.

"No trouble," said Sam, reaching under the bar. She looked about as threatening as a Smurf.

"Yo," called Linc, "leave him alone, cueball. We jus' having some fun."

Mung rotated towards Linc. "What the fuck did you just call me?"

The door opened and two people walked in. It was a man and a woman and they were both wearing wolfman masks—black-tipped noses, poofy Michael Landon hair, Elvis sideburns. The woman had a revolver. The man was gigantic, so huge he moved awkwardly, as if each part of his body had its own brain. Bonnie and Clod.

Oges," I said, thinking of the three thousand green beauties tucked away in the lining of my suit jacket.

Clod stayed in front of the door. He was taller than the door, almost as wide. Bonnie hopped down the short flight of stairs and came over to the bar. She was carrying a frilly white basket with her other hand.

"Hands up, bitch," she barked at Sam. She pointed the revolver at the pool table. "Get over there." She swung the gun towards Doris, then me. "You too."

Sam did what she was told. So did Doris.

I stared at the hole at the end of the barrel for a long tick of eternity. My body turned as cold and empty as the distance between stars.

"*Now!*" roared Bonnie.

I backed towards the pool table, joining Sam and Doris. Sam looked like she was going to cry. Doris was hugging her sack purse. The only colour in her face was the black eye.

Clod took one giant, stilted step and hauled Linc out of his chair.

"Yo, take it easy, Jack," cried Linc.

"Shut up, bitch," said Clod.

Linc's forehead wrinkled into angry lines. "Who you callin' a—"

Clod shoved him towards the pool table.

45

"Get over there!" Bonnie barked at Mung, who hadn't budged an inch since the arrival of our two trick-or-treaters. She set the frilly white basket on the bar and leveled the revolver at Mung.

"Or what?" snorted Mung. "You gonna *cap* my ass with that thing?" He turned his back on Bonnie and pointed at Clod. "I don't care about the size of you, bud. Get in my way and I'll make you eat that stupid mask." He flexed his bulbous arms as he strode towards the door, bald head glistening, acid-washed jeans swishing.

Bonnie didn't shoot him. What had Mung said? *You gonna* cap *my ass with that thing?* I squinted at the revolver in her hand. It was a cap gun, a toy. I slipped my fingers under the left cuff of my suit jacket. My three thousand green beauties weren't going anywhere tonight. Thank you very much, Mung.

Clod blocked Mung's path. Mung never hesitated. He swung one bulbous arm, ramming a fist up into Clod's face. If Mung had hit me like that it'd all be over. My face would be an eyesore. I'd never get another client.

Veins were rising all over Mung's arms and scalp. You had to hand it to him. He looked sort of . . . transcendent. He launched another fist but Clod's boxcar arms shot out and yanked Mung into the air. Clod whirled and threw Mung towards the PacMan table. Mung sailed across the room, bounced over the table, knocking it on its side. The PacMan table made an electronic burp and the blank screen filled with glowing yellow dots and chomping ghosts.

Linc said, "Holy croak."

Sam started crying.

My fingers turned to icicles and fell out of the sleeve of my jacket. It didn't matter that Bonnie's gun was a toy. Clod was a weapon.

Clod went over to Mung, picked him up by his wide leather belt and carried him down the hallway to the ladies' room. He kicked open the door and tossed Mung inside.

Bonnie and Clod kissed, tongues slurping. Bonnie strolled off towards to the washroom. Clod came and stood in front of the pool table. He crossed his arms and loomed.

"Hey Jack," said Linc, "here, you can have it, man. It's all yours." He was holding out a greasy brown wallet; crumpled paper, bus transfers, a TOPPS baseball card were sticking out of it.

Clod regarded the wallet.

"Take it, Jack," said Linc. "There's three Mastercards in it and two Visa. They still good."

"I could open the safe for you," offered Sam. She had stopped crying. Her mascara had run, leaving big, sloppy purple runnels down her face.

Oges

A scream came from inside the ladies' room. It was a chorus of all the worst things in life—profound agony, hopeless pleading, abject fear.

The scream stopped.

Sam started crying again.

Clod watched our faces, his gigantic body shaking with laughter. "You can keep your money." He pointed at Sam. "We want you." Then Linc. "And you." Then Doris. "And you."

Then me.

"And you."

Clod patted his belly and smiled proudly. "She's eating for two again. Another bun in the oven."

Sam bent forward and puked. Clod looked down at the mess, nostrils flaring in disgust. Linc took off, darting forward and ducking under Clod. Clod lunged for him but he was too late. Linc's basketball afro was already bouncing through the mismatched tables and chairs, his lumberjack shirt flying back like a cape.

"See ya, Jack!" cried Linc as he hurtled towards the entrance. Clod turned to follow, tripped, caught his balance on the bar. For a moment, Clod's mammoth back was to me, as wide and inviting as a door. My fingers tensed, ready . . .

But what if you miss?

Clod went after Linc. He plowed through tables and chairs, making them spin and wobble. But Linc was quick. He was already springing up the entrance steps, lumberjack shirt flapping.

Don't look back, don't look back.

Linc reached for the doorknob. He didn't look back. That's why he didn't see Bonnie. She slammed him into the door. She tore at him, shredding his shirt. He fought wildly, punching her, kicking with his platform shoes. Then Clod joined the tangle. Linc tried to keep fighting but Clod was too much for him. Linc never screamed, never made a sound while they killed him. I don't know why. Whether he didn't know what was happening or was hurt too badly to scream or just wouldn't give them the satisfaction. His afro had been snatched bald in places.

I didn't remember the emergency exit at the end of washroom hallway until they were finished.

So what? You going to run for it? Like Linc? Long odds and you've never been one to risk your pretty face, have you?

Bonnie and Clod walked back to the pool table.

"Who's next?" said Clod.

Sam puked again. Nothing came out this time but a dribble of complete terror. Doris clutched her sack purse.

"How about you, bitch?" said Bonnie, flicking a finger through Sam's red hair.

I stepped forward, away from the pool table, into a vast, desolate place. Bonnie and Clod both glanced at me in surprise.

Take it back, take it back. You don't protect women. That's not what you do for women.

"What do we have here?" said Clod. "A hero? Perfect hair and big green eyes and sooo brave?" He turned to Bonnie, grinning. "Isn't that just so sweet?"

I felt something take form inside me, something clean and dense with potential. An ember of rage.

"Hey Rover," I said to Clod.

They stopped laughing.

"Bite me," I said.

Doris inhaled sharply. Sam looked up at me, purple eyes wide.

Clod roared as he took one giant step towards me. He picked me up and shook me until it felt like my skeleton was liquifying. He carried me over to the washroom hallway. He kicked open the door of the ladies' room and threw me inside. I covered my head and gritted my teeth, bracing for impact. But I landed on something soft, was grateful until I realized what it was—Mung. Sort of.

I scrambled off him. I saw why Mung had screamed the way he had. She had eaten him.

I closed my eyes, to keep the sickening, pulsing soup inside me from boiling over into the room and dissolving the world. I turned away from the sort-of-Mung sprawled on the drenched floor. My hip bumped into something hard and my eyes opened. I was at the sink.

They ate him, she's going to eat you, eat you while you're still alive, Linc never screamed, Linc fought them with his platform shoes—

I splashed water on my face, hid in its simple cold wetness.

The door opened and Bonnie sauntered in. "Hi there," she said, smiling. She came towards me, hips swaying. She raised her long arms, stained hands reaching for me.

"Wait," I said, smiling with all the heat and smoke in me, as if I had the sun hidden behind my eyes.

She paused. "Are you going to beg for your life, pretty little dinner?"

I almost lost my smile. The sickening boiling pulsing soup tickled the back of my throat, scratched at the edge of my mind, wanting in. But I kept smiling, giving her everything I had.

She swayed toward me.

Oges

"I know how to touch you," I said. I caressed my fingertips over the back of her hand.

She stopped. She stared at the goosebumps on her hand.

"Let me show you." I slid the tip of one finger across her palm. She shuddered. I traced intricate, spider-leg patterns over her wrist and down her forearm. I brought up my other hand and did the same to her other arm, leaving a trail of shivery goosebumps.

"I could touch you other places . . ."

She moved closer. "Oh, such a clever little dinner."

I made a circle with thumb and forefinger, floated the circle towards one of her breasts. She arched her back. I paused. She buried her stained nails into the palms of her hands, waiting, waiting for my touch.

I gently flicked my forefinger across her nipple. She groaned. I flicked again, harder, the shock of the pain exaggerating the pleasure.

"Take off your shirt," I whispered.

She grabbed at her black turtleneck and tore it open.

I gazed at her dark, avid eyes, promising her ecstasy. I drew an S down one breast, ending at the straining nipple. She wasn't wearing a bra. She locked urgent fingers around the back of my neck and pulled me to her. My head lowered to her breast and—

Oges.

Her breast was covered with wavy, brown swirls of hair. Fur. Light and downy, but still fur. From this close, I could see individual follicles coming out of the pale, blue-veined skin. Her nipples were a deep satiny black.

She dug her nails into the back of my neck. "What's wrong, bitch? Why have you stopped?" Her nails burrowed deeper; blood trickled down my neck and nestled in the collar of my shirt.

And you know something else, don't you? You'd already figured out that something wasn't right about Bonnie and Clod. You knew when you saw what they did to Mung. So what are you waiting for?

I placed both hands on Bonnie's muscular back. I pulled her to me. I put my mouth over one of her nipples.

The first woman who'd actually paid me cash money had been nursing her firstborn. I'd watched him feed, learned to imitate the motions of his tiny mouth. I improved on it, adding innovations of tongue and lips and breath. For that, and the other things I learned to do, she'd begged me to marry her.

I tried to make Bonnie do the same. I almost wrenched my head away from her breast when I felt something hot squirt into my mouth. I swallowed, knowing the only thing keeping her other appetites at bay was a flimsy gauze of bliss.

At first, I thought it was my own blood, that I had bitten the inside of my mouth when Clod was shaking me. But the taste was wrong. Sweet as a soft peach, smoother than hundred year old scotch, radiant in my belly, spreading glowing tendrils throughout my body.

Not human, hot but not human, sweet and delicious but nothumannothumannothuman

I almost let the boiling pulsing soup inhabit my mind but my mouth, trained and obedient all these years, kept trying to make her forget anything else existed in the world but ecstasy.

And it worked. Because she was still groaning with pleasure while I slipped my fingers under the left cuff of my suit jacket, drew Mac out of his sheath and thrust the knife into her back.

I'm good at two things. One I use to make money. The other thing I use, every once in a while, to make sure no one takes my money away from me. To make sure no one takes *anything* away from me.

"I just killed you," I said and shoved her away from me.

She looked at me, panting, breasts heaving. She hadn't realized she wasn't in ecstasy.

I held up Mac—his serrated blade glistened with her life. She bent an arm around behind her and touched the hole in her back. Her eyes were confused, clouded with imminent agony.

"Pretty little corpse," I said and cut her neck from Elvis sideburn to sideburn. She staggered away from me, tripped over Mung and fell into his contorted embrace.

I went over to the sink, stuck two fingers down my throat and emptied my stomach onto the cracked porcelain. I rinsed my mouth out with cold water. I walked across the drenched floor and opened the door. Clod's massive, shaggy head turned towards the washroom hallway as soon as he heard the door open.

"Hello, Jack," I said.

He actually did a double take, eyes bulging out of his inhuman face.

"Surprised to see me?" I ambled down the hallway. "Oh, by the way—" I held up Mac. "I made lamb chops out of her."

"Marsha?" said Clod. He shook his head then clawed at his cheeks, leaving tears of blood. "*Marsha . . .*"

I stopped at the end of the hallway. Marsha?

Clod bent his head back and howled.

I waited.

He charged, bounding across the room. Each leap toppled mismatched tables and chairs. His last jump flattened a table decorated with pink flamingoes. I threw Mac. Clod saw the knife flickering towards his head

50

and raised his arms but Mac dipped suddenly and thunked into his chest. He spun past me and crashed into the PacMan table.

I'm good at two things. Sometimes I'm very good.

I went over to Clod. He was still alive. But the only place he'd be going any time soon was to meet his maker.

And who would that be? Who made him? And who made the other one, lying on the floor with sort-of-Mung, deep black satiny nipples, milk like the birth of the universe?

I looked away from Clod, over at Sam and Doris. They were frozen, as still and unreal as a portrait—Two Astonished Women.

I walked over to them. I smiled nonchalantly. Damned if I didn't wink, too. "Boy, I could use a—"

Neither woman was looking at me any more. Another portrait—Two Petrified Women. I didn't bother turning around. *Can't kill one that easy, dummy.*

I took off for the bar, hearing chairs toppling behind me, snuffling breath. I dove over the bar, one elbow sweeping a peanut bowl into the air. I plunged to the mucky floor in a shower of cigarette butts and peanut shells. I scrabbled on all fours over to the spot where Sam had been when Bonnie and Clod came in. I flung glasses off shelves, searching for whatever weapon Sam had been reaching for under the bar.

Clod landed on the bar over my head, splintering wood. He lowered one boxcar arm towards me. Mac was still sticking out of his chest. I found what Sam had been reaching for—a cellphone.

Clod latched his hand around my neck and dragged me towards his maw. I tried to scream but something else came out.

"She was mine before she died!"

Clod hesitated, maw stretched wide open, as if he were going to say ah for some obscene doctor.

"Can't you smell her on me, Rover?" I said.

His black nostrils flared then quivered with the shattering knowledge he was inhaling.

"No . . . Marsha would never—"

His head exploded, coming apart like a jigsaw puzzle tipped off its table. Slowly, limb by limb, his freight train body toppled down behind the bar. I slid away from the mass of hair and muscle and gore. I climbed to my feet using a Guinness spigot as a handhold.

Doris was standing in front of the bar, sack purse in one hand, a very large, very shiny silver handgun in the other.

"I think," I said, "I love you, Doris."

She nodded grimly and lowered the gun. "Storm," she said. "With an h."

51

"Storm?" I said, glancing up at the ceiling, expecting to see dark clouds. "With an h?"

"My name's Storm," said Doris. "With a silent h on the end."

"Oh," I said.

She leaned over the bar and looked at Clod. One of his boots was stuck in the bar sink. Clod had worn a size eighteen. I tugged Mac out of his chest.

Monsters roam the world, eat you alive, knife in the chest won't kill them, deep black satiny nipples, milk like the beginning of life.

"Sorry it took me so long to get him," said Doris, no, Storm with a silent h on the end. "I never had a chance to do anything until you distracted him. Thropes are way too dangerous to take on alone." She shook her head, making her pigtails swing. "I came here as an afterthought. I've always had a bad feeling about the other bartender. Tonight confirms he's a collaborator."

"Thropes?" I said. "Bob's a collaborator?"

"As in lycanthropes." She nodded, mouth tight. "And I think it's a certainty that *Bob* was part of this."

"What are you talking about?" said Sam. She had floated over to the bar and was looking back and forth between us.

Stormh frowned, tugged on one of her pigtails. She pointed at Clod. "Him and his mate were skinpoppers."

"Huh?" said Sam.

"Werewolves," I said. "Just like in the movies. American Werewolf In London, I Was A Teenaged Werewolf, Abbot and Costello Meet The Wolfma—

"Yes, yes, that's right," said Stormh. "Just like that. Give or take a few details." She tapped the shiny silver gun on the sole of Clod's boot, like a professor pointing out some fascinating concept on a blackboard. "We think they're using some kind of mutagenized transgenic retrovirus."

"Ah," I nodded. "*That* explains everything."

Stormh gave me a hard look hovering somewhere between impatience and ire. She turned to Sam. "Could you make us some coffee? I think we could all use something hot to drink."

Oh no, none for me, thanks. Had enough hot drinks to last a lifetime.

Sam said, "Okay, sure." She floated down to the end of the bar.

Stormh picked up the frilly white basket on the bar—the one Bonnie had brought into this fine establishment—and set it in front of me. I peered inside. There was a baby inside; pudgy face, fresh baby smell, big saucer eyes, two white teeth poking through pink gums, as sharp as pins.

"Give me your knife," said Stormh. She held out a hand.

Oges

I looked up. "What?"

"Give me your knife. I have to finish the job."

"It's just a—"

She slammed a fist on the bar. "It's an *abomination!*"

A sound came from the basket. "Blug," said he, she, it, I don't know. I poked my head inside the basket. The baby was smiling.

"Blug!"

"Don't worry," I whispered. "Don't worry, little . . . guy."

What are you doing? You hate *babies. Woman cooing over them because that's what they're supposed to do. No past, no mistakes, only a coddled present, a rosy-cheeked future.*

"Get away from it," said Stormh, raising the silver handgun.

"Are you serious?" I said.

She didn't say anything. The answer was in her eyes.

I said, "You get that shiner battling werewolves? Like you did tonight? Watching while other people fight and die?"

She stared at me, eyes steady, gun steady.

I backed away from the basket. "Are you going to shoot me? After I saved your life?"

"Mogl!" said the baby.

Sam came back carrying a tray with three grubby mugs of coffee and Kit Kats that had been broken into individual fingers.

"I made some coffee," she said.

"Thanks," said Stormh and shot the baby.

Monsters roam the world, beasts with Elvis sideburns and Michael Landon hair and—

Stormh pointed the gun at my chest.

Pigtails.

"I wouldn't do that if I were you!" she said.

"What?" I stared at the maw at the end of the shiny silver barrel. "Do what?"

"Put the knife down," she said. "I don't want to hurt you."

I looked at Mac, surprised. He was by my ear, throwing position.

"Okay, take it easy." I slowly lowered Mac and slid him back in his sheath. "I won't do anything stupid."

I turned to Sam. She was crying again. I squeezed her shoulder and since I couldn't think of anything else, I said, "Your mascara's running." I walked out from behind the bar.

"Hey," called Stormh, "where are you going?" She followed me as I headed towards the washroom hallway. "We need to talk. Bane could use someone like you."

I passed the shattered PacMan table.

"Are you just going to leave?" she said. "You've seen the face of true evil and now you're running away?"

I went down the hallway to the emergency exit. I looked back. Stormh was glaring at me, shiny silver handgun resting on her shoulder like a rifle. Sam was still holding the tray. The frilly white basket had a gaping black hole.

"What's your name?" I said to Sam.

"Joanna."

Joanna . . . Jo. I smiled at her, no heat or smoke. A real one. She tried to smile back. I opened the emergency exit and stepped out into the narrow alley.

"We'll be seeing you again!" yelled Stormh. "That's a promise!"

The alley stank. The dumpster near the exit was a lodestone of foulness, drawing and magnifying every horrid odour in the alley. A host of stenches clawed at my nose—rancid oranges, maggoty fish, the sour old stink of a man's running shoe, wet moldy cardboard, the sickly sweetness of sun-fried cola—

A man's running shoe?

I stopped. I stared at the dumpster. How did I know there was a man's running shoe in there?

Something moved on the other side of an old car halfway down the alley. A padded, stealthy movement. Mac leaped into my hand. I crouched low, waited. A cat dashed out from under the car, a pudgy, nutmeg-colored tom.

You drank some.

There were no lights in the alley. The surrounding buildings were high enough to block out the streetlights. But I could see the raised letters on the crumpled hood of the old car—A M E R I C A N. I could see the color of the fleeing cat. I could smell the piquant vapors of the tom's fear, the tart hone of its sex.

You drank some.

I ran down the alley. I passed the cat before he reached the street. The tom froze, looking up at me as I bounded over him, fur bristling, ears back. The scent of its terror reminded me of Glenfiddich.

My car was parked beside the mouth of the alley. The fumy cloggy metal smell of the Porsche made my empty stomach churn. I unlocked the door and got in. The inside of the car smelled like blood. I snatched Mac back out but the car was empty. The blood smell was coming from me, from my suit. I breathed in the sweet, narcotic aroma.

Not human.

Oges

It reminded me of Glenfiddich that had been aged since the birth of the universe. I gulped down the aroma, couldn't stop sucking it in, until the car began to turn to mist and the only real thing in the world was Bonnie and Clod, their hot, warm, smothering nectar.

I ran Mac across the palm of one hand, grasping onto the sizzling pain, the private, comforting smell of my own existence. When the car started to feel solid again, I put Mac down on the passenger seat, tugged off my tie and wrapped it around my bleeding hand. I jammed the Porsche in gear and pulled away from the alley.

I glanced up at the moon. It was a crescent, as fine and bright as the blade of a scimitar. Shouldn't it be full? Wasn't that one of the rules?

When there was half a city between me and the Oges Tavern, I took the flask of Glenfiddich out of the glove compartment. I took a long, long swig—or started to. I opened the car window and spat out the foul liquid. It tasted like distilled poison.

I looked up at the bright crescent moon and decided Storm with a silent h at the end had been right when she promised I'd be seeing her again. I would definitely be seeing Stormh and her Bane, whoever or whatever that was, again. And Bob. Bob the collaborator. And . . . Sam. Joanna. Maybe I would call her some time and ask her how she's doing. Maybe ask her if she wanted to go for a coffee.

But I wouldn't be seeing Mrs. Welton again. I was through with trick or treating.

Ashes to Ashes
by
Sheri White

"It was a beautiful service, Dear. Greg would have loved it."

Tanya gaped at the old woman and held back a sarcastic reply. But she knew Greg's great-aunt meant well. Platitudes were spouted when people died; nobody ever knew the right thing to say.

Tanya realized Aunt Abigail was waiting for a response. She forced a wan smile and patted the old lady's hand. "Thank you, Auntie."

She tried to make her escape, but Abigail grabbed her arm.

"Why won't you bury my nephew properly? I hear you're going to *burn* him." The old lady stared accusingly at her through rheumy eyes.

Christ. Tanya had already been through this with her mother-in-law. Thankfully Greg had written the cremation into his will when they realized he wouldn't go into remission after the last round of treatments.

"It's what Greg wanted, Auntie. Oh, excuse me. There's someone I must talk to." Tanya quickly walked away before Auntie could say anything else. She just didn't have the strength for it. She wanted to go home and cry.

These people never liked me. I don't want to share my grief with them.

Tanya decided to say her good-byes and leave. She'd never see Greg's family again anyway.

*

Her footsteps echoed through the empty house. Walking in the front door was different this time. When Greg was in the hospital for his regular treatments, she knew he would be coming back home. Now, however, their cozy little house seemed cold and foreign in its emptiness.

Tears welled when she entered their bedroom. The bed was messy; she hadn't had the time or energy to make it since Greg's death.

She curled up on the bed and hugged Greg's pillow tightly against her body. She could still smell his scent in the sheets and pillowcase. She cried herself to sleep.

Ashes to Ashes

*

Several days later, she decided to put the urn in the bedroom. It sat on her nightstand next to a picture of Greg before he got so sick. Tanya found herself talking to the urn before she went to sleep at night.

"Maybe I'm going crazy, Greg. Talking to you like this. But God, I miss you so much." Tanya choked on the words as she tried to hold in a sob. "I want to make love with you and be held in your arms."

With a heavy sigh, she undressed and slipped beneath the sheets. She still couldn't bear to change them. Greg's lingering scent in the cool cotton against her skin provided a bit of comfort.

Tanya lay there in the dark, thinking of the last time she and Greg had made love. They both knew Greg didn't have much time left, and the sex was tender and bittersweet. They cried when it was over. The next day, Greg made his final trip to the hospital.

Tanya could feel wetness between her thighs. The thought of making love with Greg had aroused her, and she ached for release. She reached down under the covers and began fingering her clit. She gasped at the waves of pleasure that raced through her body. Her orgasm was quick and strong, and she yelled out at its intensity.

Then the emptiness came rushing back.

*

She trudged through her days, only going through the motions at work. Her coworkers gave up trying to invite her to lunch or happy hour. Tanya always refused or just stared into space without acknowledging she'd heard the invitation.

She heard the genuine concern in Jerry's voice and fought back tears. "I'm all right." She offered a slight smile and wiped away a tear.

Jerry got up and sat on the edge of his desk in front of her. "Look, Tanya. I think you should take some time off. You're obviously still very distressed, and rightfully so. Frankly, I'm surprised you came back as soon as you did."

She shrugged. "I guess I thought keeping busy would help. I'm sorry my work has been so poor lately."

Jerry dismissed her chagrin with a wave of his hand. "Don't even worry about it. Take a couple weeks or so—a month, if you need to. You've been through hell."

Tanya stood up and smiled gratefully. "Thank you so much. I really appreciate this." She reached out and shook his hand, then left quickly so she wouldn't cry in front of him.

*

"It's not getting any better, Greg." Tanya took a sip of scotch from the bottle on the nightstand. The sheets were beginning to smell sour, but Tanya still couldn't bring herself to change them.

"I miss you so much. I *want* you so much. I'm ovulating—remember how badly we wanted a baby? I'm so wet and so horny, and I need you so badly." Tanya took a drag of her cigarette, then put it in the ashtray on the bed next to her.

She grabbed the scotch and took another long pull. Some of the amber liquid leaked from the bottle and dripped onto her breasts. She traced the wet trail with her finger.

"You would lick that off if you were here. Remember I'd pour scotch on your cock and suck it off? God, you loved that."

Tanya took another drink, then poured some of the alcohol over her body, splashing the bed. She rubbed the warm liquid into her body. She arched her back, letting the small pool on her stomach run in slow rivulets down to her pussy.

"I wish I could feel you against my shkin—*skin* right now." Tanya giggled. "I guess I'm a little drunk, Sweetie."

She let her hand wander between her legs as she drank from the bottle. She slowly stroked her clit, slicking her fingers with her juices.

Heat rushed through Tanya's body. Her nipples hardened and her breathing quickened. She took one more drink, then let the bottle fall onto the bed, soaking the sheets with the remaining liquid.

Tanya gently stroked her clit, moving her hips as she imagined Greg on top of her. She put her fingers in her pussy, but cried out in frustration. She wanted to be filled with Greg's hardness. Desperately she grabbed the scotch bottle and inserted the neck.

The bottle filled her physically, but it wasn't enough. Tanya still craved Greg. She needed to feel him warm against her skin. She took the bottle out and threw it against the wall, barely hearing it shatter.

She looked at the brass urn on the nightstand.

"You don't belong in that cold jar." She leaned over to pick up the urn. She held it tightly to her chest, smiling through her tears. "You belong with me." Tanya opened the urn and upended it, sprinkling Greg's ashes over her body. She dropped the urn off the side of the bed, then began rubbing the ashes over her sticky skin. Patches of gray ash decorated her breasts and stomach.

The ashes felt coarse against her smooth skin. She imagined Greg's face, rough with stubble, scratching her as he kissed the length of her body.

"I want you inside me," she whispered. She rubbed ashes onto her clit, then scooped some onto her fingers. Slowly Tanya let her fingers glide into her wet pussy. She ignored the coarse texture of the ashes and pretended she was feeling the bumps and ridges of Greg's hard cock.

"God, that feels good, Greg. You're such a good lover." Her hips moved quickly as she fucked her fingers. She closed her eyes and imagined him leaning over her, his hard cock thrusting in and out.

Tanya clenched the sheets with her other hand, not realizing she had bumped the ashtray, knocking her smoldering cigarette onto the bed. She didn't notice the growing heat next to her writhing body. Her orgasm was quickly approaching. She fucked her fingers faster and harder, picturing Greg naked and healthy on top of her.

Suddenly she arched her back and cried out as her orgasm ripped through her. She withdrew her fingers and sucked on them. She used to do that to Greg, suck his cock right after she came. But the taste of ashes mingled with her pussy juices jolted Tanya out of her fantasy.

She began to sob. She covered her face with her hands and shook her head from side to side.

"I can't live like this. I can't."

Abruptly she gasped in pain and opened her eyes.

"Oh my God!" The sheets had caught fire. The flames licked her breasts.

Yet she didn't try to escape. She knew she should get up and run for the extinguisher; instead, she welcomed the pain. Her skin began to blister. She closed her eyes to listen to the crackle of the fire, sure she had heard a voice whispering to her. The flames kissed her stomach and legs.

This is where I'll find Greg. This is where I need to be.

She reached between her legs once more to stroke her herself. With a deep breath, Tanya embraced the fire. Embraced Greg.

As the flames licked and devoured Tanya's flesh, she felt herself approaching another orgasm. Her skin blackened and peeled, yet she kept fingering her clit. She made love to the flames, and screamed in pain and ecstasy when her orgasm tore through her body.

"I love you," a voice whispered—and before she lost consciousness, Tanya couldn't be sure it was hers.

Ratz and Snalez
by
Peadar Ó Guilín

Another sweet day; a perfect yawn and stretch. Sunshine and sweat like my drool on a lover's back—and I will be a lover soon! I will! She, Dympna, my love, my beauty, She . . . has agreed to a date. The eighth, that is, of April. Tonight that is . . . Tonight!

I lance a few boils in front of the mirror, taking time over the ritual. Beats the hell out of working . . . I linger. I imagine her reflected beside me in the looking glass, lancing them for me, delighting in their ripe juiciness, their gay colors.

"Men," she chirps, "men! Do you have to do this every morning? It looks so painful! Can I—could I put on your cologne?" And then: "Does it sting, dear?"

Yes it stings. It really, really hurts.

My fantasy is beginning to fall apart. Something has been prodding me in the leg continuously for the last five minutes. I look down. It's only my dog, Lovable Spot, trying to impregnate my boot again. I kick out hard and he flies through the air to crash against the lamp-stand. He clings to it like a limpet and never stops pumping.

Ahhh. Lovely day. I'm so glad now I forgot to get the car fixed. I can walk to the office in the sun. Sure beats all those traffic jams, it sure does, although it was a pain not having transport all winter. This year, I decide. This year the car shall be mended!

Exercise has helped me. I have noticed that walking five hundred yards (each way!) to work has improved my standing in the community and substantially contributed to of my career as a detective.

But what's this? The Square is usually the second place I stop for a quick breather on my way to work. Something is wrong, though. A crowd is gathering. Smug, sweating men, vomit stains on their lower lips, sundried snot and designer lice as big as your thumb; slender females, elegant as they step around mounds of droppings left by those males too vulgar to use their pants.

Ratz and Snalez

I push my way to the front of the crowd, bursting through and stepping on the man's corpse that had drawn them here in the first place.

"Back!" I command. "Everybody step back! I'm a detective on the job!" To prove my point (for the crowd seems mutinous), I remove the safety catch on my pistol and wave it about.

I fire a few warning beams over their heads, rejoicing at my power, blowing out windows that are tinted the wrong color. The people at the back are curious to see if I would really use my gun on unarmed civilians as I've been known to do in the past, so they push forward against the ones at the front who are screaming and madly trying to get out of the way. Police arrive before I can be put to the test. The mob scatters, leaving a few crushed ones behind it amidst the mounds of shit and vomit pies

"Awndray Vile, you old devil!" Peeair Horrid, the sergeant stumbles over to me from the squad-pod. I know him well; we used to be partners before I retired from the force, disillusioned as I was by corruption and incompetence in all ranks.

He slips on a turd (left by the killer?), recovers, and staggers over to flop down beside me on the corpse. It has obviously fallen from a great height and the two of us, sitting on it, crush it further. Peeair is out of breath.

"I don't believe it!" he says, "you got the drop on me this time Awndray. How the hell did you find him so fast? Share a secret with an old partner, won't you?"

"Sorry, Peeair. Have to protect my sources, ye know?"

He gives a low whistle and absently wrings out the armpit of his shirt, licking his fingers. "Shit," he says, "I have to admit—you know—when we were partners and you were told to take a walk for accepting bribes and all . . . well you can see how I must have felt. I guess you've made me and the other lads eat our words. You've finally become a good detective."

I accept the recognition as my due but refuse to take on the case of the murdered man or that of the other twelve or so killed by what Peeair says is the same crook over the last few days.

I'm still holding out for that very special case which is going to come along any day now and make my reputation. In the meantime I refuse to be distracted by just any old thing. Besides, it's not even opening hours for me yet.

As I stand up I notice a message written in blood beside the corpse. The words are spelt way wrong and the letters are strangely formed, but I can just make out: "Ratz aned snalez aned puppee dogz talez . . ."

The very thought of it makes my stomach growl and I have a terrible urge to snack. I head for the nearest café.

61

Soon I have forgotten the murder and my mind is filled with thoughts of Her. Dympna. Tonight . . .

*

She's late.

She hasn't come and there's no reason why not because there sure is nothing wrong with any of my features. Sometimes—I know it can happen—your skin can clear up without warning and you're stuck in the house then for a week eating chips and praying a glass of cola will do the trick. But this sure isn't one of those times.

I check myself in a mirror behind the bar.

There is a delicate caking of mucus on the end of my nose, like icing. I am tempted to try and reach it with the tip of my tongue but I need to keep that for her, for Dympna. I have spent too much time perfecting that look . . . Perhaps just one lick.

Salty.

*

Still she does not come.

I have more beer. I adjust my pants to make sure that just a hint of bum-crack is peeping over the edge. How could she fail to be enticed? Why must she torment me so?

*

She is now three minutes late. "More beers . . . and put some vodka in. You're looking at a man who's been stood-up . . ."

But the barman catches his breath and forgets to serve me. There is a gust of perfumed air. A Presence invades the room.

Dympna smiles. "I hope I'm not late."

"Hell yes, you're late." But I can only whisper it for she is a vision. My stubby fingers reach for her thigh but don't quite touch. I am afraid that if I pinch her I'll wake up and it'll all have been a dream with my pajamas even more badly creamed than usual.

She misinterprets the intention of my outstretched hand and takes it in hers. I see a twinkle of pearly teeth and shiver as I imagine them nibbling the sores on my genitals. Ooooh . . .

"I brought along my notebook," Dympna says brightly.

What's this?

62

"I can't wait to start," she says, "I'm ever so excited about the investigation . . ." I am on the point of taking her right here, right now, when I remember that I've promised to make a detective of her. This was the excuse she used for wanting to see me, but she obviously enjoys fantasy and wants to play this thing to its final conclusion. I sigh as I realize that my virginity is doomed to last another hour at least.

"I have a lead on the 'Puppy Dog Tail' murders," she says, "You know about them?"

Of course I do. Didn't I find one of the victims myself only this morning?

"They've just found another corpse," she says. "It was on a tennis court over at the Police station. There was the usual message in blood beside him and he had a tennis racquet embedded in his skull. Isn't that ever so creepy? If we knew who he was playing tennis with we would have the killer . . ."

I'm already getting bored with this. It is hardly a case to tempt even the most mediocre of detectives but it may be the only thing that will allow me to give Dympna what she *really* wants, so reluctantly I ask her about her lead. She smiles.

"I want you to meet my friend," she says.

"A girlfriend?"

"Oh, yes," giggle, giggle, "a girlfriend. I want you to meet her. And she wants to meet you ever so much."

This is not quite the date I had expected. I imagined that tonight we would get to know each other. Just the two of us, intimate and candlelit with romance lighting up our faces. However, since she is obviously so eager for a raunchy threesome who am I to question? In my trousers there is no question whatsoever. I am dribbling already. Besides, Dympna's friend does sound as if she sure is ready for anything.

"She dresses like a man . . . And she says she comes from a parallel uni-. . . uni-something or other."

"University? Universe? Unicorn?"

"The second one," giggle, giggle, "She says she was in the army in the parallel unicorn . . . as an explosives expert!"

"A woman explosives expert!" I hoot, "More likely she's just a man who blew his own balls off! Not much of an expert, that!"

We both have a good laugh while Dympna takes off her friend using a twangy accent I've never heard before. Apparently, among all her other mad claims, this woman also pretends to know the identity of the killer but she will only tell it to somebody who is officially investigating the case. Just for tonight, that's going to be me.

Here she is, now, Dympna's friend. Men's clothes all right. Combat gear; big boots and a camouflage jacket. But then there's her face . . . No boils or gently leaking pustules. This is either a eunuch's face or a woman's.

"Miss . . . uh, Miss Ann Tropé?"

"*Mizz* Ann Tropé." she corrects, rather rudely for a woman. Whatever about her parallel universe bullshit she is definitely a foreigner. She speaks our language awkwardly and she has a bizarre first name: 'Mizz'. How could anybody do that to a child, even if it is only a girl?

She is a strange woman. She has cropped her hair and practically hidden her body deep in the depths of a combat jacket with 'US Marines' written on it in funny lettering. I don't know what a marine is or who US is, but she must know that she is asking, practically begging for such a jacket to be removed.

"I know who the killer is."

"Oh yes?"

Time for a few notes, I guess, but as she begins to speak her jacket parts just enough, just *almost* enough . . . Something bobs around inside. Something round and warm, I don't doubt. Bob, bob, bob, she says, bob-bob, bob-bob. An invitation if only I were man enough . . .

". . . and that," she concludes, "is the identity of the killer."

She looks me straight in the eye, "What are you going to do about it?"

My throat goes dry. How wonderfully brazen. Oh God! My notebook slips from my fingers. She bends down to pick it up for me and as she does something falls out of her inside jacket pocket. We both stare at it in shock, for it is not a breast at all, but a tennis ball with specks of blood on it! Of all the lousy tricks! She isn't even embarrassed and has the nerve to ask if I've seen enough and if I want to "take" her now! As if I would want a woman who was almost a man even down to fake bouncy breasts!

"I'd rather die!" I say.

"That can be arranged," and now she is the one who looks annoyed. Good! It serves her right!

I head out into the night in search of Dympna to continue the date but the whore is nowhere in sight and has obviously run off with another man, or men, most likely. I hope she doesn't think she's going to get away with this.

*

The day goes by slowly in the office and the strangest thoughts pass through your head. Like, maybe Dympna left last night in a fit of jealousy.

64

After all, I was alone in a room with another woman. If the foreigner had been as red blooded a woman as I am a man, the inevitable was bound to have occurred. For a moment I wish it had . . . Mizz Ann Tropé. The name has a certain romance, and her twangy accent while strange, has a breathless, husky quality . . . I have no doubt now that she wanted me desperately—why else tease me with the tennis ball like that? The problem is simply that a man like me cannot possibly feel attraction for a woman who cuts her hair like a man, dresses like a man and wants to do a man's job. The thought is scandalous but it keeps coming back again and again. Her throat, not manlike at all. White, slender. I imagine my lips on it, her chin raised. And my hands, slipping inside that combat jacket over tiny breasts which are smaller than any tennis ball. I tremble at the touch of her nipples. They're real, so real, as hard now as the plastic ones I keep for fun, but warm. Deep in her throat a gasp.

Dympna is there too. She helps with the buttons of the combat jacket like she can't wait. The white shoulders of Mizz Ann shrug free. She pulls Dympna close, slides in a quick tongue. Then it's my turn and it's her hands, brazen whorehands down my pants as three of us fall to floor. Mizz Ann Tropé, shoves Dympna aside. "Awndray," she breaths and spreads her bony hips to straddle me backwards so I can't see her breasts. She squeezes tight around my shaft. Boils burst for lubrication and then she pistons up and down, grunting like a tattooed builder. Oh God! Oh lordy! This is better than the time with the donkey, better than when Lovable Spot licked off the ice-cream. She bucks, she howls. Dympna bends over my face to kiss me. She hides the sight of Mizz until I push her away.

Then it's just me and her again. She arches back, sinking deep into my belly, nails everywhere, hurting and tearing until I can't stand it any more. A buck, a thrust. Three in a row, convulsive; sweat and heat where our bodies touch.

Then, my virginity blasts free throwing Mizz Ann three feet into the air, spraying Dympna who is left in the corner wringing her hands.

"I thought you wanted a woman!" she cries.

"I do, Dympna! I . . . I . . ."

She flees in tears without even bothering to wipe off my love.

I need new pants.

I'm too tired to change today. Since there are only a couple of hours to go before lunch I decide to knock off for the day and go home.

I see a crowd in the street on the way back. I push to the front but it's only another one of those 'ratz aned snalez' corpses again. A big fat man who had been battered to death with a dainty little combat boot, a child's perhaps, which was left on the scene by the killer. The boot reminds me so much of Tropé and the events of last night that I don't have the heart to stay around and discipline the crowd. I'm too depressed.

Further down the road there is a much smaller crowd staring at a new and very bizarre poster. It shows a woman lying down with her face in the mud while a large man has his foot on her head to keep her there. While such things can be quite titillating, I don't think a public street is the right place for them. I rip it down to the great disapproval of the onlookers. The women in particular are annoyed, but I keep my disgust at their open wantonness to myself.

I keep the poster too. I imagine myself as the man with Dympna prone before me. But in my mind her hair keeps shortening, her dress becomes a pair of pants. I rip the poster to shreds.

*

Home at last. Before opening the door I can hear a ticking noise coming from somewhere within my apartment. Strange, that. I open the door, walk inside and fall flat on my face. I have slipped on my own excrement again. I don't get up right away. Now that I'm here perhaps I'll snooze or . . . wait! If I wasn't on the ground I wouldn't see it, but there appears to be a string tied across the door to the kitchen just where I might trip over it. It passes over the frame of the door and into a small black box I've never seen before. That's the source of the ticking noise. Second by second the noise becomes more and more urgent and suddenly . . . pain explodes in my head! Something collides with my right eye-ball and begins to batter against it again and again without mercy.

But it is only Lovable Spot, my pooch, rather inappropriately displaying his affection. I rip him from my face and fling him away. He lands on the string across the door to the kitchen and his head disappears in a flash of blood and light. The rest of his body lands against a table leg to which it clings convulsively. It is some hours before it stops pumping.

I haven't got the heart to pull him away.

Being a born detective it doesn't take me long to figure out that someone has broken into my apartment and planted a bomb there. But no matter how much I tear my hair or grind my teeth, there is still one thing that I cannot explain: why would anybody want to kill my dog?

*

It's strange, but now that I'm no longer in the police force, the only one I can turn to who claims to know anything about explosives is the Tropé

66

woman. It's unsettling having to ask a woman for advice, but what choice do I have?

I phoned Dympna's home just now. She wasn't in but I spoke to her father. He is very worried about her. Apparently she said she was going to some kind of party with some of her friends, only she had called it an 'open air meeting'! The meeting was to be held in Patterson Square . . . I thanked Mr. Turred, and left immediately to find her. I knew that in spite of the jealousy that existed between them, Dympna would be able to lead me to the man-woman Tropé.

*

The streets are strangely quiet for this time of the evening although, every now and again, the grunts of couples courting in alleyways floats to me on the breeze.

Soon I reach the small square where Dympna was to meet with her little friends. There are quite a lot of them; forty, maybe fifty or a hundred. They are all sitting on their coats on the ground, fanned out in a circle with—and this is the stunner—Mizz Ann Tropé standing at the center, directing all the gossip around her!

I fart politely at the edge of the circle but they are all so intent on their gossip that I get no reaction. I am forced to fart again, this time loudly but firmly. Incredibly, they still don't hear me. No matter, Tropé is the one I've come to see and I *will* see her. I push my way through to the center of the circle and all the twittering little voices falter in my wake.

Tropé's eyes go wide when I appear. From the crease between her eyes and the muscle which takes to twitching in her jaw all of a sudden, it is clear she still desires me.

"Have you come for me at last, Mr. Vile?"

"No . . ." I say, but I feel a wave of confusion come over me as the word leaves my mouth. It's Dympna I want. Dympna. A woman like Dympna who used to play with dolls and couldn't climb a tree if her life depended upon it.

Mizz Ann Tropé is exotic. That's all. Once I've had her the novelty will wear off. Still she insists on teasing me. She is only wearing one of her little combat boots, the other foot is bare—ripe for a man's tongue.

Sooner or later I will have to give into one of her constant demands for sex . . .

"I wanted to ask you some questions about . . . about . . ." Oh hell! What on earth was it I had come to ask?

"I see," she says, raising her voice to reach all the young girlies around us, "but I refuse to answer any of your questions until you answer one of mine!"

There are murmurs of agreement from the crowd and for the first time I see Dympna, sitting just behind Tropé. I'm amazed I haven't noticed her there before.

"One of our members," Tropé continues, "saw a man beating a woman today in the street. In broad daylight. In front of everybody and nobody lifted a finger to help her. What do you say to that?"

An expectant hush falls. At first I don't understand the question, but then in a flash I see what must have been bothering her.

"Oh don't worry," I assure her as best I can, "I'm sure they were married."

They are all staring at me in total and utter silence. I am filled with bashfulness as I feel their lovely eyes upon me, each of them wondering no doubt how it would be to feel the weight of *my* hand in an argument; and the lightness of its touch afterwards as we made up. My shyness forces me to adopt a mask of nonchalance. I mumble something about having work to do and make my exit.

Mizz Ann's eyes bore into my back, undressing me from behind! Dympna's eyes are there too, and all the others'!

I float home on a bed of warm, perfumed air.

*

I've been at home the last few days or so waiting for one of the women in the group to give me a call. No luck so far, though. It would seem that while in one way my sexual charisma must make them yearn for me, in another, the sheer power of it must be terrifying. Like being swallowed by a hurricane.

*

Still no news. Dympna at least should have called. I phoned her father last week to let him know she had just been gossiping with her friends.

"A meeting, they called it! Next thing they'll be wanting the vote!"

"Not my daughter," he said proudly.

Tropé doesn't have my number, of course. Not that it matters to me—I need a real woman or nothing at all. I don't expect to be kept waiting long.

*

Ratz and Snalez

Time passes so slowly by the phone. I get hungry, but I can't go into the kitchen as the weather sure has been torrid lately and even I can't stand the smell of Lovable Spot's corpse which is still lying there. With all that's been happening I just never got around to putting him into the ice-box.

My belly thunders but I can't leave the apartment in case I miss one of the phone calls. Luckily, I always have my old force training to fall back on: I put my fingers down my throat and am soon rewarded by the arrival of an instant snack. I pick out the choicest morsels. Meat always tastes better the second time although vegetables tend to be too soggy and acidic to make them worth the effort. I sure can't complain, though, this is one way you can eat to your heart's content and never gain so much as a single kilo!

A troublesome carrot falls behind my chair. As I bend to retrieve it, I hear a boot in the hall outside my apartment. Just one boot, and one bare foot. I stumble to my feet, but I just have time to see a piece of paper slide under the door. The footsteps run off—clump, slap, clump, slap—before I can get there to see who it is.

The note sure is strange. The hand-writing seems vaguely familiar. A lot of the words are spelt wrong and the letters are badly formed:

Deer Missteer Viel,

letz meat fore sex toonite inn thee shipyord. I wont u to treet me like ane objekt aned yuse me to satissfy all yore sexual dezires whyle ignore-ing my needz intirely az I dezerve,

  lotz ov love (casual, widout comitment)

  yore sex slayve,

  Dimmpnah.

My hands tremble. No wonder none of the others had telephoned! Dympna had laid claim to my wobbly body and, like a tiger protecting her kill, would scratch the eyes from anyone who tried to take her man. Actu-ally, it's easier to imagine Tropé scratching somebody's eyes out . . . I shiver deliciously, but put the thought away immediately. I run into the bathroom and block up the bath with a plug of my own hair. I open all the bottles of cologne and pour them in one by one. They are expensive, but what the Hell! I am celebrating the coming end of my virginity and I sure intend to smell juuust right!

The night is crisp and dark. Sounds will carry tonight, which is good because I want the whole world to know about me and Dympna. The streets are strangely nervous, as if they know about us already. Men seem to be few and far between, but there are small knots of women huddled everywhere on street corners. No doubt they are whispering some delicious piece of gossip to each other. Sometimes as I pass by in a cloud of after-shave and pheromones they stop to stare at me. At any other time I might have made it my duty to move them along home, but not tonight!

I pass down by the docks. I spy a pair of giant cranes in the distance and my heart begins to thump in my chest. She, shesheshe is there now; waiting for me to take her to Paradise. I can feel her hair on my thighs, the sting of her tongue on my sores.

I arrive in the shipyard. Dympna is nowhere to be seen and I am required to search for her. It is a difficult task although I am considerably well aided by a lovers' full moon. Everywhere I search, I seem to hear the whispering voices of women. I feel as if a thousand pairs of eyes are watching me, but I see no one. After a few hours of wandering around, I lean in exhaustion against the base of a crane. Something metallic and spanner shaped flashes just in front of my face and clangs noisily into the ground at my feet. I look up to see who has been trying to attract my attention: it is not Dympna, but Mizz Ann Tropé herself! She is standing on one giant arm of the crane, silver in the blazing moonlight.

"Mizz Ann! Where's Dympna?"

Tropé just laughs at that for some reason. Her hair is disheveled and wild. She is wearing the same T-shirt she's had on since I met her. It is stretched at the neck line so that it hangs a little off one slender white shoulder. She is beautiful. I sure must be sick to find her so when she dresses so blatantly like a man . . . but I figure, there'll be plenty of time to see a psychiatrist *after* she gets what she so plainly needs. It's a mission of mercy, really—she might even go back to real clothes again.

She chooses foul language for her come-on: "Get up here you fat bastard!" she screams. All thoughts of Dympna disappear from my mind. Forever. I scramble up the ladder, sweat pouring, nectar for her tongue when I reach her. She's babbling now, about sisters about . . . about women being on top at last!

"Do you hear me, fatso? Wait 'til I get my hands on you! I'll give you something that'll have you moaning and rolling on the floor! I'll teach you . . ." Is she trying to give me a heart attack? I'm already climbing as fast as I can go! My gun slides from its holster and falls to the ground way below. I couldn't care less: I want her as much as I've ever wanted *every* woman. Soon. Soon I will be able to look with scorn upon all virgins.

More spanners begin to hurtle past me. Hey, maybe she really was in an army: her aim must be brilliant to come so close without ever hitting me.

Ratz and Snalez

At last I reach the top. I slide my belly onto the platform but I'm so excited it turns out to be quite a struggle to drag my bottom half onto it as well. I need tighter trousers.

She has backed away from me as if in fear. She is trembling and a sheen of very unfeminine sweat glitters on her skin in the moonlight. I am disappointed to see that she has no more spanners left, but I am as good as any woman when it comes to improvisation. As if by magic, a pair of handcuffs appear in my hand.

Tropé backs away even further, out along the arm of the crane with the ground yawning beneath her. She has to walk carefully especially as she is still only wearing one boot. I follow with my handcuffs, admiring her spirit.

"How long have you been after me?" I ask her.

She has a lovely sneer. "Any man in this world is fair game . . ."

"So why is it me you want?"

"I needed to protect Dympna, goddamn you!" Does she know about the letter Dympna has sent me, then? Does Tropé honestly believe that after I have had my way with her I won't be man enough to show her friend an equally good time? She is sadly mistaken there.

". . . and the others, all the other sisters. Tonight I was going to show them how to stand up for themselves but you have the devil's own luck. Don't think I'm gonna let you arrest me—" Suddenly her eyes widen in shock, "Oh my God! What's that behind you?"

As I turn around, she accidentally pushes against me and I fall over into the void. Somehow the open handcuffs latch onto one of the girders that make up the crane and 'though my arm is nearly wrenched from its socket, I manage to hold on. Is it my imagination? Can I hear excited women's voices coming from the ground below?

Mizz-Ann Tropé is standing above me. She is so kinky that this life or death situation actually excites her. She is magnificent. She jabs the foot with the boot on towards my head, presumably so that I can grab it to climb up to her, but when I do she actually looks surprised and plunges off the crane and tumbles a few times before splattering into the concrete. What a terrible waste! And I still have that annoying erection!

I hear hushed voices on the ground below me but I can't look just yet. I swing my legs up onto the gantry and manage to drag the rest of me after them. I am surprised by a scene taking place underneath: women, thousands of women are gathered around Tropé's body.

My surprise at seeing them there lessens considerably as they begin to mop up her blood and brains. Of course! How they love to clean things up! Gently, some of them wrap the body in cloth and carry it away, singing.

They leave flowers behind where she has lain. Others light torches and follow the corpse but there are still a few who stay behind.

These stare up at me. They seem to have found Tropé's spanners and my gun. They tap the palms of their hands with them. Surely they intend to finish the good work Tropé started! In spite of my many bruises, excitement begins to mount again. I scramble back to the platform and rush for the ladder. I'm thinking that with so many women in one place at one time, surely, surely tonight of all nights one of them will be mine!

He Who Increases Knowledge
by
Wrath James White

I never believed in God. And if I had I'm quite sure my response to a Supreme Being would not have been to prostrate myself before him and offer myself up as his eternal slave, renounce all reason and autonomy to become his unquestioning, submissive yes-man, one of his mindless cattle. I could never have offered him my throat to crush beneath his heel and my backside to kick. The very notion offends me. I might have sought to study him, after he'd been captured and caged. Run him through a few IQ and physical dexterity tests before vivisecting him and examining his organs through a microscope with thin slices of his brain laid out on slide trays. Worship? No, I would want to own him; claim his power for myself. Pretty soon, I was hoping there really was a god, actively searching for him. If such a being existed, there was hope that I could usurp its power.

It was this search for God that led me into the sciences. I studied everything from bio-chemistry and quantum physics to astronomy, psychology, and socio-anthropology. I sought him in petrie dishes, in electron microscopes, in radio telescopes, in chemical and mathematical equations, in ancient crypts and burial mounds, and in the minds of men, but he eluded me. I then took all the traditional routes. I went to churches, mosques, temples, and synagogues. I went to sights where miracles were said to have taken place. All I found were more deluded sheep following a shepherd who was nowhere in evidence. Until the day I was led, as if by fate, to a whorehouse in Mexico.

A man I'd known for some years had come to me with a tale I'd heard many times from many men but had never found so thoroughly convincing as I did hearing it from him. He told me that he'd found heaven . . . between the thighs of a woman. He told me that he'd touched God.

Big Willie was six-foot-five, two hundred thirty-five pounds of muscle bound lady-killer. Every common epithet used to describe a notorious womanizer applied to him easily. The same women who called him a no good dog still called him every night. His friends lived vicariously through him, recounting his infamous exploits while seated on bar stools and

73

knocking back forty ounces. "Pimp" and "Player" were titles he wore with pride. It made no sense to me at all to hear him talking like this.

"I found an angel. Her pussy is paradise!"

"Okay, so which deluded little slut might this be?" I asked, not just skeptical but downright hostile. I had listened to stories of his various conquests since our days in high school together and I no longer found them amusing. I felt as if he told me these things merely to feed the jealousy he knew I already had for him. My entire sexual history was barely a weekend in his life. But then, I'd never heard him lavish such praise upon a woman after he'd already slept with her. Generally he would become obsessed with some woman or other but then once he'd had her he would immediately loose interest. Once she was demystified and revealed as a mere mortal, his disappointment would become immediately apparent. I often wondered if perhaps Willie was looking for God too but just taking a different approach in his search, seeking him in the flesh. Perhaps Willie sought the goddess.

As unusual as it was to hear him talking about a woman like this, I did not regard his comments as anymore than the inevitable downfall of any man, even an unrepentant pussy hound like Willie. I assumed that he'd simply fallen in love, that this man for whom passion was a sport had finally found his competitive equal. It was only when he began to elaborate was my curiosity piqued.

"Man, I'm tellin' you, this ain't what you think. It ain't like I'm in love or nothing. I'm tellin' you, this woman's pussy is like the gates of heaven! I was fucking her and man I was like teleported straight to paradise! I saw the face of God! I could feel the entire universe!"

"In some bitch's pussy?"

"Yeah!"

"Well, what a fool I have been! Here I was looking in churches and books and all the time all I had to do was find the right piece of tail!"

"Bro, I'm not bullshitting you. Her pussy is like some kind of portal to another plane of existence! It's true! She works in this whorehouse in Tijuana and everybody down there knows about her. She's like a legend! They even pray to her! Women send their husbands to the whorehouse to fuck her as part of a religious ceremony. They call it getting "the blessing". There's even some big controversy with one of the local churches down there because they want to take her out of the brothel and put her up in the church, make her a saint and put her up on the altar. They want to make her part of the communion! But the brothel owners don't want to lose her because of the money she brings in."

"You have got to be full of shit."

He Who Increases Knowledge

"Bro, I ain't even creative enough to come up with some shit like this if I tried! You've got to come down there and see for yourself!"

So I went. On the slim chance that it was true I had to go see. I knew it was ridiculous but I was intrigued. We lived in Los Angeles so it was only a short drive to Tijuana. We jumped in the Honda Civic hatchback and made a run for the border with images of the sainted whore dancing through our minds.

The den of holiness and iniquity where the holy slut lay on a bed with legs akimbo, was a dingy little place that featured a live sex show in the basement in which women demonstrated one of the acts that had made the city famous, fucking a donkey. The upstairs lobby was littered with last ditch whores who wreaked of infection and disease. Many of them were missing teeth and had black eyes or busted lips and a profusion of other scrapes and bruises, mostly on their knees and elbows. Many of them were smoking crack pipes and shooting themselves up with heroin right there in the lobby as they sat on battered lice-ridden couches waiting for the next trick. They all had vacant eyes and hopeless expressions like prisoners at a death camp. This was the end of the road for the world's oldest profession. The place where whores came to die. I could only wonder what the hell had brought Willie here.

Willie could have anyone woman he desired. He had a way with women that went beyond his rugged handsomness or chiseled physique. He knew all the right lies to tell. Women looked into his soft brown eyes, followed the movement of his heart shaped lips, and believed every word that came out of him. Willie could make a woman feel like the most beautiful woman on the planet. Yet for some reason he had chosen to pay for sex with prostitutes that would have made the elephant man lose his appetite. The only thing that struck me more odd than Willie having been there was the site of the long line of respectable looking gentlemen of every age from nineteen to ninety-five waiting to get into a room somewhere in the back of the establishment. Every now and again a man would step out of the room and genuflect with one hand while zipping his fly with the other then the next man would cross himself and enter for his turn. Everyone in the line seemed to have a look of solemnity and piety and many of them carried bibles. This was some weird shit.

"Willie, how the hell did you find this place?"

"A cab driver brought me here. I told him I wanted some pussy and you know, I thought he'd bring me to a dance club or something. He tells me that he knows where there's some pussy like nothing else in this world. So I said, well fuck yeah! Take me there! Next thing I know we're darting through dark alleys at like eighty miles an hour and we wind up here."

"Okay, so why didn't you just turn around and leave when you found out what the place was?"

"Do you want to leave?"

I looked at the long line of men waiting to get into the room. They looked more like they were waiting to enter a confessional than a whore's bed. My curiosity was roiling like a furnace. No, I didn't want to leave. I wanted to uncover the mystery. I had to find out what was behind that door.

Another man came out with his eyes glazed as if in a religious rapture. I grabbed him and asked him what he'd seen. His eyes stared straight up at the ceiling and did not even turn my way. When he didn't reply I shook him and repeated my question in Spanish.

"*¿Qué viste?*" ("What did you see?")

"*¡Vi a Dios! ¡Vi la eternidad!*" ("I saw God! I saw Eternity!") he replied.

"*¿Quién es ella? ¿Quién es aquella mujer allá adentro?*" ("Who is she? Who is that woman in there?") I asked.

"*¡Es la puta de Babilonia! ¡María Magdalena!*" ("It is the whore of Babylon! Mary Magdalene!") he replied again, nearly swooning as he spoke in a tone that could only be described as reverent.

The whore of Babylon, the woman who'd been afflicted with seven different demons whom, according to the bible, Jesus had exorcised with a mere touch. The woman who'd watched as Christ was executed and who'd been the first to witness his resurrection, over two thousand years ago. These peasants believed that she was still alive, or had been resurrected herself, and was now throwing her legs up for money in the filthiest brothel in Mexico. I searched his eyes and the eyes of those who stood around me, mumbling prayers and clutching bibles and crucifixes to their chest as they waited to be perhaps the one-hundredth man that day to fuck the same ho, and I could see not one shred of doubt in them. Whatever lay beyond that door, it had convinced them all. This was either the crowning example of man's absolute superstitious idiocy or the most profound leap of faith I'd ever seen. More than likely, it was both. I kept thinking about a quote I'd heard years ago: " The world holds two classes of men—intelligent men without religion, and religious men without intelligence." I'd seen nations, entire cultures comprised of the latter. It should not have surprised me at all to find a brothel filled with them.

There was no way I could have left at that point. I let the man go and watched as he stumbled past me, out the doorway, and off into the shadowy street, already growing dim as the sun set and twilight slipped into darkness. He shouted something as he staggered down the street with his head pointed heavenward. Loosely translated it was something like "I have been saved! I have seen God!" Whatever it was that Willie had experienced in that room, between that woman's thighs, it was not, it seems, an isolated occurrence.

What he had told me about the locals treating the place like a house of worship was by far an understatement. Even children walking by stopped and crossed themselves. As the man who'd just left the tiny room made his way down the street people rushed out to touch him for good luck. How a prostitute could become an object of worship was completely beyond my comprehension. I had to know what it was about her that could cause such a reaction in these people and even in my own friend.

I'd spent nearly every year since high school chasing miracles and messiahs around the country. I dropped out of UC Stanton one year before achieving a doctorate in Science and Philosophy just to pursue my quest for God and have never regretted it a single day. I have seen bleeding statues of the Virgin Mary. I have seen infants worshipped as the resurrected Messiah. I have seen stigmatics bleeding with the wounds of Christ. I have seen Buddhist monks levitate and voodoo priests possessed by demons. Still, this was the most bizarre religious experience I had ever had and it had not yet even begun. Ignoring the *I told you so* look on Big Willie's face, I took up my place in line and watched as the men kissed their crucifixes and hugged their bibles while waiting in line, in a whorehouse, to pull a train on a living saint.

Nearly an hour had gone by before it was my turn to enter the little room. The man who'd gone before me was kind enough to hold open the door for me. The first thing I noticed upon entering the dingy little room were the candles. White candles by the dozens filled the room casting shadows everywhere. The second thing I noticed was the smell. The overpowering odor of semen and stale pussy hung in the air like a fog and fired in my nostrils like a mentholated nose drop, causing my nose to run and my eyes to water almost immediately. The source of the malefic stench lay unmoving on the bed with her blank weeping eyes, white with cataracts, staring vacantly at the ceiling.

She was little more than a skeleton with wrinkled and mottled flesh wrapped loosely about her brittle bones. Her hair was all but gone save for a few white follicles clinging stubbornly to her crinkly liver spotted scalp. Her mouth was a hollow crater devoid of teeth and with gums that had shrunk back against her jawbone. Her withered breasts drooped like two empty bladders from her chest and were draped on either side of her ribcage. Her ancient thighs were a maze of varicose veins from which shriveled skin sagged loosely like gooseflesh. Between them was a raw and angry gash, a worn and shriveled vagina that looked like an infected hatchet wound, leaking a steady stream of semen from the countless dozens of men who had visited her this day, if not from the hundreds and possibly thousands who had visited her over her lifetime. Her labia hung like dried and wrinkled curtains from the ghastly orifice that so many men had come to worship.

I stepped closer to the bed and leaned over the impossibly ancient woman who looked more like a mummified corpse than a living person. I whispered softly to her some stuttering greeting. There was no reply. I raised my voice slightly and shook her bed. Still she did not move or respond in any way. Her skin looked as dry and brittle as an autumn leaf but when I reached down and pinched her on the thigh, it felt tough and oily like a wallet I'd once owned made out of eel skin leather. She still gave no indication that she was even aware of my presence. The woman was catatonic. Her brain was completely gone. I lifted one of her tiny hands and felt for a pulse. It was feint but present and you could see her bird-like chest rising and falling ever so slightly as she inhaled and exhaled. At least she was alive. How could Willie have fucked this half-dead thing?

I looked back down between her thighs and could see a feint light emanating from the hairless slit. Her vaginal fluids seemed to have a chemical luminescence. I tried to approach the experiment with clinical detachment but the unctuous cocktail of fluids still weeping from her loins made the very thought of entering her a repulsive and abhorrent prospect. Still, I had come for revelation, to capture God in a bottle, and if this was the vessel he was hiding in than I had no choice but to go in after him. If all those other guys could do it than so could I. In the interest of science, I dropped my pants and mounted her.

I wasn't really too fond of missionary position but I thought it might have been somewhat blasphemous to bend her over doggy-style. I took myself in hand and masturbated to semi-erectness, imagining a naked Naomi Campbell giving me head while Pamela Anderson licked my balls and tried my best to ignore the putrescent odor emanating from the brainless vegetable I was about to fuck. As soon as I squeezed my near flaccid penis into her I knew what Willie had been raving about, what all those superstitious peasants had been so awed by. I was awed by it too. My manhood surged growing massively erect as all the blood from my body seemed to suck down into it. My very consciousness seemed to have relocated to the tip of my swollen cock. But there was no way I could have been conscious. I had to have been dreaming. Because what I was experiencing was beyond anything imaginable.

He Who Increases Knowledge

Entering her was like falling from a great height. No, it was like hurtling through space at the speed of light. I saw world's rush by as my dick slid into her sopping wet snatch. My head was filled with images that belonged to nothing on or in sight of earth. It exploded with color that I'd never seen before and that I could not describe to you now. It was just like Willie had said. I'd entered a dimensional doorway and I was as far from earth as the sun is from the nearest quasar. The harder I pumped into her the faster the universe flew by. The experience was exhilarating. It was like fucking on the head of a comet! My body was on fire with sensation. My every nerve ending was electrified! Soon I found myself at the very end of the universe, looking at it from some perspective beyond space, outside of existence. What I saw was astounding.

An amorphous semi-organic organism that seemed to be composed of living energy, stretching to infinity in all directions, so impossibly vast that the entire universe nestled within it. As I watched, entire galaxies emerged from it and others dissolved down into it. Planets formed and life emerged while other planets winked out of existence and were re-assimilated back into it, broken down and recycled into new planets. It was like a program stuck in an infinite loop of wanton destruction and recreation. I somehow found myself in some type of telepathic connection with it or rather I became aware of the connection that had always existed. I was in touch with its mind and there was not a single discernable thought. It was all thought merged into a screaming cacophony of white noise, an endless riot of thought with no order or cohesion. The voice of the entire universe in one inarticulate stew, incomprehensible except for one powerful drive—survival, continuance! But it was not concerned with the survival of any one person, or species, or world, or galaxy, but simply that something survive, that something continue, that life in some form continue to exist. Endlessly it recycled one species and created another from its ashes, an endless continuum of emergence, evolution, and inevitable extinction leading back to the emergence of new species, new planets, new solar systems, and galaxies. This was the very force of creation, the source of all life. I had found God and it was all voracious appetite and mindless creation. Not a being but a force. A force that could not be pleaded with or appealed to. A force that did not share any of the concerns of mankind. A force that could never be captured in a book or in a laboratory or in any one man's mind or heart. This was the face of infinity and no finite being would ever be able to fathom but the smallest iota of its depths. Suddenly I understood man's place in the universe. We were not the favorite children of a "Supreme Being" in whose image we were created, we were just one finite part of an infinite creation. We were grains of sand in a vast beach among countless billions of beaches. All of man's religions appeared as childish and ridiculous fairy tales and flights of presumptuous vanity compared to the reality of this.

I don't remember screaming but I must have, and the screams must have been terrifying, because Willie came rushing into the room calling my name and looking at me as if he were afraid I was going to drop dead on the spot. I turned to look for him in the doorway but all I could see was a vast sea of stars. Then the orgasm came thundering through me with the force of an exploding sun and my entire being nearly flew apart.

My body convulsed so violently that Willie had to grab me and hold me down to keep me from breaking my own neck as cataclysmic explosions went off in my head and shook me to my soul. I was abruptly jerked backwards through time and space, back to the filthy little Tijuana whorehouse where I lay weeping atop the withered husk of a two-thousand year old vegetative prostitute whose pussy was the gateway to truth, with my seed running down her inner thigh and my tears running down her cheek. I had found God. I had seen the mysteries of the universe revealed. And I wished that I had been smart enough to have left well enough alone.

I looked about me at the men who still stood in line, holding their ridiculous religious trinkets, and wondered why none of the other men who'd come into this room had been so struck by what they'd seen. Then, when I looked into their vacuous exultant faces, I knew the answer. They'd had their faith to shield them from the truth. They'd gone into that room already knowing what they'd find and no matter what they experienced their answer would always have been the same: "I have seen God!" Their God. The Christian God. There was nothing else they would ever have allowed themselves to see. Faith had blinded them to even this awesome experience. I had gone in unprotected. I reached out and took the bible from the man's hand who stood waiting to enter after me. I kept thinking about what the philosopher, Arthur Schopenhauer had said nearly a century ago—"He who increases knowledge, increases suffering. Man has but two choices, to be a happy animal or a suffering god." I should have listened. I did not want to know what I now knew. I did not want to suffer. I wanted to believe. I wanted to become one of the mindless sheep, to be a happy animal, unaware of the absolute insignificance of every breath I inhaled.

I cracked open the bible and began to read as Willie helped me out of the brothel and back into the hatchback. I read passage after passage as we traveled back up the road toward Los Angeles. I read about Adam and Eve and the Garden of Eden. I read about Moses and the Ten Commandments.

He Who Increases Knowledge

I read about the birth of Christ and the resurrection, and I began to laugh. All I could see where those planets being ingested into that mindless pitiless mass. I knew now what had sent the old prostitute into that mindless fugue. She had seen the truth. It didn't even matter if she was really Mary Magdalene or if she was actually two thousand years old or not. I would never be able to believe in anything again. The truth had set me free.

DANCING BAREFOOT ON RAZOR BLADES
by
Randy D. Ashburn

It's another one of those eight days no sleep, lotsa crystal meth, fast forward blur kinda evenings. Not that you've had a *whole* lotta experience with that sort of thing—or any?—how the hell are you supposed to remember the past when the present keeps tripping over its own fucking feet trying to become the future?—but you sure as shit have never been in this particular bar before.

Maybe.

The little girl's screaming the loudest—mommymommymommy—over and over and over again until they're just sounds, not words any more, just sounds strung together like barbed wire. One of the tall ones (gender choice c: None of the Above) slides up to her quick, quick, nice and slick, and snatches her tongue right out of her mouth. Her whole head is nothing but blonde curls and empty mouth, silent scream, bubbly gurgles now, so another one rushes over and smacks a big old kiss on the gaping hole of her face, catching the gush of blood—waste not, want not—before it hits the piss-sheened bar floor.

Vampires are so damned cool.

At least they *said* they were vampires when you met them last week— why would anybody wanna lie about something like that?—and besides, you've seen so much blood that there couldn't possibly be any other explanation.

Could there?

Anyway, they're all over the little girl now, tiny limbs jutting out in strange directions from a black-clad ball of mob, and her mama's trying to rip her own arm out of the socket and leave it dangling from the handcuff, but daddy's got no fight left 'cause they did the baby with most of it still strapped into the car seat half an hour ago, and that pretty much sent him down for the count . . .

One, two, buckle my shoe; three, four, out the door—try that particular trick and you're one dead mother fucker—*five, six, pick up hicks; seven, eight, it's way too late; nine, ten, let's do it again.*

Dancing Barefoot on Razor Blades

. . . down for the Count. Vampires. Get it? Nothing like that old two o'clock on a Saturday morning, black and white monster movie kinda humor, and you'd be laughing your fucking head off if you could just stop throwing up.

But soon enough you're through, and they're through, and sure as hell the little blonde is through, and most of them stroll away from the corpse so you can do your thing, take care of business, justify your presence at the night's festivities. But two of the women—used to be women? once-women? were-women? no, that last's too lycanthropically confusing—are still standing there pointing at the brown smear on her little yellow dress and arguing over whether she "shat" or "shit" before or after she died.

Shit, shat, chew their fat, a-hangin' off the bone . . .

And you must've said it out loud since one of the was-women is calling you a poet—hell yes you know it!—as she's slapping you on the back, red nails drawing blood, drawing hungry glances all around.

You raise your hand—didn't you used to have *five* fingers back before you met your new friends?—but they all keep right on coming your way, big, big, big toothy grins shining from every direction. And you can't believe you're giggling just because Dandy Don's crooning inside your head, "Turn out the lights, the party's over . . ." when the Dark Lady, Head Honcho, Queen of These Particular Damned, steps in between you and the rest, giving them all one of her patented slam-your-balls-against-the-roof-of-your-skull stares.

So they back off and all's quiet again, which is to say very, very, very loud, what with Marilyn Manson cranking full volume from a dozen different Dolbys, the now resumed and ever-escalating shit-shat chit-chat, and mama—once mama? was-mama? oh, screw it!—carrying-on while she carries on her late daughter's role as the festivity's official non-stop scream machine. See, some time when your back was turned the bald-headed vamp with the goofy grin tried out an amateur-hour mastectomy, and he's wearing her left boob like a party hat while he does his damnedest—huffing and puffing, grunting and pumping—to *earn* the name "mother fucker". Only, mother doesn't quite seem to get the joke. If you had time you could explain to her that it's nothing personal—just part of their unnatural nature, inevitable as sunrise and crucifixes, 'cause after all, when you shovel through all that scared-of-his-own-cock Victorian symbolism bull shit Stoker piled on top of it, even Dracula was just another rapist.

The vamps give you a very wide berth as you plop your dreaded Scooby Doo backpack next to the little girl's body. *Doctor, Doctor, give me the news; Got a bad case of exsanguination blues.*

83

And if you sang it out loud again, at least nobody mentions it this time.

You usually put the communion wafer under the tongue, but seeing as how that's not exactly an option this time—vampires are so damned cool—you stuff it into her cheek instead. "Just a pinch 'twixt the cheek and gum'll do ya," that old television cowboy—was he the one who was president?—cackles at the back of your mind, spitting a hunk of slobbery tobacco and cancerous flesh into the campfire.

Next comes the garlic.

You pack it in nice and tight, no longer amazed at just how much shit you can cram into a human mouth; 'course it never should've been a surprise in the first place considering just how much shit can come *out* of a human mouth. Stitch the dead white lips together with course black thread—mustn't drool, baby, mustn't drool—such creative needlework.

But why the hell are so many of them snickering behind pale, thin hands like you're the funniest goddamned thing in the place? Can't they see this is serious work? After all, you're running this little un-birth control clinic for *everybody's* sake, aren't you? Mr. Community-Fucking-Service, that's you! Somebody's gotta clean up the mess, after all, and we can't have just everybody who gets the Dark Kiss coming back, now can we? Without people like you, the predators would soon outnumber the prey, and then we'd all be screwed, 'cause the whole fucking world, human and vamp both, needs you, man. They all need *you.*

So why won't everybody stop laughing?

You slide your fingers through your hair and don't even want to think about what that slimy shit you feel there might be.

Just saw, saw, saw at the neck gristle—can't somebody shut her goddamned mother up?—and for christsake don't slice your finger and bring them back over here all hungry-eyed, sharp-toothed, curled-taloned, maybe-she-won't-be-able-to-stop-em-this-time insatiable. Chop, chop, chop with the meat clever at those stubborn neck bones, and you know there's a joke in there somewhere but you just can't seem to find it as you stare down into the head-sized hole between the little girl's shoulders; wide as a door, deep as a well, and for goddamned sure twill suffice, twill suffice indeed.

Whoever said we're all pink on the inside never went to the right parties. All you've seen inside these eggshell thin skins is bright, bright red, and you wonder why there's still so much blood left when the feeding's over. But the vamps, you imagine, they gotta be solid white through and through. Perfect as alabaster. Eternal as marble.

Undead, undying, un-fucking-touchable.

And that's what you really want, ain't it self-sacrificing, save-the-world Brother Bull Shit? A long-shot at immortality explains how come you fell right in line with the program when you met them last week—"Hey, college boy, wanna come to a real Fucking-A, blow your mind out your asshole kinda rave?"—and maybe they never actually *said* they were vampires, but you knew, you just knew—so, *of course* it was all your idea to learn to "live" on crystal meth so you could stay awake all night to clean up after them, and all day to make sure no Buffy-wannabes go poking their stakes where they don't belong, but they agreed quick enough, didn't they? You finally get a chance at fitting in somewhere, and God what a kick in the old corduroys when that somewhere turns out to be the same black satin and absinthe world of immortals you've always dreamed of. Reality really is stranger than fiction, huh?

So, they should just stop all the fucking laughing already.

It's not like you don't know they're probably lying about turning you into one of them. Like you—*you* of all people—really deserve to stalk the Night Everlasting. Probably just use you till your goddamned heart explodes like an over-filled water balloon from all the drugs, then suck you dry just for the buzz they'll get from the meth-laced leftovers.

But maybe, just maybe . . .

Hey, a person's gotta have faith, don't he? Otherwise, why bother?

And who really gives a flying fuck if they can't—that is, don't, *don't*, not can't!—change you into an all-powerful creature of the night? You're worm chow anyway. Tonight or half a century from now, what the hell's the difference?

You sprinkle holy water and try to hum to the rhythm of your hammer on the stake, but this time the tune just won't come. Grab a fistful of blonde curls and shove the little girl's head into the trash bag. Just try not to notice the even tinier head you put in there earlier this evening.

You're dry, used up, crashed while the night's still young. They're wet, blood-flushed, and about to start in on mama with that game where they pull the intestines out through the belly button like a straw. You know, it's funny, but until last week you'd always figured the only bodily fluid vampires were interested in was blood, but real ones don't seem nearly so finicky. Red, brown, yellow, creamy white, all seems the same to them so long as it flows when the switchblades dig in. Only, no matter how much they look like it, those aren't really switchblades, goddammit, they're fangs—six inch, pearl-handled, shiny silver metal *FANGS!*

And when they're done using them on mama, there's still daddy left to go. It's those quiet ones that always surprise you the most. Maybe there'll be one of those surprises tonight. Never know.

Just gotta have faith, remember?

Queenie runs her cold, sandpaper tongue deep inside your ear and her hand's on your crotch, going at it like she's kneading bread, only your cock seems to have forgotten what it's supposed to do at times like this. Stupid cock. You'd think it'd remember something as simple as that—even though the rest of you is having trouble focusing on Queenie's moist pink instead of all that red.

So much red.

'Course, it's not like that should come as a surprise. News flash, genius: shit like this hurts. Bad. Just what did you *think* was going on all those times you were jacking off to streams of blood dripping down Ingrid Pitt's tits? Holy Hammer horror flicks, Batman, they're monsters! And monsters are just so un-be-fucking-lievably cool.

Aren't they?

You shiver as Queenie finally releases your sore, limp dick and tells the others to stop laughing, 'cause you're doing a *good* job, and just one more night, maybe two—maybe—and they'll be about ready to turn you into one of them. But that just makes all of them start laughing again like she's told the funniest goddamned joke they've ever heard, and even she chuckles a little as she pops a couple pills between her black painted lips.

And even though the pills are red, it's getting kinda hard to believe her when she says they're really just blood clots.

You should be happy, having the chance to live out these Anne Rice dreams, but all you know is you're still so damned empty, and God you need another hit of crank *right now*, 'cause when the world's moving this slow it's too damned easy to start seeing answers to all those questions you wish you'd never asked in the first place.

Cold Plastic
by
Mark McLaughlin

The bank was downsizing, which was just a tidy way of saying that soon, heads would roll. Forty-five employees took early retirement; twenty-three were pink-slipped; and one had his hours reduced by half. That one was me, a graphic designer/copywriter in the marketing department. Mrs. Karr, the office manager, smiled as she told me the news. At the time I told friends, good thing they only cut my head halfway off. Ha fucking ha.

To augment my income, I began looking for part-time and/or free-lance work. I updated my portfolio, bought a couple suit coats, and began making calls.

After I lined up a few appointments, I mulled over whether or not to cut my hair. I lived in the Midwest, where a thirty-three-year-old man with a seven-inch ponytail is considered, at best, eccentric. The only reason the bank never groused was because I was cloistered away in marketing, where the customers never saw me. Finally, I decided to let the ponytail live: weren't creative folks supposed to be a little *avant garde*?

In the next few weeks, I visited a print shop, a graphics production studio, and three ad agencies. Unfortunately, it was mid-January, and all of these business were experiencing a winter business slump. At least, that's what they all told me.

In addition to my advertising work, my portfolio also included a few illustrations I had worked up in my spare time for some small press magazines. These illustrations depicted space ships and some rubbery-limbed aliens—nothing especially freaky. And yet, judging by the responses of the folks at those businesses, one would have thought I'd shown them snapshots of my most recent bowel movement. They would look at me with my long hair—then at the illustrations—then back at me. They wouldn't say anything, but their silence told me all I needed to know.

Eventually I took the sci-fi art out of my portfolio, and that helped. Soon, a three-person ad agency (a new business with a very relaxed atmosphere) gave me a few projects to work on. Still, I thought about the people who had stared at me and my illustrations. They worked at different companies, and yet they'd given me the same look. And they were all very corporate sorts: men with tasteful ties and forty-dollar haircuts . . . women with silk scarves draped over their stiff shoulders.

One night, my girlfriend Maggie stopped by my apartment to show me a small ad in the local newspaper. It read, PART-TIME COMPUTER GRAPHICS FOR VIDEO COMPANY. MUST BE EXPERIENCED. PAY NEGOTIABLE. SEND RESUME, followed by a P.O. Box.

"Have any idea who they are?" she asked.

I didn't know, so I shrugged. "They probably want somebody who can do computer animation."

Maggie's sculpted eyebrows scrunched together in her puppy-like Worried Face. "So you're not interested . . ?"

"I'm not really sure what they're looking for. Why?"

She gritted her teeth in an apologetic smile. "I already sent them your resume. I'm sorry. I saw the ad this morning and thought you'd want them to have a copy as soon as possible. You're the one who's always saying, 'Strike while the iron is hot.'"

A few weeks earlier, I'd given her a copy of my resume to get her thoughts on some of the wording." You don't have to headhunt for me," I said. "I can take care of myself." I suddenly realized that I was being too hard on her—she had been trying to help—so I took her hand. "Don't worry. They probably won't even call. So—do I really say that 'iron' thing a lot?"

*

Three days later, someone called at about ten-thirty p.m.

The voice on the phone was deep, but undoubtedly female. "Is this Randy Buchanan?"

"It depends," I said. "Who are you?"

"My name is Amanda Rogers. I'm with HouseCat Productions. You sent us your resume. I like your credentials." She laughed, low and throaty. "Does anyone ever call you Randy Buck? You should change your name. Randy Buck—I like that."

"Thank you, I guess." The woman's friendliness was kind of nice, but also kind of weird. "This is about the job, right?"

"Yes. We haven't filled that opening yet—" She laughed again, very softly. "—and we wanted to see if you were interested in the position."

Certainly this woman had to know she was flinging out cheesy double entendres. I wasn't sure about the job, but I thought it might be fun to

Cold Plastic

meet this strange, giddy lady. "Did you want to set up an interview?" I said. "I'm free Thursday."

"De-lish. Shall we say two-thirty?"

I said, "Sure," wondering what sort of person included *de-lish* in their business vocabulary. Amanda Rogers gave me the street address of HouseCat Productions. She added that it was on the second floor of a brick building, over a vintage clothes shop with lava lamps in the windows.

*

I arrived at the brick building about fifteen minutes before my appointment. I wanted to see if the downstairs shop had anything Maggie might like. She had a thing about campy old clothes and hairstyles. She wore her fine brown hair long and straight, with 70s-style moussed-up bangs.

The clerk was a red-haired man in his late twenties, wearing bell-bottoms and a tie-dyed T-shirt. "Peace, bro," he said to me with a goofy smile.

I smiled back. "I can dig it." As I looked over a shelf of granny glasses, a *thud* sounded on the ceiling, followed by several more. *Thud-thud, thud-thud, thud-thud.*

"What's going on up there?" I said.

The clerk's eye grew wide. "I don't know. I think they make porno movies up there. They're always banging around like that. Wouldn't it be funny if I walked outside and like, somebody shot a big wad out the window and it landed on me?"

"Hilarious." I checked my watch. It was time for my appointment.

I went to my car, took my portfolio from the trunk, and headed up the wooden staircase that led up the side of the building. The steps brought me to a sky-colored door marked with the words, HOUSECAT PRODUCTIONS: ENTERTAINMENT FOR A BLUE TOMORROW.

The waiting room of the production company had been painted light blue, with accenting purple picture frames and lampshades. The receptionist, a young Asian woman with platinum-blonde hair, glanced up from her magazine—*Biker Bondage Boys.*

"Oh, hi. You must be Randy." So saying, she took me by the hand and led me into the pulsing heart of HouseCat Productions.

What can I say? The clerk had been right. A low-budget porno movie was in full swing in the next room, which was actually three rooms with most of the walls knocked out. The stars of this production included a

89

chubby woman dressed as a stewardess, albino twin brothers, and a three-pronged, lime-green dildo.

"I can come back later," I whispered.

The receptionist giggled. "Don't be silly! Just ignore them." She nodded toward a purple door in the farthest corner of the makeshift studio.

I crossed to the door, trying to keep out of the cameraman's sightlines. I knocked, very lightly.

"Come inside," said the deep but undoubtedly female voice from that phone call.

I entered, and found Amanda tapping away at a word processor. She was a big woman: not fat, but tall and large-boned, with black hair and startling green eyes. She had high cheekbones, a long, thin nose, full lips, and a perfect alabaster complexion. Agewise, she could have been anywhere from twenty-five to forty.

The room was filled with work stations: desks covered with editing equipment, a nice graphics system with scanner, a laser printer and more. Amanda pointed to the nearest chair. "Sit down," she said. "but first, give me your portfolio."

I handed her the large leather case and took my seat. Amanda unzipped the case and fanned through the pages of printed pieces. I started to tell her a bit about my career, but she didn't appear to be paying any attention, so I shut up.

Finally she zipped up the portfolio. "Looks good. You're not a cop or a religious freak or anything, are you?"

"Nooo . . ." I didn't know how to phrase what I wanted to say next. Finally, I decided to just speak my mind. "But I don't know if I want to work for a dirty movie company."

"You'll be designing the boxes for our videos. Twenty hours a week, and you get to pick your own hours. We have all the equipment you'll need —" She snickered. "—and we'll pay you twenty-five bucks an hour."

Twenty-five dollars an hour! My mouth went sandpaper-dry. The bank paid only fourteen. And what's more, I could easily hold down both jobs at the same time.

In the other room, somebody shrieked with ecstasy.

"When do I start?" I said.

*

Working at HouseCat Productions was about eight-million times more fun than the bank. Soon, Amanda let me write the copy for the video boxes. My empurpled prose can be found on the packaging for *Blow by*

Cold Plastic

Blow, Bi and Large, Sex Toy Fever, The Adventures of Sir Pump-A-Lot, Johnny Cum Greatly and many more.

Eventually I told Maggie about the job. At first she was upset, but soon, she realized that I wasn't about to throw off my clothes and join the fun. Every now and then, I'd buy her something wacky at the downstairs store. She loved all the retro goodies I bought—plus, she was thrilled by my newfound sexual inventiveness. To discover some new and titillating erotic technique, all I had to do was watch a few minutes of the production du joir.

As I was designing the box for *Dildo Divas*, a thought occurred to me. I turned to Amanda, who was typing up the script for the next movie, and said, "These sex toy movies. Do they sell any better than the others? We seem to be putting out a lot of them."

Amanda turned to me with a raised eyebrow. "Dildos, pumps, love-dolls—plastic sells."

"Oh?" I hadn't realized that the toy-vid market had such an eager audience. "Why's that?"

Her eyebrow raised a bit higher. "Plastic makes some people hot. And vice versa."

I was still in the dark on the matter. "I don't understand."

She sighed. "It's just too hard to explain. And you probably wouldn't believe me anyway." She paused, and then said, "You've been doing some pretty good work, Randy. Starting next month, I'm raising your pay to thirty an hour."

*

The next day I had to work at the bank, and I found myself thinking about what Amanda had said about plastic.

Mrs. Karr came to my desk carrying one of my layouts. "Mr. Henderson has some corrections on the billboard," she said. "He wants you to add more information on home improvement loans."

I glanced at his 'corrections,' scrawled in red ink across my design. "You can't put that many words on a billboard." I said. "People won't have enough time to read it as they're driving by. Besides, the TV and radio ads have all that facts."

She sniffed sharply. "I'm not going to argue with the vice president of marketing. Obviously he knows what he's talking about."

"And I don't?"

Mrs. Karr flashed a stiff little pseudo-smile. "Just do as you're told. Is that clear? You're just lucky they don't have you scrubbing the toilets."

91

I studied her perfect makeup, her designer outfit, her frosty expression, and thought, *This woman is like a mannequin. It's like she's made out of plaster. Or plastic.*

As she marched away from my desk, she glanced back at me over her shoulder, and the look she gave me was like the one all those business-types had given to my sci-fi art. An aloof, suspicious look. As if—

As if I were the enemy.

*

"So tell me more about plastic," I asked.

It was a week after the Mrs. Karr incident, and I was at my desk, working late. Amanda always stayed late—he practically lived at the studio.

She had opened a bottle of wine to help her to get through her paperwork. She shot an odd glance my way. "It's waterproof and easy to clean."

I shook my head. "Plastic makes people hot. Remember?"

Amanda finished her third glass, which also finished the bottle. She opened the desk's bottom drawer. It was filled with videotapes, and she fished one out from the back of the drawer.

She then crossed to a combination TV/VCR, popped in the cassette and hit PLAY. I swiveled my chair to face the screen.

"Over the past few years," she said, "I've taped over three-hundred people having sex. This tape is a compilation of some scenes I've had to edit out. You'll see why in a minute."

On the screen, a well-muscled blond man doggy-styled a red-haired woman while an Asian woman stood by, rubbing her crotch as she watched. I recognized her as the production company's receptionist.

Suddenly, a length of what appeared to be a neon-pink dildo shot *out* of her vagina a few inches, and then slid back and forth as she climaxed. The plastic then returned inside completely.

Another scene: a fiftyish man pulled out of his partner, a much younger man, in time to ejaculate blue spunk across his back. The fluids then coalesced into a slender, semi-solid tube that slid all the way into the younger man's ass.

Scene three: Two women appeared to be fellating a double-headed purple dildo.

Suddenly they brought their heads together along the plastic tube. At last their lips met: when they separated, the dildo was gone. Both of the women then turned toward the camera. With a jolt of surprise, I recognized one of them as Amanda.

92

Cold Plastic

Amanda turned off the tape. "So now you know. Satisfied?"

"But—I'm not sure what happened." I gestured frantically toward the screen. "What that some sort of special effects? What about that stuff coming out of those people? Out of *you*?"

"At some time in all of our lives, some form of plastic is—introduced—into our bodies." Amanda removed the videotape and returned it to the desk drawer. "Contact lenses, prosthetics, birth control devices, sex toys, you name it. Sometimes we ingest bits of plastic by accident. Kids swallow little toys all the time. Usually, the plastic allows itself to be removed, or expelled. But sometimes, some of the plastic will stay inside. And grow. Almost everyone has some form of plastic living inside of them. And most haven't the slightest clue."

Lifting her leather mini-skirt just a little, Amanda straddled me on my chair. She then cradled my face in her hands. Suddenly I realized that my pants zipper was being pulled down.

"What are you doing?" I whispered.

She drummed the sides of my face lightly with her fingers. "Good question."

I sat up just as—something—grabbed at my cock. Amanda fell off my lap, and for a moment, I caught a glimpse of her crotch. There, a little purple hand waved to me, just before popping back into its nest of dark curls.

"I have more control over my plastic than most," Amanda said matter-of-factly as she straightened her skirt. "It's tricky stuff. It can move . . . hide . . . masquerade as real flesh. There are two kinds of the stuff out there—I call them Hot and Cold Plastic. If you have any at all, I'm sure it's the hot kind. That's why I was flirting with you on the phone when I first called. To check you out. People with Hot Plastic are usually . . . Wacky. Fun-loving. Adventurous."

"But—" It dawned on me that I was still staring at her crotch. So I looked her in the eye. "How come coroners don't find all this stuff in dead bodies?"

"Maybe they do, and they're not talking: a cover-up. Or maybe the stuff abandons ship when we die." She put her hands on my shoulders. "Now. Shall we find out if you have any plastic in you . . ?"

I squirmed away from her and took a step toward the door. "I don't think I want to hear any more. This is all just too damn freaky. I just want to go now."

"But I haven't told you about Cold Plastic yet. It's different—"

"I don't want to know," I said. On the way out.

*

I spent the night with Maggie. On the way to her place, I decided not to tell her what I knew. As I made love to her, I tried to feel around inside her with my cock. Searching for plastic. She had no idea what I was trying to do, but she loved it.

In the morning, she made scrambled eggs and served them up on plastic plates, with plastic forks. Without a word, I transferred our breakfasts to china plates.

"That's sweet," she said as I handed her a silver fork. "Making our breakfast so romantic."

At my job at the bank, I watched Mrs. Karr as she walked her pigeony little walk around the office. I figured that whatever Cold Plastic was, corporate types had to be full of it. That, I decided, was why they hated my long hair, and my drawings of rubbery, sinuous aliens. Those things reminded them too much of Hot Plastic.

Mrs. Karr marched up to my desk. "Will you please stop staring at me?" she hissed. "I will not have you undressing me with your eyes, you—you disgusting *hippy*." I noticed that all the other anal retentives in the office were staring in my direction. Even jowly old Mr. Henderson was there, watching from behind the water cooler.

"Frankly, Mrs. Karr," I said, distractedly, "I only wish that my eyes could put more clothes on you. I'm tired of looking at your droopy Cold Plastic ass."

As Mrs. Karr's face twisted into a mask of rage, I felt my heart rise up in my throat. What had I just *said*?

She turned toward the others in the office. "*He knows,*" she rasped. Her voice sounded like broken glass being ground underfoot.

"*He knows!*" Henderson hissed. His hands shot up into the air, fingers curled into talons.

"*HE KNOWS!*" the Marketing Department cried in unison. "*HE KNOWS! HE KNOWS! HE KNOWS!*"

As I watched, all of those corporate tight-asses *broke down* into foot-long scarlet grubs with mandibles and tiny pellet-eyes. Soon their clothes were scattered about the floor like discarded husks. Mrs. Karr's head turned into a fat grub covered with thick bristles. Out of Mr. Henderson's pants crawled a smooth, tubular grub—the head of it was shaped like a misshapen helmet. The penis-grub grunted at me and began to spit thin streams of greenish venom.

The creatures sprouted dozens of spindly legs and scrambled toward me. Some of them grew wings and soared around my head. I grabbed one

94

of the grubs out of the air and threw it against a copying machine. It cracked in half—its shell was only brittle plastic—and began to leak yellow steam and thick gray slime.

I picked up the computer keyboard from my desk and began smashing the monstrosities, one by one. They shrilled like dying birds when I crushed them. I chased the horrible creatures all around the office. A few of them raked me with their claws, but within a few minutes, I knew that I'd won the battle. The last one to die was the penis-grub: I tipped over the water cooler on it, and the ugly thing burst with a satisfying *splat.* The creatures had made a big mistake when they changed form: they may have been ugly and vicious, but they were also awkward and laughably fragile.

I heard raised voices and footsteps out in the hall. Snatching a special little souvenir off the floor, I left the building by way of the fire escape.

*

That evening, I stopped by the production company to talk to Amanda. I wasn't too surprised to find two people making love on a mattress in the studio—until I realized they were Amanda and the clerk from the clothing shop.

Amanda disengaged herself and gently pushed the smiling buffoon to the side. "What's up?" she said.

"Oh. Um . . ." For a moment, I'd forgotten why I was there. "Just wanted to let you know that—Well, I'm okay." I didn't know how much to say in front of the clerk. "I'll be back to work on your boxes in the morning."

"I'm glad to hear that. I was afraid I'd scared you off." She smiled crookedly. "I came on pretty strong. Won't happen again. Unless, maybe, you want it to." She reached for a wine glass by the side of the mattress and took a sip of chablis. "See you tomorrow, bright and early. We're starting production on *Meter Maids in Heat.*"

I nodded and backed out. The clerk nodded back, like one of those wobbly-headed toy dogs people keep in their cars.

Over the next few days, I watched the TV news and read the papers, but the incident at the bank was never mentioned. No mention of the missing employees or the dead insect-creatures. A cover-up? No big surprise. Ah, well. At least I have my souvenir: a segment of bristly scarlet shell.

I use it to scrub the toilet.

Sacred Mutations
by
Richard Gavin

She's left the room again. I reached my hand to her side of the bed, hoping to meet with the cool softness of her back, but I find myself alone. The clock on the bedside table reads three-seventeen am. The streetlight outside my bedroom window casts an austere band of yellow light across the otherwise unlit room.

I can hear the sound of running water coming from the bathroom down the hall.

She must be at the sink again. Scrubbing it away. Cleaning it. Sculpting it anew.

My head feels heavy. Too much vodka again tonight. I have to piss but I refuse to walk into the bathroom. I stumbled in on her like that once before, purely by accident. She'd been in there for so long that night that I thought she had passed out, perhaps banged her head on the sink. She could be in there bleeding to death. All of these thoughts raced through my mind as I pushed the bathroom door open.

The harsh light from the naked bulb stung my eyes and I instinctively squinted them shut. But not before I saw her sitting, one leg prostrated on the porcelain tub, the other stretched out straight in front of her. The hem of her silk robe had fallen away, exposing the naked body beneath. I caught her just as she was reaching for the small sewing kit resting on the basin. There was a scream, but I can't recall if it was hers or mine.

I didn't sleep for three nights after that. My insomnia was partly due to the horrors I'd stumbled upon, but due more so to an overwhelming sense of guilt. I knew that it was all my fault, that I had driven her to this extreme.

*

The light has gone off in the bathroom. The door's groaning open. I can hear the faint, measured taps of her bare feet against the hallway floor.

Sacred Mutations

Roll on my side. Eyes closed and face complacent. Please God, don't make me feel her again.

She must be standing in the doorframe. I can sense a shape looming over me. A creak of the floorboards, a rustle of cloth as her robe crumples at her feet.

My name is being whispered. I struggle to maintain the illusion of sleep.

Her knee presses down on the mattress.

Fingers slipping underneath the sheet, peeling it back, slowly, erotically, as if it were some kind of foreskin. Her breath is hot and moist against the nape of my neck. I groan as if suddenly awakened.

Her mouth feels familiar against mine. After nineteen years it should. I recognize so many things about the woman who now straddles me in the darkness. I savor the scent of her favorite flowery shampoo as her mane sweeps across my face. I love the feel of her breasts as she presses my palms against them. I want so much to love *all* of her, but I cannot. There are aspects of her that I do not recognize.

*

I don't know how long she knew about the affair. Perhaps she suspected my infidelity long before she found any proof that her fears were anything more than a wife's protectiveness. But my inadequate lies eventually unraveled under her astute questioning. The affair lasted only five months, but I know that my wife and I will both suffer eternally for it.

She'd asked me why, and the only reason I could offer was vapid and hollow. I was bored, restless. That was all.

She cried for days, threatened to divorce me along with all the other reactions one would expect. But when she called me home from work early one afternoon and began to tell me that she knew the affair was all her fault, I could do little more than stare at her both in horror and in pity. I can still see her all balled up on the living room sofa, tear-soaked tissue clutched in one fist, babbling about how her body had become "so grossly familiar" to me.

That's when she promised me she would change.

It started innocently enough: dying her hair a bolder shade of red, buying revealing negligees. But she quickly tired of these techniques and feared that I would do the same. She constantly asked me if she felt any different to me. I innocently told me no, but that I loved her as she was.

My answer did little to ease her paranoia. In fact it seemed to intensify it.

She began to re-form herself. Night after night I hear her sneaking away into the washroom. I cringe every time I hear her scrounging through the sewing kit in search of needles and thread, or trimming scissors, or stickpins. She wants me to feel as though I'm in a different woman every night. Wants to eliminate any desire to stray from her.

*

I can feel myself growing erect. A biological reaction, one I cannot fight, no matter how I try.

She hisses as I slide inside of her. Tonight she's stitched up, tight and virginal. Other nights it feels like a great open wound, or the intricate folds of some fleshly flower.

Every night she re-sculpts it for me.

Every night I find a stranger in my bed.

Mournful Tune
by
Teri A. Jacobs

He straddles her face and rubs his hard cock against her luscious mouth, those lips redly stung with her arousal.

Slip of her tongue, she teases him. Round his head, making tiny wet circles. Up, down and across the vein of his erection, flicking pleasure. Her hand grips and guides his cock into her mouth, and he watches her lips encircle his width, watches his length slip into her moist hollow. Throat opened, she takes his entirety in. His dark pubic coils tickle her nose; his balls hang against her chin.

And hungrily she sucks. That tongue still toying with his shaft, building him with slow, aching strokes.

He pulls back a bit, then thrusts into her mouth, into her throat. Into the musical vibrations of her moans. Again and again. Her Aegean-blue eyes glisten with desire, and her long fingers dig into his hips, urging his rhythm harder, faster, deeper.

With abandon, he fucks her mouth.

Her beautiful, warm, wet, suckling mouth.

"I want to cum on your face," he groans, feeling the incredible charge of his cock hammering against the back of her throat, his orgasm coaxed on the edge by her moist friction.

She giggles her *yes*.

Delicious tremors of her want titillate him.

And he withdraws at the last second. His cock pumps salty cream onto her face. Semen splashes across her finely sculpted cheeks and dribbles down the sides into the strands of her black-velvet hair. Happily she licks the slick spill off her lips.

Then licks his cock again, until he stiffens for another performance.

She spreads her legs, offering her gaping pink sex.

Knelt between her thighs, he inhales her musky perfume and, with his talented fingers, strokes her clit. Gentle as if caressing with tulip petals. Her breath catches, then quickens, and her pelvis lifts toward his fingers. He increases the pressure and pace. Across her chest, passion's blood

99

flushes her skin, plumps her breasts, and darkens her hardening nipples. Fingers tickling her soft labia, darting into her quivering quim, he bends down, takes a nipple inside his mouth and nips the bud. She murmurs lasciviously.

He slides his fingers from her silken sex. Glosses her lips with her own inner lubricant. Wraps those fingers around her neck and thumbs deeply the cords of her throat as he enters her.

Beneath him, her body tenses. She clenches her legs around his waist and drums her hips against his, mouth gasping for air, fucking in breathless carnality. He squeezes his hand in concert with her tightening vagina.

She shudders.

Her undulating orgasm kicks off his own, and he spends himself within her before collapsing beside her and releasing his hand. She gulps in shivery breath.

"You just played me like a fine violin." She reaches for him, but he's already moving away from her and putting on his robe.

"I guess you weren't paying too much attention to the orchestra because I play the cello, a 1673 Jacquline du Pre Stradavarius." He sways to the music in his mind. "*Concerto in D Minor for Cello and Orchestra*. I think Edouard Lalo knew one day I would be born to play that solo."

"You were magnificent! You played with such passion."

"My critics say I'm an exuberant performer, matched in talent by no one. Superbly in tune to the very heart of music." He closes his eyes and hums.

"And what made the great Carl Mantel want me?" Leaning back against the pillows, she cups her hands over her breasts.

"I need the heart put back into my music," he says, brushing the wisps of distinguishing gray hair from his eyes. "Like Orpheus, my Eurydice was taken from me forever."

"How poetic," she sighs, like they all do when he tells the story. Orpheus could lull a dragon to sleep with the power of his lyre, but he couldn't quell the desires of love struck women. When Carl worked his fingers and bow fast enough to make the cello sing as sweet and high as the tender-stringed violin, women swooned in the audience. All soft bosom bodies with hard, wanton eyes.

The women of Thrace repaid Orpheus' heroism by tearing him to pieces. All because he couldn't stop loving his dead wife.

"My cello won't make a sound after a performance unless I give it a new voice." He slips the sash off his robe and wraps it around her right wrist. She giggles.

Mournful Tune

"How do you give it a new voice?" They all ask.

He ties her other wrist and fastens the binds to a leather strap attached to the bed.

"I will show you later, but the more important question is why does my cello turn silent?" He covers her mouth with his hand and pinches her nostrils together. Her eyes open wide, two musical notes under a deep line in her brow. With his other hand, he plays between her legs, his fingers conducting Gershwin's *Rhapsody in Blue* inside her. He removes his hand from her face, and she sucks in the air between gritted teeth. Her nearing orgasm steals her breath this time.

"When my wife died, she haunted my cello. You know how I knew?"

She shakes her head, and the scent of coconut drifts up to him in waves.

"It would play no other note besides E flat. I always played a certain piece for her in E flat, so I knew my Zoe was with me, and I could almost hear her lovely voice singing. Something I hadn't heard since she was attacked." Carl withdraws his finger abruptly from her, and she makes disappointed sounds, her voice as grating as an untalented flute player showing off.

"What happened to her?" She pulls on the knots above her head, but they don't budge.

"Zoe was an international star, a soprano singer." He stops and remembers the first moment he saw her perform, in Rome outside at the top of the Spanish Steps. She sang in sotto voca. He fell in love with her voice, and he couldn't understood why Odysseus would plug his ears not to hear the sirens sing and sail his ship into the crags. Carl would've gladly met any rock face just to listen to Zoe's melodious tune. It was at that moment that Carl knew music in his soul.

When he played his solo that night, with the Pope in the balcony, he played to her voice. Each note on his cello carried her breath. He closed his eyes and allowed her to guide his fingers. It was his most brilliant performance, and he had never even met the woman who could bring out his greatest talent. She was his Muse.

He attended the Pope's reception for the orchestra, but Carl was hopelessly distracted. He nodded his head when spoken to and smiled, and everyone had assumed he'd drank too much; although, he carried the same flute of Dom Perignon the entire night. He thought only of her, her golden tresses and a beauty fashioned after Aphrodite, her glorious mouth spilling out song like the sun shines life to the earth.

Around midnight, like some phantom of the opera, Zoe sidled to his side and took his arm. They didn't exchange a word, but their glances contained every epic of intense love ever imagined. They left for his room, cheeks ruddy with anticipation, eyes gleaming. Once upon the bed, she spoke.

"Play Bach's Hercules at the Crossroads, 'Chorus of the Gods.' I want to sing for you. I want to make you feel as much as you made me feel tonight during your solo."

The height of her voice piqued his ears, and he wept, for he found heaven's bliss. Only then did she kiss him. Their bodies fluid together while they made love, the most beautiful music.

"Carl? What happened to your wife?" A blaring mistake of a note.

"She had stopped off at the bakery. She loved Italian Biscottis. On her way to her car, a man grabbed her from behind and put a knife to her throat. Zoe handed over her purse as he asked, but then he got a different idea and ripped her pants down. She fought him." *My brave, stupid Zoe.* She should've let him penetrate her with his dick and not his knife, he thinks as he always does at this point in the story. The cruel Fates wouldn't allow it. "The man stabbed her in the throat, but he didn't kill her. It was a shallow strike, and it went into her voice box, severing all her sound. I wished he had cut her eyes out. A blind world she could've lived with but not a silent one."

"Oh, how horrible!" They exclaim, skimming only the surface of how horrible it really was.

The siren's wail was empty. Zoe thrashed in the hospital bed, her mouth wide open in silent screams, the veins popped out above the bandages from straining. Her lips had turned blue from lack of oxygen and tears flowed from bloodshot eyes. If Carl had the option of not looking at her, he wouldn't have tortured himself with her anguished face, but he was drawn to her like Orpheus to Eurydice. He couldn't help but look before they made it out of Hell.

He read in her eyes that she hated the pity she received from well meaning friends and family. He read in her eyes the depth of her sorrow, a mirror to his own.

"Zoe killed herself the first day after they released her from the hospital. The reddish fluids hadn't even stopped soaking through her bandages yet," he tells the stranger on the bed. "She swallowed the entire prescription of Demerol. She didn't even say goodbye to me." Carl laughs, scaring the woman. She's the first not to find his laughter endearing, and maybe he wonders if his mania shows through. "She couldn't say goodbye. The irony of it. She didn't even think to write a note!" The tears come now, racking his body with old mourning.

"I'm sorry," she whispers.

Mournful Tune

"Do you know what it's like to lay in bed at night, knowing the warm body you used to hold is cold in a grave? Six feet of dirt and worms separate your arms from your one true love. I can't fall asleep because I'm afraid if I die, then I will lose her. I'm afraid of oblivion and all the darkness that would suffocate my memory of her. I don't know if I believe we will be together again in the hereafter. It frightens me to lose her forever. I've already lost her once, but she's with me when I play." Carl rises from the bed and heads for the closet. He drags out his cello. "In my mind, I can hear her singing every note I need to play. My Muse has never left me, but she needs to replenish her voice."

"I don't understand," the voice on the bed says.

"If you listen to the cello, it sounds like a woman's cry. I've discovered if I fill my cello with a woman's cry, then I will have my Zoe's voice singing again for me. I need to keep her with me. It's all I know to do."

Carl stands on the bed above her, holding the cello up so that its stand centers on her throat. The woman screams, her voice strong. He shoves the cello down as if he were on stage, and the platform of her neck accepts the stand's sharpened point. The woman's blood and cries spill.

"Such a mournful tune," he says as he picks up his bow and plays Chopin's "Nocturne" in E flat. His song for Zoe.

Pieces of the Game
by
G. Durant Haire

Cameron admired himself in the hall mirror. He adjusted his breastplate and straightened his cape. The only thing he didn't like about the costume was the tunic; it reminded him of a dress. He had no idea why those hard-ass Roman soldiers wore the silly looking things.

A horn blared from the driveway. He popped an Altoid in his mouth, grabbed his plastic helmet, and proceeded out the door.

"Sixteen-fourteen Tremont," he told the driver. "The Mythic Club."

He'd decided to go to the Mythic's Halloween costume party. Gothic dance clubs weren't his thing, but he was feeling wild tonight, hell, he was wearing a dress for God's sake, and he wanted to try something a little different. And the Mythic was definitely that.

It was six when he arrived at the old brick warehouse that housed the club, and already the crowd was growing. He paid the cover charge and stepped into another world.

Eerie dance music throbbed in the background, and strobe lights fired like stop-frame machine guns, making everyone move in slow motion. He stood in the smaller of the two main rooms that made up the club. The larger room reminded him of a vast cave full of pounding rhythms and pulsating bodies.

As he squeezed past all sorts of ghouls and creatures he noticed the decorations. Baby dolls, smeared with what he assumed to be red paint, hung by their plastic feet from the ceiling. Life-size skeletons stood cruci-fied to the corrugated tin walls, and hideous jack-o-lanterns grinned from every corner. They had the place done up right, but he suspected it looked this way year round.

Cameron pushed his way to the bar, ordered a Killian's, and began searching for tonight's lucky woman.

Several vampires looked promising, one of which had enough cleavage to hide in, and he noticed an especially hot mummy whose bandages hung loosely over all the right parts. But nothing clicked; he didn't feel drawn.

Then, as he turned to get another beer, he saw her. A tattered red sofa supported her thin figure. The spot to her left vacant, as if she had been

104

saving it just for him. She wore a black dress that looked like it had been drawn on with a black marker. Ample breasts strained against the tight fabric, nipples erect. Long hair the color of midnight draped her shoulders and touched the small of her back. Her makeup was done to make her look pale and gaunt, but she was beautiful. Elvira had nothing on this girl. Something clicked and he was drawn.

She smiled at him, the corner of her mouth and her eyebrow rising at the same time as if attached by an invisible string. He returned the smile and walked to the couch.

"This seat saved?" he asked, motioning to the empty spot beside her.

"Saved for you," she said. "Sit."

"My name's Cameron," he said.

"I'm Sindy."

"Pleasure to meet you Sindy. Can I get you a drink?"

"Why, yes," she replied slyly, "I'll have a Bloody Mary."

"Don't go anywhere, I'll be right back." Cameron smiled as he got up and headed to the bar.

Cameron returned with the drinks and began the small talk. He was the manager of a video store and lived in a nice apartment east of the club. She owned an antique store downtown. She inherited it and her house when her mother and father died several years ago.

It was after eight now and the music, the crowd, and the smoke were increasing. Cameron was about to hit her with the "let's-go-somewhere-quieter" line when she beat him to it.

"Listen, I hate to be so forward, but do you think we could go somewhere a little less . . . congested? I've got a thing for soldiers in skirts."

"Uh . . . yeah, sure, did you have any place particular in mind?" Cameron felt that warm, tingling sensation begin in his groin.

"We could go to my place, if that's okay with you," Sindy replied, flashing a wickedly sexy smile.

"No, that's fine by me," he said, stoically controlling his excitement. "I've got a thing for pale women in black."

"Oh, one thing I forgot to mention. My girlfriend, Eva, will be there. She gets a little jealous if I don't share my men with her. I hope you don't mind."

Cameron's reply caught in his throat, or more correctly, his crotch. *Did he mind? Was she kidding?*

"It's fine by me," Cameron replied, his mind already creating sexy scenarios.

Sindy smiled and Cameron thought he glimpsed something in her eyes, something feral, predatory. He knew his intuition might be trying to sound an alarm, but he wouldn't listen. There was just no way he could pass up a three-way with two hot women.

*

The cab came to a stop in front of Sindy's estate. A huge, weathered Victorian peered from a shroud of trees, and an ancient iron fence encircled the grounds adding further atmosphere and seclusion. Cameron was impressed; her parents had probably left her a pile of money as well.

He paid the driver and they ascended the creaking steps to the front porch.

"This is a beautiful house," Cameron said, admiring the imposing structure. "Do you live alone?"

"Yes, I do," Sindy said, unlocking the front door, "but it's not so bad. I've managed to keep a few friends."

"And speaking of friends, when will I get to meet Eva?"

"Soon," Sindy said.

The door swung open, and she invited him in.

Just as Cameron stepped into the foyer, he smelled something foul, a rotten sweetness. But it only lasted for a few seconds before the musty odor of the house absorbed it.

Sindy led Cameron down the hall a short way and into a den off to the right.

"Would you like a beer while you wait?" Sindy asked.

"Wait?" he replied curiously.

"I've a few things I need to attend to. I need to make sure Eva is ready. I won't be a minute."

She brought him a beer and disappeared up the stairs.

Cameron sipped the beer and looked around the room. The inside of the house looked as impressive as the outside. A huge chandelier hung from a nine-foot ceiling. The furniture was old and expensive. A fireplace gaped on one wall and resting on the grate, instead of wood, was an obese jack-o-lantern. Flame flickered brightly through its triangular eyes and jagged smile.

A Bosch hung above the mantle, and Cameron walked over to get a closer look. He saw agony in the inhabitants of the painting, and as he moved closer, it seemed he could hear their suffering as well. But something was wrong. The voices weren't in his head; he could actually hear them. He took a step back and listened. Coming up through the fireplace were low, tortured moans. Puzzled by the sounds, Cameron bent down and leaned in close to the fireplace.

Pieces of the Game

"It's the wind."

Cameron jumped, startled by Sindy's sudden appearance.

"Damn, you scared the shit out of me."

Sindy took Cameron's arm and led him to the couch.

"I thought I heard voices coming from the fireplace."

"Just the wind. It happens frequently. That fireplace is connected with one in the cellar. When the wind blows it acts like a huge whistle."

Sindy took Cameron's empty beer bottle and blew into the top making a deep whistling sound.

Cameron wasn't totally convinced. What he'd heard sounded more like voices than wind. But, after seeing the way Sindy's full lips caressed the bottle, he had to give her the benefit of the doubt.

"You need to relax," she said, reaching down and massaging his crotch through his costume. "Would you like me to help you?"

Cameron simply nodded.

"Then follow me."

He followed her up the creaking stairs, enthralled by the rhythmic sway of her hips. He imagined Sindy on her hands and knees offering that beautiful ass to him. He imagined sliding himself into her while he watched Sindy lick her girlfriend.

He felt himself getting hard and chased the thought from his mind. He wanted this experience to last as long as possible.

Sindy led him into the bedroom. Candles littered the room and smoking incense swirled the scent of sandalwood into the air. He took note of the sparse but elegant furnishings.

A dresser stood against the wall to his right, and he noticed a door in the left wall that he assumed to be a closet or bath. Positioned in the center of the room was a large canopy bed. Cameron had never seen a bed like this. It reminded him of a tent. The dark, lacy canopy rose to a point over the center of the bed and hung down to drape the entire structure. A single nightstand stood to the right of the bed supporting many dripping candles. The only thing missing was Sindy's girlfriend.

"How do you like it?" Sindy asked, taking hold of one of his arms and pulling him toward the bed.

"It's cool, very unusual," he replied, offering no resistance. He couldn't wait to put the bed to good use.

She stopped him at the side of the bed, and began to undress him.

"Lets get these silly props off so I can see what I've got to work with."

"Where's your girlfriend?" Cameron asked, trying to mask the lust in his voice. The thought of doing two women simultaneously nearly drove him crazy.

107

"She's just down the hall. Don't worry, she'll join us shortly. But for now, I'm going to take care good care of you."

She looked deep into his eyes as she removed his helmet. He saw that predatory look again. It almost unnerved Cameron, but as she unbuckled his sword belt, he dismissed it.

She walked around behind him and pulled off his cape. It fell between them and she reached under his arms and pulled herself close into his back. He could feel the heat coming off her as she caressed his breast-plate. She moved back in front of him, popped off the plastic armor, and began licking and his neck.

As her wet tongue ran up and down his neck, Cameron could feel the blood rushing to his groin, and a thickening in his briefs. He moved to embrace her, but she quickly seized his arms and forced them down to his sides.

"Not yet, we're not ready for that. First, we've got to play a little game," she said, pulling off his tunic. She grabbed his briefs and slowly pulled them down, freeing the throbbing prisoner within.

She knelt and took him into her mouth, sucking fiercely. Her head pistoned back and forth as she glared up at him. A few seconds later, she stopped as suddenly as she started.

"Shit, don't stop," Cameron said, tearing off his undershirt.

"What did I tell you? We've a game to play first."

"What kind of game? I don't know if I can take much more of this teasing."

"Just think of how much better it'll feel when you finally get to push yourself into my hot pussy, while you watch me take care of Eva." Sindy pushed him back onto the bed.

Cameron let himself fall onto the bed. He drew in a deep breath of sandalwood. Listening to Sindy's dirty talk made his balls ache. He imagined sharing the women as they shared themselves.

Sindy turned and slinked over to the dresser. She pulled out two scarves and went back to the bed.

"You going to tie me down?" Cameron asked, putting on a sultry voice. "Kinky."

"I'm glad you approve. Appropriate for Halloween, don't you think?"

She pushed him back down on the bed and straddled him.

"Only, I'm not going to tie you, I'm going to blindfold you. I'm using two to make sure you can't peek. But, you won't be able to touch either. It's part of the game. You have to keep your hands to yourself. It amplifies the desire, the lust. By the time I'm through with you, you'll be ready to

Pieces of the Game

scream. And I'm serious, I'm in charge. You play by my rules. If you touch, you won't get any. I'm sure you wouldn't want that, would you?"

"No, oh no, I'll be a good boy, I promise. Why don't you ask Eva to come on in?"

"Patience dear, patience."

She tied one black scarf a little higher than the other so she was sure that he couldn't steal a peek.

"Now just relax, I'll be right back."

"Where're you going?" he asked, lifting his head and staring around blindly.

"To get Eva and the pieces of the game," she said, pulling the door closed behind her.

Cameron lay there, his heart pounding and his dick throbbing. He reached down and gave it a few strokes. He didn't mind a little kink in the name of fun, but he hoped she didn't get too wild. He didn't know what type of game pieces or toys she had, but he didn't want her trying to stuff a ten-inch dildo up his ass. There were lines he wouldn't cross. Of course, he couldn't wait to make it with two women. He'd been waiting since puberty to cross that line.

He heard the door swing open with a moan followed by a squeaking noise that reminded him of bad shopping-cart wheels.

"I'm back," she said, pushing a cart to the end of the bed.

"What's that noise?" Cameron asked, once again looking around blindly.

"It's my cart, saves me from having to carry all the stuff in here."

"Damn, how many toys do you have?"

Sindy giggled in reply, and Cameron felt the bed sink as she climbed on.

"Where's Eva?" Cameron asked, tilting his head back trying to see beneath the blindfold.

"She's here, but just as you, she's incapacitated. You'll experience her when *I'm* ready for you to, not a moment sooner, understand?"

"Oooh yes, mistress, I understand."

"Good, boy. Now this is how the game works. I'm going to pleasure you with an object, and you have to try and guess what it is. No touching, no peeking. I can send Eva back as easily as I brought her."

"Okay. But just remember, I can only take so much teasing."

Sindy took the first item and folded it around his hardened gland. She slowly began moving the object up and down, squeezing with her hand to increase the pressure.

"What is it?"

The object was warm and slippery, but he could tell what it was by the clumsiness of her attempt.

109

"It feels like someone needs a lesson in how to jack a man off," he said with a chuckle.

"A hand, very good," Sindy said. "Now for number two."

She set the first toy aside and grabbed the next one with both hands. She placed it over his dick and began pumping again.

This one was tight but unsubstantial. It had a familiar feel, but not complete enough for him to place.

"And this?"

"I don't know what this one is, but I do know that you're turning me on."

"Guess."

"Okay, a cheap sex toy, a pocket pussy or something."

"Close, but no."

"Well, what is it." Cameron started snaking a hand down to investigate. Sindy slapped his hand away.

"No touching," she snapped.

Cameron couldn't remember when he'd been this horny. The suspense was driving him crazy. He felt ready to explode. And what she slid onto his engorged meat next pushed him to the edge. It was hot and tight. The game was about to be over; he couldn't hold back any longer.

"What is this one?" Sindy asked, rapidly pumping the thing up and down Cameron's straining dick.

Cameron answered with a violent orgasm, moaning and shooting loads of semen into the object. As his heart pounded and the final ripples of pleasure escaped his body he tore off the blindfold, dying to know what had caused such a powerful orgasm.

The first thing he saw was the blood. Sindy was covered with it. She sat back on her heels, grinning like a demon; a large serrated knife in one hand, the other behind her back.

Then he saw the body. It lay on the cart, glistening crimson in the candlelight. Time seemed to slow, images flashed before him like scenes from a low-budget horror film.

It was female minus the head, pubic area, and right hand. A ragged hole gaped in the chest.

Cameron fought to close his eyes, but it was too late. He saw the hand and vagina on the bed next to him. He found the heart impaled on his rapidly shrinking dick. For a fleeting moment, he thought it might just be a Halloween prank, but the metallic smell of blood had over powered the dying incense, and he realized this was no game at all.

Now more beast than beauty, her eyes burning with insanity, Sindy moved her hand from behind her back and held the head out to Cameron.

Pieces of the Game

"Cameron, meet, Eva. She's been just dying to give you head."

Cameron let out a horrific scream, ripped the gory heart from his penis, and leapt from the bed. He slipped in blood and slammed hard into the closed door. He pulled frantically at the knob, but it was locked.

Cameron spun and ran for the door across the room. He slipped again, falling against the cart, upsetting Eva's remains. He collected himself and dashed out the door that he had previously assumed to be a closet. It led to another hallway.

Sindy sprang from the bed like a crazed ape. As Cameron frantically searched for an unlocked door, she crouched in the doorway rubbing Eva's face against her crotch.

"Cameron, where're you going? Don't you want to fuck us!" Sindy screamed, her voice full of broken glass and nightmares. "I'm hot as hell and Eva's still warm!"

Cameron ran down the hall trying each of the doors. They were locked. All except the last one. He jerked it open and stared down at a flight of stairs. He looked back. Sindy was waving the knife and violently pumping her hips against Eva's head. He thought about attacking her, but in the hands of a psychopath the knife would be more like a chainsaw. Cameron had no choice. He bounded down the stairs, praying that it would lead him to a way out.

As he reached the last step, he heard the door slam and the lock being set. It was dim and cool in the cellar, and the rottenness he'd smelled before hung thick in the air. He heard the desperate moans that he'd listened to upstairs, and walked toward the sound. He found a man and woman huddled in a corner. They were naked and gaunt, lying on a pile of filthy linen. Food scraps and feces lay all around. Their eyes were vacant and hopeless; their voices truly nothing more than wind.

Cameron searched for a door, but found only stone walls. He'd been trapped like an animal, and as Sindy's depraved laughter echoed through the house, Cameron realized that he would soon be the next supplier of game pieces.

Soft
by
C. C. Parker

Mother's naked breasts sagged a little and the nipples were scarred from too many sucklings. What can I say? I was dissatisfied, even sickened. And her vagina was a gaping, tangled mess of puffed out labia and whitish pubes.

"Miles? Where are you going?"

"I don't know," I said.

"But I'm hungry for it."

I hated when she talked that way. It made me want to vomit. It made me want to run as far away as possible. Still, I knew if I tried that I would always return . . . always. She was my mother, and I her son. My father, her husband, had died so many years ago that he was nearly gone for good.

"I'll be back," I said.

"First," she said, rubbing the clitoral protuberance jutting from the leaky mess.

"Maybe when I get back."

I also hated when she pouted, complained, bitched. She killed father with her bitching, and I knew that she would kill me too. Not even Jesus Christ would have been able to withstand it.

We found dear old dad bathing in a pool of alcohol, urine, and vomit. I can't say I really blamed him. Dad couldn't run away either. It's just not as easy as that.

I'm angry at mother, but I don't hate her. I don't think I've ever hated her. Actually, I think she's kind of pathetic, like an animal that never grew to full size. She mewls like a wounded beast, and cries like a infant. I would kill her, but I know what that would mean . . . the world would dissolve slowly, like a corpse in solvent.

So I leave her in that house all alone, and I drive down our hill toward the city. There's a lump in my throat that won't go away, but I don't have a problem being sympathetic toward myself. I tell myself that it's okay; that the way in which we live and breathe is wholly based on individual contention. Dad drank, but it's never been that easy for me. It never has. I guess it's her thick skin, massive skull, and course hair. Like I said, I don't hate her, but I hate some of the things she makes me do.

*

I cruise the suburbs. That's where most of them reside.

Long, slender necks and perfumed throats. There skin is always fair because they are rarely seen in the day. They huddle up in malls, their shiny, flitting eyes seeking anything that will provide attention. They are like soft, exotic birds strutting through the neon infrastructure of America's ground zero. They are all that is left in an otherwise decrepit garden; fourteen, fifteen, sixteen . . . any older and they are clearly dying off.

I take their pouty smiles home, and I cannot sleep. I masturbate, but still can't sleep. I keep bottles of their perfume tucked underneath my bed, but it is their skin, their essence, that give these fragrances life.

The contours of their bodies and the lean, soft limbs tapering down to twenty elegant toes and fingers . . . pert breasts and silky vaginas . . .

I've read Nabakov's Lolita dozens of times, but now it just depresses me.

I always knew that it would come to this.

*

If I took one home to mother she would bite their head off. She would be cordial at first, but that would just be part her game. And then she would punish me after; would make me wallow in her bodily secretions for as long is it took for me understand that we belonged to each other, alone . . . that the world could be ours if we wanted it.

Mom liked to stroke my hair and call me 'baby', but only after I had pleasured her. Everything had a price, including motherly love.

I wouldn't dare hurt her, even though I knew she needed to be hurt. Someone needed to be cruel with her, but I just wasn't the one to do it. Someone needed to scold her; to make her sit in the corner and think about what she was doing, and what she'd done.

Christ, I'm only twenty-eight years old.

"Please Miles. Please put it in me."

Twenty-eight and helpless, fucked, insane.

"Miles?"

I close eyes and try to imagine that she is one of them, but it is useless; she is too awkward, and she smells like sweat. Maybe if I doused her in a bottle of their perfume, but even that would be a futile attempt to make this more bearable. Besides, she would know. Mother could always see though my mind and into my sickness. It was the same thing with dad.

Anything that could make my life more bearable she will instinctively destroy. It is a dance of wills, but mine has always been weakest. Mother is strong inside her shell, and her shadow is everywhere. Every wall of my psyche is shrouded by her wanton desire for control. Her voice is a harbinger for my guilt, and I am the one who is dying.

I dream the taste of girl-flesh, and I wake up with the taste in my mouth. Mother is coming and I am inside of her. She rapes me in the morning, and I'm still dreaming. Give me the girl-flesh so I can be alone. It is everything she isn't, and everything I am.

It is a portent of safety; and I can only save myself.

*

I knew my life was grotesque at an early age, and maybe that's why.

I am practically an only child. I say practically because of a sister that came into this world when I was twelve, and left it when I was thirteen. She died in her sleep, but I've known all along that it was mother. Her grave is derelict in an overgrown cemetery down the road, but I visit her at least once a week: Susan Michelle Daniel. Mother never visits.

"The child was too perfect for the world," Mother says. "God took His angel away. It was never meant to be ours anyway." And then acts like Susan Daniel never existed.

Before father died he visited the grave of Susan Daniel every day. He knew exactly what he lost, and he wanted it back. I also think he knew what I knew; that mother was responsible for Susan's departure.

"You have to go on Hank Daniel. There's still Miles to think about. Susan is with God now."

Mother's words lingered contemporary.

God give me the strength to hate her.

*

I sit on a bench in Zenith Mall and suck down an Orange Julius. The drink leaves a bad taste in my mouth, and I'm uncomfortable here. The lights glare down hot and persistent, while smatterings of inane conversation leave me dumb. The voices move like water around me, and I feel like I'm stranded on a toy island.

A group of them walk by, and one of them looks at me. A slender brunette with hazel eyes and purple lipstick. They all smell like candy so I can't tell which one she is. She smiles, and I could be stranded on a toy continent. My wrists become hot with pulse and my cock is alarmingly erect.

The shimmy of their asses side by side, and the laughter.

There's another group behind and another one in front, but I throw away my cup and follow the one who smiled because she's still smiling. And it's when I can sense the smile growing around my cock that I feel the most insane. I consider masturbation, and I think of mother; she is also smiling, but cruelly.

I feel like I'm swimming. My body is bent because of the erection I'm hiding, and my throat feels tight. If I don't watch it I might suffocate here—the undertow of plague-like plasticity. My head feels light, and the faces around me grow pale and distant. I am alone, but I am not alone. I am a survivor.

"Wendy," she says.

"I thought you were somebody else," I say. "A cousin." My hands sweat inside my pockets.

"Is she cute?"

"I haven't really thought about it."

"Oh yeah?" she says, between smacks of fruity smelling gum. Her whole body smells of fruit, and spice. She is like a piece of candy.

Her friends stand around her, as if pretending to be part of some candy-tribe. They look at me, and look away. From the corner of an eye I see one of them mouth the word 'gross', but I would never be able to hear it . . . not in a billion years. It is of an elite tongue, one that only little, cruel girls can spout. Still, I can feel the degradation.

I feel like I might black out, and maybe I want to.

"Well, I hope you find her," says Wendy.

"Yeah," I say.

And they're gone . . . all except for their smell—their candy smell.

I masturbate in a nearby bathroom, and I think of killing them, but not just the ones that mocked me directly . . . all of them. I snap back their long, slender necks and slit their flawless throats. I lie them side by side in a cracked-sky desert and watch them fade. The sand glows dry-purple around their heads where their blood has baked, and the semen between their legs gives birth to darkness. Vultures pick at their sweet meat until their hollowed out skulls are grimacing at the sun. Over the centuries their bones turn to dust, and nothing at all has changed. I'm still as confused as ever.

Mother, please hold me.

115

*

"That's it Miles. Just like that."

My head is trapped between mother's varicose thighs. My fingers struggle toward and around her breasts and she asking me to stick my tongue in her asshole, but I have not yet removed myself completely.

"Oh Miles! I'm coming!"

I am in outer space, and my body is cold. Mother is a planet very far away, and maybe she isn't my mother at all. I am God and I have created everything my vision can pick out. There are too many ghosts inside my brain, but they are silenced before the voice of God: "NOW HEAR THIS!!!" There is nowhere at all for the ghosts to go, save for deeper into the darkness. If there is anything for the them to know it is that I am God and that they should have no other God before them.

But it is Susan Daniel's little planetary ghost-face that forces me to acknowledge that I'm hurting badly.

And the shit taste in my mouth.

My cock wilts in silence.

"Oh Miles . . . I love you."

My head is pinioned against her sweaty, heaving breast . . . her elephant heart pounds against my ear. Her breath stinks of amniotic fluid and death, which turns my stomach, but I'm careful not to vomit. I nearly tell her about my trips to the mall, but it would only hurt her and, in turn, hurt me.

*

I return to the Zenith. I want to find Wendy so I can tell her my dream. I dreamt that her and I killed mom and ran away together. The dream is not concretely fixed in my mind, but that's what I remember. Mom was covered in blood, her eyes livid, and everything smelled of candy. I don't know if you can smell things in dreams, but that's what I remember.

In the dream, Wendy told me it was okay. Mom would not be missed. She killed your father, your sister, and now she was killing me.

And then we fucked. Wendy's soft skin next to mine. Her smallish breasts and rose bud nipples, and the soft down of dark hair settled between her legs—the vulva opening like a flower, and scentless. *Nobody will ever hurt you again.*

Wendy's face is my greatest creation.

But I couldn't find her. There were many girls who looked like Wendy, and even laughed like her, but none of them came close. They all carried the same oversized shopping bags, and their skulls were flawless around their eyes. Their hair had been shampooed several times, I could tell, and they always smelled like candy. Their asses shimmied, and that was great, but none of them could save me.

At the end of the dream I was invited inside Wendy's womb. It was unflawed, and the passage closed behind me. I curled inside the purple-warmth of dawn, and felt the thing inside me growing—until it was out of me and I was looking in Susan Daniel's eyes. I said something, but my mouth was flooded with amniotic fluid. I said the word 'STAY', but Susan Daniel never heard it.

*

I went home and went to my room. When mother knocked on the door I told her I was busy. She asked me if I wanted some lunch. I said I wasn't hungry.

I went into the bathroom and masturbated to Wendy. She was crouched over me, her lips moving wetly over my cock. I came on her brain and the image dissolved. I spent some time feeling guilty, and then I went into the living room.

Mother sat on the couch with her legs sprawled out in front of her. The television was on. It was very loud, as usual, because of mother's bad hearing.

"There's still some lunch in the kitchen . . . if you want it."

"I'm fine," I said. "I'm going for a walk."

When I kissed mother on the cheek she grabbed my balls.

"Not now."

"When?"

*

I walk to the bottom of our hill, along a shallow ravine, and across a weathered bridge. Gravestones are sticking up through the tangled land, and there is the usual lump in my throat. I follow the narrow trail down through the dead, but I always know where I'm going.

Susan Daniel's grave is underneath a weeping willow. Her name is scrawled unevenly across course marble, and the date is barely readable.

I sit in front of the stone, my legs crossed. Wisps of sunlight slant down through the tree and I say, "Susan."

She would have been about as old as Wendy, and just as beautiful I'm sure. But instead I imagine a tangle of infant bones that reveal nothing of the future.

How did mother kill you?

Did she suffocate you with a pillow? Did she poison your milk? Or did your heart simply fail because you knew?

Father's grave is a few feet away. At least mother had the decency to bury them next to each other, I thought. Besides, she must have known that he wasn't to far behind. She must of known a lot of things.

I tell Susan "I'm sorry", just like I've done a thousand times. I say it for mother, because she can't, and I say it for the world, because it is hanging by such a tattered thread. I would say it for father, but he has said it enough himself.

I say it over and over, and maybe one day the word will lose meaning and I can get on with my life.

But for now mother is waiting.

Mother is always waiting.

Goodbye.

Mushrooms from Outer Space
(With a Side of Pepperoni)
by
Sue D'Nimm

It was far fuckin' out.

Of course, Apple Annie was missing it as usual, having long ago gone inside to burn her incense and chant her incessant mantra.

But not Billy Deerfriend. No siree Bob. He was lying out here under the stars enjoying the show. The clouds had finally cleared and the best Leonid meteor shower in three decades was in full bloom.

Billy took another deep hit off his joint. There must be a thousand of them coming down an hour now, just like that manicured weather dude on TV said there would be.

Some weather. Rocks falling from outer space right onto your doorstep. Another one of Billy's patented shiteating grins came over his face, as the weed permeated his brain, shutting down those troublesome higher centers once again. Those centers seemed to be reviving with alarming frequency between tokes lately. Billy was beginning to think that Captain Happy might be starting to step on the dope he was selling Billy. The weed did seem to exude a troubling aroma reminiscent of eau de oregano. Billy thought he might be better off putting it on his salad than into his brain. He was going to have to confront Captain Happy about this. Either that or look for a different connection.

But those troubling higher centers were basically all shut down now, and Billy felt that he was communing with those shooting stars from outer space, that he was reading their thoughts and they were reading his. He sent out a mental greeting to his asteroid friends and felt a warm glow as his greeting was returned in kind. Right on your damn doorstep, he thought. Wouldn't that be the cat's pajamas. Even better yet right into your skull, man. There would be no troubling signals from his brain's higher centers then. No sirree Bob.

Suddenly one of the shooting stars seemed to turn in Billy's direction.

"Far out," Billy whispered in appreciation to the night sky.

The meteor grew even brighter.

"Far out," Billy reiterated, his verbal capacity, never large to begin with, further diminished by the weed.

Unlike Billy, the meteor grew brighter and brighter. Somewhere deep in Billy's limbic system, a primal brain center finally activated. Suddenly Billy knew where his meteor pal was headed.

"Oh shit!" said Billy in a rare moment of enlightenment. He rolled quickly to his right as the scream of the meteor finally reached his ears. There was a tremendous crash to his left, at the approximate location that his head had just occupied. A spray of dirt and turf clumps covered Billy's face and chest.

Billy slowly rose to his feet and crawled to the small crater in the lawn where he had just been lying. Smoke and steam were still rising from the ground. Billy looked at the glowing rock that lay in the middle of the crater. It seemed somehow alive. He thought he could see things moving in its pores. The rock seemed to send out a mental greeting that warmed his brain, once again happily suppressing those nasty higher centers.

"Far out," said Billy, and reached down to lift his new friend from outer space out of the hole it had dug for itself. He was rewarded with an intense pain and the smell of burning flesh as the two thousand degree heat of the rock incinerated the flesh on the palms of his hands.

"Oh shit," Billy said.

*

Later they sat as usual on the kitchen floor, both naked as the day they were born, a candle burning beside them. Apple Annie sat in full lotus position, Billy with his legs and ankles crossed. Beside them, the meteorite still steamed in the wheelbarrow they had used to drag it into the house.

Also as usual, Apple Annie had Billy's throbbing shaft firmly grasped in her right hand, squeezing it while she traced the fingernails of her left hand up and down its length. Billy sighed helplessly as her left hand reached down to grasp his balls firmly, squeezing them alternately in turn as her right hand began to pump his stiff organ mercilessly.

"I want to test your control tonight, Billy," she said in the pseudo-spiritual whispering voice she saved for such occasions. "I want you to take my breasts in your hands while I try to milk you tonight. Don't disappoint me, Billy. We are never going to get to the next step if you don't progress."

Obediently, Billy reached out to seize both of Apple Annie's firm and magnificent globes with his bandaged hands. His palms ached at the touch of her flesh, but he slavishly began to knead her tits with his relatively unscorched fingertips as best he could.

In the meantime, Apple Annie leaned forward to take Billy's earlobe in her mouth. She tugged it back and forth and then ran her tongue around the inner workings of his ear, all the while pumping his stiff organ harder and harder with her right hand and squeezing his balls brutally with her left.

"Remember, Billy, the secret to tantra is control. If you want to progress to the next step, to have your lingam in my yoni, you must exercise complete control."

Billy's cock was throbbing now and his balls, squeezed ever more tightly in Apple Annie's teasing hands, aching for release. He did not know how much longer he could hold out.

Despite his best effort, Billy felt a drop of precum emerge from the tip of his shaft. It was immediately detected by Apple Annie's right thumb, which was rubbing its way back and forth over the offending opening in Billy's tool, monitoring him for the first signs of a spiritual transgression.

She immediately withdrew both her hands from Billy's genitals and her tongue from his ear, then held her right thumb in front of his face so that he could witness the offending drop for himself.

"I am very disappointed, Billy. I thought you were progressing faster than this," she told him harshly. She rose and stormed from the room, her naked butt swaying tauntingly back and forth as she climbed the stairs.

Billy's balls ached and his pulsing organ throbbed, pleading for full release.

Suddenly, Billy heard a high-pitched voice somewhere to his right say, "Eat me."

"Excuse me," Billy said, turning his head to the right. He saw a small group of mushroom-like fungi standing next to the meteorite, apparently growing directly from the metal of the wheelbarrow.

One of the mushrooms opened a tiny little mouth. "I said, 'Eat me!'" it yelled in a tiny little voice.

Billy was reminded of *Alice in Wonderland* and the dangers inherent in eating things that invited you to do so.

"What did you say?" he asked incredulously.

Suddenly, the mushroom was transformed into the fictional redhead that was the perpetual subject of Billy's masturbatory fantasies.

She rose from the wheelbarrow, her firm breasts jutting out, her finely defined calf and thigh muscles flexing as she stepped down from the wheelbarrow. She lay down on the kitchen floor and spread her legs, splaying herself wide open for Billy's entertainment and enlightenment.

121

"What part of 'eat me' don't you understand?" she asked him.

Billy thought he got it now. She was like that mushroom-induced hallucinatory god Mescalito who was the subject of that renegade anthropologist Carlos Castaneda's Don Juan tetralogy. Billy knew a little something about anthropology, having spent two months as pre-anthropology major over at Clearwater Community College before that bastard Professor Thornstein had failed him on the third retake of the first hour exam, forcing Billy into his present career as a Delivery Associate at Pizza King. Billy thought he knew a few things about hallucinations, too. And at this point, there was little about the phrase "eat me" that he didn't understand given the present context.

He crawled over to his masturbatory fantasy made flesh, dragging his still-throbbing genitals along the tiles of the kitchen floor until he reached the object of his masticatory desire. He took her mound in his mouth without hesitation, as she reached down to grab the sides of his head, shoving his mouth more tightly against her crotch.

She swung her hips up over him to ride his face, grinding her mound into him as he eagerly lapped her cunt. That cunt was so sweet and so warm and so wet and tasted so delicious (dare he say mushroomy?) in his deprived state, that he began to eat it as if there were no tomorrow.

The girl began to rock on his face as he tongued her, lapped her, sucked her and chewed her for all she was worth. She came several times, gushing a pungent fluid all over his face before she lowered herself on him.

Billy could feel the protruding erect nipples of her breasts as they contacted his lower abdomen, sending an electric thrill running through his body.

Then she took Billy into her mouth and began to suck him as he had never been sucked before. Her hunger seemed insatiable, and her mouth strangely talented. It was as though she had two or three tongues, each one capable of independent and very rapid movement. And each one very skilled and thoughtful in what it did. And her mouth seemed impossibly long as she took in Billy's full length and then kept it in without even gagging once. The walls of that mouth seemed to adjust to the exact size of Billy's prick, squeezing it and caressing it alternately as he began to fuck the redhead's sweet mouth for all it was worth. And after Apple Annie's torture, it was worth a great deal.

The mouth and tongues continued to milk him as the girl began to grind her cunt into his mouth even more vigorously. She seized his balls in her hand, using them as a makeshift saddle horn while she rode him like a wild cowgirl. Billy, who began the encounter with a prick already throbbing from Apple Annie's masochistic religious ritual, could hold back no longer. He felt the pressure building in his balls, which were being cruelly squeezed in the redhead's hands. He felt the jism shoot out of him, the redhead's supernatural mouth sucking every drop of fluid from his balls. He bit down on her clitoris in appreciation, but soon found that his mouth held only . . .

. . . a mushroom. The girl was indeed Mescalito after all.

He looked around at the kitchen floor. There were mushrooms growing everywhere now.

*

When he whipped it out to go to the bathroom in the middle of the night, it felt a little strange. The hood seemed larger than usual, almost (dare he say it) mushroom-like. His burnt hands, however, seemed to be miraculously healed.

When Billy arose for his morning piss, his worst fears were confirmed. His organ had indeed been transformed into a mushroom. A rather large one though, thank God. That was at least some consolation. And as the urine streamed out of him, he thanked God again for the fact that it still worked. No reason why it had to. Would have been a bummer if it didn't, he thought, the idea of vomiting his urine out through his mouth not a particularly appealing picture.

He supposed he had better make yet another appointment with Dr. Peterschticker. Peterschticker had been the one who got him through that urinary tract infection last fall. Not to mention the gonorrhea back in '99 and the clap in '97. Or the herpes infection and the wart situation and his recent problems in properly performing Apple Annie's increasingly exacting tantric rituals. Peterschticker was the go-to guy, all right. He would know what to do in a situation like this.

When Billy went down to the kitchen, most of the floor and walls were covered with mushrooms. Apple Annie was sitting at the kitchen table, nude as usual, munching down her granola. She didn't seem to notice a thing.

*

Later that afternoon, at the pizza shop, he noticed Gina Ferrilli, the owner's daughter, looking at him strangely. Her massive tits were hanging halfway out of her peasant blouse as usual. How he longed to hold those jugs in his hands and mouth and run his fingers over her sweet olive skin. But Gina wouldn't give him the time of day, preferring the company of that borderline cretin and Harley-Davidson owner, Rocky Gambino.

Today, however, seemed different. Gina was eyeing him up and down as she rolled the pizza dough, stopping occasionally to wipe the flour off of her hands and onto the already well-decorated upper hemispheres of her sizable breasts.

Finally she wiped all the flour off her hands onto those magnificent globes and her apron, with a final dusting on her very tight and pleasantly ample ass.

"Come in the back room with me, Billy, I have something to show you," she said in that sultry voice of hers.

Billy went into the back room without resistance.

"I think maybe I've been underestimating you, Billy," she said, suddenly reaching for his crotch and grabbing his gonads tightly in her hand. You are a man of greater magnitude than I have given you credit for. I never really noticed this huge bulge in your pants for some reason."

She began to unzip him. Billy's higher brain centers suddenly recovered enough to remember the current state of his organ and he reached to stop her, but he was too late. The cat (or rather mushroom) was already out of the bag.

"Oh my," she said, looking up at him with tears in her eyes. "I have never seen anything like that before, Billy."

Billy was touched by Gina's concern and reached down to stroke her hair.

"I mean it's magnificent, Billy," she whispered. "The most magnificent I have ever seen."

Suddenly, Billy understood. Gina wasn't seeing the mushroom thing that was in fact growing from his crotch, but the massive fourteen inch cock that was the subject of her fantasies. It was the Mescalito thing all over again, only this time Billy was starring in the role of the mushroom.

Gina took him in her mouth and began to suck him like a toddler reunited with a long lost lollipop.

Billy held the sides of her head, stroking her hair as she sucked him. This was what he had always dreamed about. Gina Ferrilli on her knees taking him in her mouth, her gigantic breasts rubbing against his thighs while she deep-throated him. Of course in those fantasies, it was Billy's own cock that Gina was sucking, not some mushroom from outer space. But Billy had to give the mushroom from outer space credit. It felt better than his own cock. He could feel every bump on Gina's rapidly moving tongue and the softness and texture of the inner walls of her mouth as they rubbed against his throbbing, albeit fungal, member.

Mushrooms from Outer Space (with a Side of Pepperoni)

The sensations were ten times as great as anything he had experienced with his own prick, despite all of the efforts of that selfless medical crusader, Dr. Jonathan Thomas Peterschticker.

Gina released him momentarily to pull her peasant blouse over her head. As he had long suspected (knew for certain actually), she wore no bra beneath it.

She managed to lose the skirt and panties and footwear without taking her mouth off of Billy even for a second.

She did finally pull her eager little mouth off, licking her way up Billy's balls and shaft to make one request.

"Billy, honey, I have something to confess," she said in a quiet voice, "I kind of like it up the ass. Would you mind?"

She climbed aboard the meat-cutting table, lay face down on the table, spread her legs and butt cheeks, and in general "assumed the position."

She looked pretty good, Billy thought, her boobs spreading out beneath her, pressed flat against the wood of the table, her long jet black hair spilling over her naked back, the red eye of her ass exposed, just waiting for him. The pupil of that eye looked a tad dilated, Billy thought, as if it had grown accustomed to such activities. Obediently, Billy climbed aboard her, his massive mushroom cock having no trouble finding its way into her seemingly self-lubricating entrance. He collapsed on her back, feeling her long Italian hair tickling his chest as he began to pump her. Her ass felt even better than her mouth did, the way it gripped him so tightly, the sphincter contracting around him and squeezing him as he battered his way in and out of Gina's helpless body.

She reached underneath him to grab his balls while he pummeled her, which increased the sensations by another order of magnitude. In response, he began to shove his throbbing morel-like member even faster and faster into her ever-so-willing ass. He felt her trembling as if in orgasm and soon the pressure grew too great and he exploded inside her as she squeezed his balls tightly in her hands, milking him for every last drop. Except it felt more like spores than drops, Billy thought. A lot more like spores.

*

Later they sat naked on the floor, Gina's head buried in his shoulder, her gigantic right breast rubbing against Billy's chest. "That was perfect, Billy. Just perfect," she cooed. "I just wish it could last forever. I am so worried, Billy."

"Why?" he asked her, stroking her hair gently. "I'm not going any-where."

"It's just that Daddy may have to close the shop," she told him. "The mushroom guys are beginning to squeeze him, and I don't think he can afford to operate much longer."

Billy thought about the present state of his kitchen. "I have an idea," he told her.

*

When he got to Doc Peterschticker's office, he was actually beginning to feel pretty good about things, considering his present circumstances.

Peterschticker was being his usual avuncular, reassuring self. "Don't worry, Billy. I've been in urology for twenty years. Nothing you can show me is going to shock me, so if you don't mind . . ."

Nurse Swenson gulped. She had seemed more than a little squeamish when Billy had described his symptoms.

Obediently, Billy dropped trou, allowing his fungal organ to spring forth in all its glory.

Peterschickter performed what the Japanese call a *bushuru* (affection-ately named for the first President Bush), fainting dead away on the floor, a long stream of vomit issuing from his mouth. So much for twenty years of urological experience, Billy thought.

It was that dark horse Nurse Swenson who proved to be the real trooper, eagerly falling to her knees, taking Billy's new and improved member into her mouth and sucking it for all it was worth.

*

Days later, old man Ferrilli had to hire hundreds of new delivery per-sons. The pizzas featuring Billy's mushrooms were selling like hot cakes, and the shop could barely keep up with the demand. Mushrooms were by now sprouting from Billy's forehead, cheeks, nipples, bellybutton and ass. The Nystantin Dr. Peterschticker prescribed for Billy's fungal infection did not seem to be working particularly well. That was to be expected, Billy thought. The treatments appropriate for yeast infections might not work so effectively on fungi from outer space, he supposed. They had of-fered surgery, but he was kind of growing attached to the mushrooms, especially to the very first mushroom that had sprouted from him. He did not know what he would do without it at this point.

126

Mushrooms from Outer Space (with a Side of Pepperoni)

No one seemed to notice the mushrooms much anyway. Hell, half the town was sporting the little critters on their foreheads and cheeks at this point. Apple Annie had especially enjoyed hers. A gift straight from Kali, she called it.

Poor Apple Annie. She had grown so tired that Billy had taken to performing the tantric rituals in her bed. Now she existed essentially as a bed of mushrooms. They grew from her body, her mattress, even the walls. Apple Annie had not moved much in the past couple of days. Billy was not even sure how much of Apple Annie was left anymore underneath all those mushrooms, if anything at all.

*

Billy was feeling kind of peaked himself as he rang Mrs. Gunnreil's doorbell. Mrs. Gunnreil was one of Pizza King's most loyal customers, and she always asked for Billy.

When she opened the door, Billy saw that she had sprouted two new mushrooms from her temples since last night. She looked tired herself.

"Billy, how nice to see you," she breathed. "Here, let me give you your usual tip." She opened her nightgown, exposing her large firm breasts, each now festooned with mushroom nipples.

She unbuttoned Billy's shirt slowly, stopping to lick his own mushroom nipples with her now mushroom tongue before she squatted to remove his pants. Each touch of fungus on fungus was the purest ecstasy Billy had ever known. She took Billy's magic mushroom twanger into her mouth and pulled Billy down beside her to the floor, where Billy began to eat her mushroom clit with his own mushroom tongue. Spores were soon flying all over the place and new mushrooms blossomed from each of their bodies, each locking its newly formed mushroom lips with those of its nearest neighbor across from it. It was the sweetest bliss that Billy had ever known. Soon his own mushroom parts were touching each other, exchanging their spores and Billy felt his state of bliss increasing exponentially.

Now they were lying side by side, he and Mrs. Gunnreil, their mushrooms interwined, cross-pollinating in a frenzy of combinatorial possibilities. Their human energy was spent, Billy knew. They were going to bed in the most literal sense. Soon they would be nothing but mushrooms infesting the rug, the walls and the ceiling in an unimaginable orgy of spore release.

Suddenly his future looked very bright indeed, Billy mused, in his last human act of cognition.

127

The Woman Beneath
by
William P. Simmons

Doris waited for Mark's touch, and tried not to think about the *thing* inside her.

For several nights after meeting Mark, sleep had refused her like those precious, warm moments of security she'd searched for since leaving home. Shifting her large feet beneath damp sheets, she would imagine the stranger

—not a stranger, no—

shifting inside, a repulsive parody of a hateful, in-complete fetus hungering for freedom. Thirsting for what was hers. Doris felt it there now, wiggling half-phantom fingers between her ribs, flexing the urgency of its desire through her womb, wedged beneath bone and skin and organs, staring with sightless eyes at the stringy, wet slopes of her insides.

Waiting.

Doris wouldn't allow herself to think for what, not even when the shifting sensation demanded to be recognized, poking up oh-so-slightly between her ribs.

Better not to think at all, or the Bitch would hear. For if it could hide inside her skin, day by day exercising its influence—moving Doris's arm here, causing a tremble to ripple down her thigh there—than the monster, that other filthy side of herself, could surly hear her thoughts, couldn't she?

No, it did no good to think!

Easier to give in to the confused, desperate sympathy of her desire. Better to simply forget the woman she'd been, and the woman she was becoming—the woman *he* was creating

Was it a creation? Or was he simply opening the way for something she'd hidden deep down inside herself? God, I don't want to lose me!!!

And who, precisely, was she?

Dependable, clear-headed Doris.

Someone who'd rarely spread her legs for a man's touch, and certainly never so easily. A mousy, reclusive girl really. Big sister, efficient secretary.

128

The Woman Beneath

Afraid of change. Nervous when people's eyes strayed too long upon her form, as though every moment Gary, the office assistant with blistering pimples on his face, or the cook at the lunch counter a block away from her office, smiled, they were taking something from her.

Doris, calling home every other night except weekends so no one would know she was spending yet another Friday alone on the sofa, shoving wads of buttery popcorn into her mouth and trying not to cry when shadow-lovers writhed in sweaty embraces. Careful to keep her eyes away from mirrors; away from the wrinkles thickening cruel nets across her face and the heavy folds of skin hanging curtain-like across bone. Doris Headley, a typical stain of blue eyes and pale face, living in a city that cared nothing for her—nothing at all for the needs she tried to bury beneath work and food and books that she sometimes brought to her bed, bending the pages as she idly rubbed herself, immediately ashamed afterwards, running to the bathroom to wash her fluid, her scent, off her fingers.

When he came to her, Doris stopped thinking. Suddenly, wonderfully, fear and memory and caution bled beneath sighs she barely recognized. She arched her back, her nerves a million delicious finger-tips bending for his warm, over-bearing hand.

The fuck!

She hated him.

She needed him.

His mouth clamped roughly over hers, tracing the meaty slope of her right thigh, a delirious, confusing explosion of forcefulness and feather-light flickering against her wetness. Beneath his scrutiny, she felt ashamed and delighted, an envelope of warmth and tension tightening from within.

Or was it the Other, scrambling for his touch?

Writhing beneath his tongue, yelping in the strange silence as he bit, she admitted the old Doris wouldn't ever have followed Mark to Harper's Mill. The furthest she'd ever been from the city was a college concert in Jersey, tagging along with two of her girlfriends *(who, of course, had had dates)* and a boy with angry purple eye bags and dirty scarf tying back his shaggy mop of black, oiled hair. A boy, she recalled, who'd stopped being friendly once discovering she wouldn't put out simply because he played in some obscure cover-band.

Nothing at all like Mark.

Earlier that morning, when he'd returned from wherever he worked *(he hadn't told her where, and she knew better than to ask)* and demanded she pack some clothes, she'd done so without question, without thought. Excited and fearful, she'd nodded, wrapped her arms around him, and whispered, "okay."

Without warning, the image penetrated her mind, as rough and thick as the length of flesh she stroked. She imagined dripping loose from her bones, forming into a new, exotic shape to be further molded in his large, manipulative hands.

The thought was interrupted by a surprising turn of his mouth. He invaded, searched, opened her further. The vicious, greedy whirl of his tongue, somehow always tasting like black licorice, made her wet as he leaned up, slipped it silently, softly into her mouth.

"Open for me!"

His voice was an earthquake moving shadows as he pinched her hardening nipples. His tongue moved from her mouth to her neck, lapping delicately across the moist geography of her insides, stopping to nibble on her clit. He fluctuated his speed, and instead of butterflies, his teeth and tongue and lips burned like starving deadly insects.

Because she feared the feeling of the Stranger forming inside, she arched her back and welcomed his renewed attack. Maybe the orgasm would drown out the whispering in her ears . . .

*

She had demanded the lights be kept off with her other lovers.

In the dark, she didn't have to feel bad for not looking at them. But the first time Mark had fucked her—her mind repeated the phrase, excited by the delicious wickedness its snake-tongue sound offered—she'd kept on the little bed lamp with the torn yellow shade. After, bruised but content, she'd tried to snuggle near him in the happy afterglow of exhaustion, fascinated as a child while delicate shadows lapped the hulking gleam of his lean, muscled chest, and legs, and side.

"I've never let anyone see me naked before," she whispered, disappointment swelling in her stomach when he didn't answer. Waiting, listening to soft rain fall against the window of her damp, musty smelling apartment, she grew drowsy, feeling the juices congeal and dry against her inner thighs, her cheek, the soft soles of her feet where his seed lay in secret pools of weakness.

Later, when he finally turned to stare at her in the lamp light, he was looking not at or past her.

"Did you like it?" She asked for something to say. Her words punched the drifting silence as she waited.

The Woman Beneath

"I can see you," he finally said, face seeming to stretch in a soft pool of light streaming through the blinds.

Laying beside him in the dark after he stretched behind him to turn off the lamp, feeling both trapped and consoled by the course hair on his chest, she sensed his mouth curl into an angry, thin-lipped smile. The next moment, he was on her, over her, *in* her with fluid savagery.

Although she denied it, she savored those moments when she lay used up beneath him, responsibility faded like old faces from a scarp book . She could almost pretend she didn't exist, didn't matter. Holding her legs apart, pinching her nipples, he'd said it for the first time, then.

"You're mine," his voice far away. A passing car's front lights drank in his pupils.

"Both of you."

*

The first night with Mark, she'd allowed herself to move—*for him to move her*—ways she'd been amazed her body could support.

She exposed the soft pink skin folds of her cunt, the dark puckered knot of her ass as he repeated, "I want to know who you really are," a strange manta accompanying their filthy shouts and the frantic, stinging slaps leaving welts across her back.

"What's that supposed to mean; you know who I am; I'm just me." She fondled his limpness, somehow reassuring in the dark on their third date.

"No," he said quietly, caressing her back, the pink folds of her vulva, the intoxicating smell of her insides filling the room.

He leaned over to pinch her nipple and smiled, then.

She remembered it so well because the grin had offered no humor, ice in the dark.

"No," he repeated, "You're not."

*

"Who do you belong to?"

She heard his voice somewhere beneath folds of shadow that would have felt sensuous if not for their thickness. The air felt heavy and cold despite their grinding skin and the whispering heating unit in the wall.

Slowly, she directed his hands over her shoulders, down past her belly, and wondered if she was directing them alone or if the other Doris had already won—the writhing, uninhibited configuration of skin and bone, blood and cum and a wildness that she'd only dreamed of since her ado-

131

lescence, when she'd watched her younger sister play men and life with a reckless abandonment she could only envy.

I'm tired, she thought as Mark nibbled her, slowly working his finger into her clenched anus. She practiced the trick he'd taught her, relaxing her muscles until the pain subsided and she felt herself open further.

God, I'm so very tired.

*

"I'm Mark," he had told her in the grocery store, the last place she had expected to find . . . was it love? No, she wasn't ignorant enough to think what they shared was love. If anything, it felt like something far stronger, far more powerful than Hallmark buy two-with-one coupon sentiment.

Domination?

Perhaps, though the word soured her mouth, not at all like the swollen head of his penis, which had filled her with an unexpected mix of comfort and apprehension as it joined their bodies.

That night, and the night after, and the week after that, they explored one anther with abandon.

After speaking at the Office Efficiency convention her employer sent her to yearly, thrilling to the spark in his ice-chiseled eyes, she'd worked up the nerve to ask him out. To her surprise, she hadn't stuttered or burped or any other of a dozen embarrassing habits that seemed to hide in wait until she tried to make a good impression. To her even greater surprise, he'd said yes.

After the movie, somehow she'd found the nerve to grip his hardness, enjoying the feel of blood hardening the meat. And, yes, it had been she who asked him to spend the night.

But, of course, now she knew better.

It hadn't been *her* at all.

*

"Oh, fuck-Jesus-you-oh-Christ—oh—GOD!!!"

Writhing her hips, mashing herself against his hips, impaling herself deeper, her insides clenching, clinging to hardness, she flushed because she'd called the lord's name in vein. That's what Baptist parents did to their children, she thought, trying to laugh through the panting need echoing her need in the dark. Did she still fear God, an entity that she'd always associated more with fear than the love her sappily smiling neighbors attributed to him?

The Woman Beneath

The night listened to their breathing, unsteady as waves crashing against rocks in the sea. She felt him beside her and turned to find his eyes.

Why was she still here, she wondered?

Why couldn't she move—act to save herself?

"I'll run you a bath," Mark said suddenly, jumping from the uncomfortable hotel bed.

"Not tonight, honey," she said, stretching. "I'm really sleepy."

"I wasn't talking to you."

She sat in stunned, hurt silence until she heard the bathroom door click.

When he returned, he waved for her. But she didn't follow him; she was sure of it. It was the other one, the Bitch inside, who forced her to stand and move.

Doris felt like an unwelcome guest in her skin. As her tears re-shaped the contours of the strange, darkly paneled room looming around them, she trailed behind Mark with the jerky, ungraceful steps of a puppet.

Across the cold, scratchy carpet.

Down the hall, past a door, perhaps a closet.

Mark had reserved a honeymoon sweet; the bathroom reflected the glamour and cost. Inside, a huge, silver lined tub sat in the middle of a polished, gleaming red floor. The walls of this room were also crimson, dripping ruby moisture as Mark turned ran the hot water. Before she could retreat, he held her by the shoulder. "No more hiding," he said. "I want to see her."

He removed her earrings and placed them on the sink.

She opened her mouth to speak but he hushed her.

"Let her out!" he urged, hands clenched into fists. Cold dread slammed her in the stomach before it subsided into an even worse tickle behind her abdomen. "I'm me!" Doris thought she cried, but it was hard to tell with the droning, excited hum filling her head.

The touch of silver against porcelain against her skin gave her goosebumps. She almost buckled over, but he was there to hold her and drag her to the tub.

"I don't *want* to!"

Dizzy now. Frightened.

"I don't care," he said evenly. Perhaps that was the worse of all. No emotion. Just his need; just his absolute control.

"NO!"

She tried to kick him, struck the soft dangling meat of his balls.

Grunting, he didn't release her. His hands tightened, grips of rage that had brought her off again and again.

"I don't want to lose . . . me." She watched the water fill the tub with a new, curious detachment, shivering as he brushed his lips past her shoulder and bent to grab a fat bar of soap.

She could have ran. She could have leaped screaming from the room, out the door, into the hall of the hotel for help . . .

But where did she have to go? How could she leave behind the woman Mark had found inside her?

Heaviness building through her thighs and belly and arms increased as something *(Someone! Oh, God, someone!)* came closer.

Mark lathered his hands with a greenish-blue bar, pressed tightly against her. "Lift your arms," he ordered.

No, she meant to say, but her lips wouldn't move. She tried to force them open, but they felt heavy, weighed down by iron clasps.

I must be sick!

In the dim lighting of the bathroom, she momentarily thought she saw something brush behind her eyes, and in the distorting shadows of the little, closed-in room, she saw, for just a moment, the horrible eyes staring back at her from her own, familiar yet terribly different, growing wider, threatening to eat her pupils.

The water, when it poured around her, felt painfully hot—tearing fingers trying to open her. Soap drooled across her shoulders, down her arms, some dripping against her toes like a teasing kiss.

"Turn around." Mark rubbed the soap delicately down each side of her face, across her neck, pressing harder when he reached her breasts.

"It's *her* time, now."

He pulled slightly at her skin, and she imagined her pale flesh removed like a coat as he worked his fingers down her back.

Pushing. Probing. Pinching.

"Our time!"

He scrubbed her with the cloth, tearing scorching trails of pain up her back, across her ass, beneath her arms.

—"Let—"

He yanked at her skin as she fought not to fall out of herself.

—"Us—"

Something wiggled beneath her chest as he scrubbed.

—"Have—"

This isn't real! This can't be happening! It isn't real! I'm me! I AM ME!

—"It!"

134

The Woman Beneath

She moaned. The sound was lost beneath the roar of water pounding against the tub. She looked to find his face, but steam swallowed vision. Her head ached. Her legs buckled.

Water, fresh and hot and clean, scalded her ankles.

He pressed her face, an artist molding some worthless lump of clay into shape.

Doris felt it immediately.

Mark looked into her eyes, and when she opened her mouth, she didn't recognize the voice that whispered the two words that froze her blood.

"I'm here."

The pain of opening was exquisite. She had time to scream, once, before the heavy, damp air was sucked from her lungs and the sensation of two wet, cold hands pushed her out of her skin with a wet, tearing sound.

Apart.

Falling.

Spiraling what felt an impossibly long time headfirst into the filthy tub water where scraps of old skin floated bloodily between her murderous lover's feet.

Landing, she tried to push herself up off her stomach. But she couldn't find her hands, or her legs, or anything at all but the murky bits of skin and dirt, grime and hair, that water and sponge and the shaping, searching hands had removed.

A pair of feet kicked her down.

Her legs, though she no longer owned them.

In a flurry of soap and light and spinning walls, she felt what was left of her old form and consciousness drowning.

There was time enough for regret. Time enough for pain and fear and rage, cold as the grave, hot as betrayal. Time enough to see Mark towering above her, reaching out for the woman who now wore her skin.

She was beautiful . . .

Doris looked up at her coldly smiling face before a final wet darkness took her—so much waste—down the drain.

Black Velvet
by
Trey R. Barker

There were so many men. And then, on a moonless night, there was something else.

Questions. Accusations.

Shouts. Screams.

Shots.

She heard them and they were her dream/nightmare.

*

The room was musty, too long closed to fresh air. The boxes—one for him, one for her—were old, soft with the basement's dampness, and came apart in her fingers. Inside were pieces of the dead.

Molly went carefully through Charles' box until she found the record. *Frampton Comes Alive.* It had been the centerpiece of summer 1977, Charles' last. In the empty basement, Molly clearly heard the music: frenzied guitar, liquid bass, pounding drums. 'Do You Feel Like We Do?' How many times had Charles sung it to her, always changing the line from 'we' to 'I', always waiting patiently for an answer?

"You came back," Father said.

Had she thought she wouldn't hear his voice? Had she thought she could come to his house and not see or hear him? She turned to him. He was cast harshly by the basement light. Eyes soft blue, hair a gentle off-brown. Though his hands were trembled by age, she was certain they could still hold a gun.

"I haven't heard from you in a while, Margaret."

"Margaret's dead," Molly said coldly. "Or did you forget?"

He frowned as though confused, then his face cleared. "How'd you know I was still alive?"

"I smelled your stink in Denver." Oh, Charles, she thought, why did you bring me here?

"Perhaps you'd rather smell me dead."

"I don't want to smell you at all."

He snorted. "Do you still fuck everything in sight?"

"Never did," she said, knowing it was a lie.

"Right, and all those high school boys were just friends. You don't lie very well. Why did you come back?"

"Tell him," Charles whispered. He stood next to her, holding her hand, reassuring her. "Tell him." His breath was warm and soft against her cheek. She flushed and leaned slightly into his comforting resistance.

"I came to watch you die."

There was nothing for a long moment. Then Father nodded. "You'll be around for a while." He headed for the basement stairs. "All kinds of boys 'round here. Maybe you can find some . . . entertainment."

Charles squeezed her shoulder as Father left. "No."

"What?"

"Just stay away from them, you're not here to get your rocks off."

"Why *am* I here? Damnit, Charles, you asked me to come here and I did. I don't want to see him die . . . I don't want to see him at all . . . hell, he's crazy . . . called me Margaret. You told me I wouldn't be alone—"

"I know what I told you. Trust me." Charles' answer was a whisper, a breeze from the tiny basement window.

She said nothing else, there was no need. Charles knew. He had seen her sitting in her garden, in her living room, watching rented movies on one isolated corner of the couch or eating lunch by herself in the park while old people talked to no one.

"You're not alone," he said. "You've got me."

She shook her head. "I haven't had you since you died."

"You've always had me."

When he hugged her, she held him longer than she should have, reveling in the comfort. When he broke the hug, she wiped a tear away. "I was never lonely when you were alive. Did you know that?"

"Yeah," he said quietly.

She didn't want to be alone anymore. She wanted a warm touch, one that wasn't attached to a cock or a tongue or an ass. She wanted to be able to lay in bed and spoon with a man, or to wake up on Sundays and read the newspaper. But what she had were men who momentarily dispelled her emptiness with their physicality, their bodies and smells and sounds. They gave her only a moment of heat, or a night's worth, but it was warmth.

Charles took her face in his hands, as he had when they were little. "Trust me. Have I ever steered you wrong?"

"No," she said with a smile. She headed for stairs. When she glanced back, the basement was empty, as though Charles had never been.

*

The Elvis/Jesus Room.

Where was the blood? The handprints? The smears and spatters?

Washed away by soap and water and years tossed out after they were used up. But she remembered the blood and how she had sat on Father's desk and cried and prayed to Jesus while Father lied to the sheriff and nervously hummed Elvis tunes.

Somewhere in the bowels of the house, Molly heard Father talking himself through his retirement. No more days on the road, no more nights in cheap motels wondering where his next sales were hiding.

We all hide somewhere, she thought.

Father used to hide—when he was home—in this room. He called it his sanctuary, where the road rolled off him.

"Goddamn room," Molly said.

The moan, the one she heard in her dream/nightmare, came to her. Soft like a lover's demure whisper. She frowned and cocked her head. Still quiet, but familiar. She leaned closer to the door to hear better, and saw the dark spots.

Dark. Like the blood had been.

She gritted her teeth. There wouldn't have been any blood had Father not come home early.

The spots grew; larger, darker.

And the smell. It had been in the room for weeks afterward. Can after can of Lysol and still it smelled. Molly's throat constricted.

—"Strip!"—

—the rustle of clothing being removed, tossed carelessly into a corner—

"Charles?" she called.

—"Kneel!"—

—the sound of flesh moving as someone obeyed the command—

She knew the room was empty, had been since Father had padlocked it. But at the same time, she knew everything was in there. Guilt and anger and pain, in there and waiting on her, laughing at her.

"No," she said weakly, backing across the hallway. "Please, not again."

—"Lick me there!"—

—a satisfied moan—

"Get out, Charles," she said urgently. "Get out now. Now!" She called him just like she had that night. Except now she stood in front of the door instead of cowering in her bedroom.

—"Please, Mother," Charles begs. "Don't—"

138

Black Velvet

"*Charles!*" Molly screamed. She threw herself at the door, smeared her fists in the blood.

Then it was over. The bloody door was again painted in nothing but dirty white. The moan was just a breeze from outside. The crying was nothing more than an animal calling from somewhere in the woods.

A tear slipped down her cheek. "Oh, God, Charles. I don't want to this . . . not again."

There was no answer. Charles hadn't come back to her since the basement; not as voice, not as dream or vision. For three days she had roamed the house, lonely and anxious, watching for signs that Father was dying. But the man was healthy and Charles had abandoned her, left alone because she had left him alone.

Hands bloody, Molly fled the house.

*

She didn't know him. He had said his name but she'd forgotten it instantly. Sitting naked at the edge of the bed, he grinned and stared at her breasts. His was not the best body but neither of them were sixteen anymore. Off with her chinos, her baggy denim shirt, her sneakers. After she unhooked her bra, she tossed him the black velvet hood.

"I ain't wearing that." He held it away from him, chin stuck as defiantly out as his cock.

"Fine." She took the hood and began to put her bra on.

"Wait, wait." From behind her, he slid his hands around, tossed her bra to the floor, and caressed her breasts. His thighs pushed against hers, his groin against her ass. "You want me to wear that damned thing, I'll wear it."

Turning to him, she slid the hood over his head. Her fingers played with the drawstring before pulling it taut. The hood tightened. Another tug and it nestled up against his neck. One more tug and it began to pinch his throat.

He grabbed her hand. "Whoa, there, girl."

A hooded, anonymous lover. Just another man—another body—she'd never played. But that was the game wasn't it? Drive away the memories and the cold by playing with warm men. Games from as far back in her past as Charles' death. Disgusting games that allowed her to lose herself in something that smelled like cheap comfort.

He slid his hands over her, sending jolts through her. Reaching behind him, she pinched his ass until he gasped. He knelt and his tongue slid through the hood's mouth hole, up inside her. His teeth gently bit her la-

139

bia, pulled and spread them, his finger—two, three, four fingers—slipped inside, touched her everywhere.

His touch, his body; so warm.

She pulled him up and ran her hands over his chest, over his nipples, pinching, pulling, until he chuckled uneasily and fell back on to the bed. She fell with him and seconds later, he was inside her. They rolled together across the bed, back and forth, top to bottom, side to side. In and out, cock and hands in dark, secret places. Fingers in mouths, tongues in ears, fists in cavities. An anonymous lover who spoke anonymous, meaningless words while his cock bumped and scraped inside her.

Lost in his warmth, she glanced at the hood.

Jesus' face.

Unsurprised, Molly jammed herself down on Him. She wanted to hurt Him, to give Him a taste of what she'd had for so many years. She wanted to jam her fist up His ass until her elbow disappeared, impale Him on her anger. She wanted to kill Him, to leave Him bloody in the floor

Jesus promised salvation but all He had ever given her were the scrapings from His shit. There was nothing good here, no ever-lasting life or sweet redemption.

Beneath her, Jesus bucked and ground against her until He shouted and seized and spurted and pronounced Himself finished.

She stared at Him and He grinned at her. Jesus, who she'd picked up in a bar, who she'd fucked for a moment's respite. Comfortable sex with Jesus, comfortable like owning two cats or a dog or mowing a lawn.

"Why'd you take him?" she asked. "Why?" She slapped Him and Jesus' face shattered, disappeared into the black velvet.

"Whoa, bitch, you watch your ass," the guy said.

Molly slid off him, turned away, muttered an apology. The sex wasn't love or even a replacement for love. It was just something to drive out memories for a short time. And now, because she'd come back to this shitty little Georgia town, it wasn't even doing that.

Now she was fucking Jesus.

"Just like Jesus fucked me," she whispered.

"Blaspheme," Charles said. He sat at the bed's edge, angry and beating one fist into another. "You know I can't be with you all the time."

"You haven't been with me at all the last few days," Molly answered.

"I know, I'm sorry. But it's not quite time yet."

"Time for what?" she asked, frustrated.

"Damnit, Molly," Charles said. "You're better than this loser. Just because Mother did this shit doesn't mean you have to. This isn't love and it won't give you squat."

"What else do I have?" She paced the room. "You told me if I came here for you, I would find someone. Well, I'm doing what you asked and what do I have? Shit, that's what. So I'll fuck whoever I want." She stared at her lover and wondered how it was he slept.

"He can't hear us," Charles said. He slid his arms around her. "When I hug you, you and I are somewhere else. Like when we were kids, remember? When Mother and Father spent the night yelling, I'd hug you and we'd be in Never-Never Land or Oz."

Tears stained her cheeks. "I miss those places, Charles."

"Shhhh. Go to sleep, I'll worry about this guy." Charles poked the man in the butt and Molly giggled.

"I love you, Charles."

He nodded softly but his eyes carried the heat of his anger.

*

Molly woke in Father's house, in her childhood bedroom. And she knew, without knowing, her lover—Jesus—was dead.

She had dreamt of blood.

And of Charles.

Angry Charles, mad that she had bedded the guy, mad that she wasn't home waiting for whatever was nearing its time.

Angry, but angry enough to murder a man?

It was such a hard word—murder. Harder than her brother, harder than herself. But things had gotten so confused in the last three days. Seeing Father, listening to him talk to himself, smelling the Elvis/Jesus Room. Maybe Charles had hardened up.

"Maybe I have," Charles said. He stood near the door as though he'd been there the entire time. "You shouldn't have nailed that guy."

"I wanted to." And she had, but now she couldn't even remember what the guy felt like inside her. Instead of memory, there was blackness, an image of the velvet hood, of the Elvis/Jesus Room.

"And now he's dead," Charles said.

"Yeah," she said sadly. "But Father's not. He's not even sick."

"Trust me." Charles came to her. She loved his touch but there was something different now. Instead of Charles' fresh, clean smell, he now smelled of her lover's blood.

"Stay here, Molly. When it's over, I promise, you'll never be alone."

There was no reading his eyes. Finally, she asked, "How come you don't ask anymore?"

"Ask what?"

She waited for him to remember. He never did. With a sigh, she nodded. "I'll stay here."

Charles kissed her forehead and was gone and she was alone.

*

The Elvis/Jesus Room . . . the Dream/Nightmare Room.

Not spattered, but covered, with blood.

—"Strip!"—

The padlock, frozen with age, key probably non-existent. Father had shouted at her when she'd asked for the key and she had slinked away, chastised by the man she hated.

She knew her peace of mind—if it existed—was inside that room. She also knew she would never get in that room again. She had lost her single chance that night.

—"Kneel—!"

Her body shook with fear. Her stomach knotted.

"Charles," she wailed. "I'm sorry, I can't help you."

—Mother and Charles, talking and shouting—

—"Mother," Charles cries. "Why do you bring them here? Don't—"

"Get out," Molly called to him. She grabbed the knob and turned, pushed and pulled. The door didn't move.

"Run, Charles." He ignored her. Or didn't hear her. How could he have when she was so far away?

—then Father is home and Molly is surprised his trips are usually longer what is he doing home?—

—he goes to his sanctuary and she goes to her bedroom and hides and cries—

—Father asks asks asks, Mother denies and denies, Charles shouts—

"Answer me, Charles, damn you," Molly bellowed. She kicked the door, rattled the padlock.

—another shout—

—Father's voice, "In my study? In my sanctuary?"—

—a shot—

—Charles' scream shatters the air like a hammer against fine crystal—

Molly yelled and banged on the bloody door, trying to beat it down. If she could get in, she could save Mother and Charles. "Don't hurt him! Kill me instead!"

—another shot—

"Charles," she cried, sliding to the floor, unable to get inside the Elvis/Jesus room, unable to help. Just like that night.

Black Velvet

—a third shot—

Jesus had never really been crucified, had He? He'd been promised His torment would end. There was no real crucifixion if you knew there was an end.

Her crucifixion had begun the night Charles had died.

Tonight, hearing the voices and the shots, as she fled, it tormented her still.

*

Anonymous face, anonymous body, from a no-name cafe forty miles from home. They sat together, hands and tongues exploring. Their clothes lay forgotten in a trail from motel room door to bed. She handed him the hood.

"Yeah, I like weird," he said, pulling roughly until she was prone. How easily his lips found hers. How easily his tongue—tasting of cheap beer—danced with hers.

His hands slid up her stomach, found her breasts. She turned toward him, easier for him to hold her, touch her. The shock erupted within her, became the warmth she desired. Fingers discovered the wetness between legs, tongues discovered navels. His chin pressed against first one nipple, then a second. The jolt touched her where he could never reach.

And then anonymity became Elvis. Pompadour hair, sideburns, glinting eyes. She pulled the hood's drawstring.

"Yeah," Elvis said. "Tighten it up, baby."

She pulled again and felt the string go taut around Elvis' neck.

"More," he whispered.

Again and now Elvis' breath hitched.

Elvis crawled down her body and ran his tongue from her toes to her knees, suckling, tickling. He moved up her body, tongue against her skin, stopping to taste the folds of skin between her legs, delving deeply. A pinch, a small bite, and warmth spread through her like a summer breeze. He continued over her belly and breasts, bit her nipple and traced the swell of her breast with his tongue. Then her neck and ear, a cold tongue warming her lobes.

"Time for the beef, baby," Elvis whispered as he pushed himself inside. She didn't feel the push or the twinge of pain, she felt only the duet. Someone was with her, someone was loving her.

"Fuck me, Margaret, fuck me."

Elvis' face faded, replaced by Father's.

Then gone and she was loving Charles.

"Charles?"

"Who?" Her lover's breath came in grunts.

"I want Charles."

"And I want Marilyn Monroe but we gotta live with each other, don't we?"

"Charles . . . where are you?"

Her lover pushed deeper until she felt the pain.

"Yeah," he howled.

"I love you," she shouted.

"Yeah, yeah!"

Then it was over. Cheap and fast and finished and already the warmth was spilling down her leg.

"Damnit, Molly," Charles said. He stood in the room's corner, watching her disengage herself from her lover. "I told you."

Molly jumped from the bed. "And I told you. I need this, I want this."

"Who the hell are you talking to?" the man asked. He lay on his side, his prick shrinking. "Get your ass back over here."

"Molly, this isn't you. This is your mother and—"

"Don't you say that," Molly shouted. "She was a good—A good woman." Molly stumbled backward into a corner of the room, racked by confusion and anger. There was no reason for her to have come home. Her family was dead, had been dead for two decades. "Why did you bring me here?"

When Charles' arms encircled her, it was everything she had ever wanted. It was the warmth and the companionship, the love and the caring. It was what Mother had stolen when she'd brought those men home, when she fucked them in Father's study. It was what Father had stolen the night he had come home early, had found Mother and Charles arguing.

"Molly, stay with me," Charles said.

"Ask me," she whispered.

"Will you stay?"

She began crying. "That's not the question, Charles. How come you don't remember the question?" More tears and finally she nodded and leaned into him. Within seconds, she was nearly asleep, listening to her lover ask her back to bed . . . demand her back to bed . . . shout . . . scream . . .

. . . in dreams, she saw her hooded lover in a haze, his mouth open, a smear of blood, spit, and missing teeth.

. . . in dreams, she saw her hooded lover in a haze, back bloody, more blood than she had drawn from him.

. . . in dreams, she saw her hooded lover die.

*

She stood outside the Elvis/Jesus Room. Though the padlock was gone, the door remained closed. Inside the room, Molly could hear Father humming his Elvis tunes.

Two men were dead and inside she was ice. What else was left?

So familiar, a bloody deja vu. She'd awakened in her bed and immediately saw the blood on her clothes. And in her head, a memory of watching through a haze as a man died.

Charles had been with her when she fell asleep. Where had he been while her lover died?

"Damnit," she shouted in the hallway. Father's humming stopped, then began again. Enough. She was going home. No more bullshit.

"No," Charles said, suddenly a few feet from her. "Stay here."

"You gonna kill me, too?"

"I didn't kill him."

"You and me were the only ones there."

"No, we weren't."

"What?" She frowned. "What are you talking about?"

Charles held her face gently. "Do you think I could hurt you? I love you, Molly, I always have. I'd rather die than hurt you."

"That's not funny," she said. "They're both dead and you were there."

"So was Father."

"Bullshit. You killed them."

"No, I protected you, Molly. No one else has been here since you left him, Molly. Father is slipping over the edge. Most of the time, he thinks you're Mother, cheating on him again. He would have killed you, too. I saved you and now it's your turn."

"You saved me? Bullshit." She kicked the door open, wished that Father and Mother could be in that door, could taste her shoe leather as it smashed them down, crushed them into nothingness.

"Molly, it's time."

"Get away from me!" She turned from him and stared directly at Father.

"Get away from whom?" Father asked. He stood near his desk, just beneath the paintings. "Talking to no one again?"

"Shut up," she ordered.

Charles said, "This is it, Molly, what I—what we've—been waiting for."

"Leave me alone. You tell me all this shit. You drag me here and then kill those men and—"

"What?" Father asked. Just above him, the paintings stared down and watched everything. As he came toward Molly, Father kissed his hand and laid it against the black velvet Jesus. "Who killed who?"

She stared at him, felt her lips pull back in a snarl. "Stay away from me, you . . . you murderer."

"Oh, Margaret." Father stopped a few feet from her, his face pale, his hands shaking. "You don't understand. You cheated on me again. I can't have that."

"Get it," Charles said. "Get the gun, Molly. You remember where."

Glaring at her brother, she backed away. "Damnit, don't say shit—just—Just leave me alone."

"Molly," Charles whispered. "I'm dead, don't you remember? He killed me. You could have saved me but you hid under your bed. Remember?"

"Shut up!"

"Molly," Father began.

"Did you kill my lovers?"

He hesitated and in that moment, she knew. "You did," she whispered. "You killed the men I loved."

"You didn't love them, you were fucking them. Just like your Mother . . . just like Margaret. They were stealing you from me."

"You never had me, not since you killed Charles."

"Get the gun, Molly," Charles whispered. "In the desk."

Father shook his head. "You don't know."

She was under their gaze, always under the gaze. Elvis and Jesus; gaudy colors on black velvet. They watched her, whispered to her.

"I love you, Molly," Father said.

"Get the gun, Molly. Kill him. You owe me."

Molly crossed the room, put the desk between her and Father, between her and Charles. "I can't do that."

"Molly? Who are you talking to?" Father stared at her, his eyes suddenly soft and concerned. "My God, you think you see Charles."

"Don't listen, Molly, he killed me." The frustration in Charles' voice rose. "I talked to Mother, Molly. She cried and told me she was wrong and promised it wouldn't happen again. She *promised* me, do you hear? She. Promised. Me."

Furious, her breath was fast and hard in her chest. Her heart pounded like the sheriff's knock on the door the night everyone had died. "You told the sheriff it was a burglar. You lied to him."

"Of course, Margaret," Father said. "I wanted to protect our family name. I love you—"

"You don't love me, you never have. You killed my brother!"

146

"I did not kill your brother."

"Then who did?" she screamed.

"Your mother."

"No," Charles said. "That's crap."

Crying, she turned to the paintings. "Why did you do this to me?" she asked Jesus. She jerked the painting from the wall and slammed it against the desk. The corner punched through and suddenly Jesus was weeping not at his crucifixion, but at the wood through his heart.

"Molly," Father said. "Your Mother was fu—having intercourse with many men, Charles found them. They were screaming at each other when I found them and confronted her—"

"Kill him!" Charles screamed. "He stole me from you."

"—and she pulled the gun."

The gun had always been in the top drawer. When Molly yanked the drawer open, it was there still. An ugly piece of machinery; steel and angles, wooden handgrips and six hunks of lead in the chamber.

"Yes," Charles said. "Do it, Molly. Make it up to me."

"Your mother was upset. She fired the gun accidentally. It killed Charles."

Molly looked at her brother. When she caught his eyes, they darted away, toward Father. Inside the trigger guard, her finger twitched. "Charles?"

"She promised me, Molly. I saved us and he fucked it up. It doesn't matter than he didn't shoot me. It was his fault. Yeah, Mother shot me, true, but what else is true? I'm the only one who loves you. That's true. I've been with you since I died. I love you. That's true."

She stared at him. Those things were true, there had been no one else since he died. But he had promised her she wouldn't be lonely, he had promised her things would be better.

Without another thought, she turned to Father and fired twice. One bullet took his jaw, the other left a red rose on his chest. His mouth dropped open, his eyes surprised. Slowly, he fell to the floor. Behind him, blood spattered the Elvis/Jesus Room door. "But— I love—"

Charles smiled. "No, I love you."

Her entire body shaking, she fell into Charles' arms. She kept her gaze away from the man she had killed. "How come you don't ask me anymore?"

"Ask you what?"

"I don't what to be alone, Charles." She looked back at the black velvet Jesus. He didn't know pain. He couldn't promise anything because he didn't know, didn't understand, real pain.

But Elvis did. Elvis knew it, understood it, had dined with it and sang about it and popped pills with it and fucked it.

"You won't be alone, Molly, I promise."

She shook her head. "It's not your choice, it's mine. And I choose— You." She raised the gun to her mouth—"Do you feel like I do?"—and fired.

sweet vagina
by
Simon Logan

The spreading of their labial folds, I always think, is like the opening of a great pink velvet curtain on the first night of a stage show. I love how the lips seem almost to pulse beneath my touch; inflating, puckering, quivering—all at once.

It's amazing how different they all are.

Most guys see, I think, what, maybe twenty different ones in their lifetime? Up close and everything, that is, not just glimpses or photos in porno mags. I mean close enough to really *examine*, to *revel* in. Because that's what I do. Revel.

How many?

Well how many do you *think* I've seen, doctor?

Okay, then—I'll tell you.

I reckon, and this is a conservative estimate, about eight hundred or so. I've been doing my current job about a year now. Get about three or four clients on an average day but most of them are repeat clients so, yeah about eight hundred or so. Possibly over a thousand.

Are you sure you want to do this, by the way? I mean, I have no qualms about speaking to you, it has to be done, but maybe if you'd prefer a male doctor to . . .

No, no. I'm fine with it. I just thought maybe you . . .

Well, okay then. Fine by me.

The detective said I was to tell you about that night but I'm guessing you want a little background first, right?

*

She liked a little role-playing, Ms. Black, and because he was being paid almost five hundred an hour he gave her what she liked. He did that for all his clients. That was his job.

The warehouse was one of many crumbling monstrosities in the middle of the chemical district, where the air was filled with a hydroxide stench,

149

where the walls were emblazoned with tag art and where there was the constant drumbeat of skateboard gangs ollying off of railings and ramps. The building was partitioned into several dozen rooms of varying sizes, ranging from the exquisite *Grand Fetische* suites on the upper levels to the ten-foot squared cells that populated the basement.

His was one of the nondescript cells but with help from some of the others he had set up the room with a desk in one corner, a computer monitor set atop it and a half-height filing cabinet next to it. He cleared away most of the tools he kept nearby—bottles, dildos, batons, plant misters, tubing—and stored them temporarily in the next room, usually inhabited by Suzie until she'd run off with one of her clients.

They were all just waiting for the news report that her body had been found to appear on the TV.

He dressed in a shiny black PVC suit, complete with plastic tie, as was expected and stood in the opposite corner to the desk until Ms. Black came in.

She wore a loose cotton skirt that hung just above her knees, tan-coloured high heels and a thin silk blouse. Her peroxide hair was pinned at the crown of her head. Dark-rimmed glasses swelled her eyes to twice their size.

She glanced at him then closed the door before sitting down at the desk.

She wasn't a devastatingly attractive women but she certainly would have no trouble finding someone to do what he was about to do for free. He'd noticed a pale band on her ring finger in the past so suspected that either she had been married recently or took the ring off before coming to him.

Many of his clients were married or in a relationship but for whatever reason their partners wouldn't, or couldn't, do oral. The smell, the taste, the hairs that linger for days. So they still came to him because of what he could do.

They came again and again.

"Ms. Black, I have a report here for you," he said, holding out a small stack of blank paper. The sound of distant machinery from the chemical factories could still be heard in the background, filtering in through the air vents, but the fantasy would not be broken.

Ms. Black looked at him over her glasses and nodded for him to put it down on her desk.

He obliged, deliberately pushing the paper too far.

It fell off the desk and fluttered to the floor at her feet, swirling around her momentarily like flower petals.

Ms. Black began to reach down to pick them up, as was the procedure, but he stopped her with a hand on her shoulder. He watched her eyes flutter in anticipation.

"Here, let me."

He came around the desk and bent down, began picking up the papers.

Then moving closer towards her and under the desk, brushing against the bare skin of her calf, tracing her ankle with his finger as he picked a sheet up, and then running it up the inside of her leg until it reached her knee where her legs were crossed. Now completely under the desk and facing her he uncrossed her, easing the legs apart. The soft material of her skirt sighed with her as his hands spread her further.

He caught the first glimpse of the musky scent as he touched the inside of her thigh with tip of his tongue, then moved further up, sliding the wet flesh up to her exposed vagina. A tiny clitoral piercing glittered inside her he touched it, tugged it. Sketching a circle around it as he breathed her in.

*

A couple of them have said it's almost like I'm looking for something, I'm so thorough.

And they're right.

*

His attentions became more frenzied when he knew the time was right, quickly changing from a brief, light tonguing to taking her clitoris in his lips and drawing on it, sucking it into his mouth. She had spread her legs further, resting her heeled feet on the edges of the desk above him, gripping his head as it bobbed.

His fingers explored, searching, because there was something there, he knew it, just a little deeper, spreading her vulva like a pathologist peeling back a patient's chest after a Y-incision, frowning as he gazed down deep into the darkness that seemed to fall into her.

He was going to see something there. It would appear to him. Any time now.

A globule of thick, clear lubrication spilled out of Ms. Black as she arched her back towards him, moaning at him for stopping and, goddammit, it wasn't there, she was empty inside, just a dark pit needing his tongue, clenching around him as she came and laughing at him for thinking it held anything more than vaginal juices.

151

*

No, she didn't have it.

No, I didn't know, Doctor. Not then. Not even sure now.

But I would know when I found it. I was certain of that.

(sigh/silence)

Yes, that would be great. Just water, thanks.

Sure I can tell you about that. But I wasn't fired. It was just a temporary leave. I guess I just freaked out.

Yeah, about a week after Ms. Black I'd guess.

Well what would you like to know?

*

She was spread before him, ankles held by leather straps, lips peeled back on themselves and so dripping with self-lubrication that they remained held fast, her pubic hair in part acting like Velcro.

She liked pain with her pleasure and so he pressed the fine edges of his upper front teeth against the potted flesh of her inner thighs, ran his tongue around the fine grooves of cellulite.

The stench that emerged from her was thick and heady, full of an olfactory weight that made it difficult for him to keep his head upright.

This was the deal—an examination chair tilted back so that it angled her towards him. Her ankles embraced by the moulded plastic braces of the stirrups, a couple of dead surgical machines hooked up to her, a tray of fresh needles to one side. His hair slicked back above the collar of his lab coat.

She made more noise as he bit her thigh hard enough to graze the skin, shook in her restraints. Started swearing at him.

He continued to nibble her, the scent coming from her vagina enveloping him like a cloud, seeming to swell within him as he breathed her in, filling his lungs with it's meaty flavour until all he could think about was pushing his tongue into her. (And keep going, tongue to chin, chin to jaw, jaw to head, pushing inside it until he was embraced by that dampness like a womb, so quiet there, so peaceful, away from this terrible world and what it had done to him—that was his *real* desire, wasn't it?)

She shrieked as he moved from her thigh to her lips, teething them gently at first, then a little harder. She squirmed with discomfort, tearing at the medical cabling, and so he nibbled like a cat upon a dead mouse,

152

gnawing at those exposed pieces of her then pulling her wider to expose even more.

He felt drunk on her flavour, her smell and her screams working him into a frenzy until once more he was gazing into a black, black hole, watching the things that moved beyond the darkness, beyond the bright red lips now spattered with blood.

He tongued the cleft at its edges, pressing hard enough to feel the bone beneath, her clitoris immense and swollen as he kissed her, making her skin flutter beneath his touch. A tiny fleshy bulb that was the centre of all this, the centre of everything, so beautiful like a gem, a precious jewel, was this it? Was this what he had been looking for?

The muskiness that emerged from her like a living thing grew stronger as her orgasm approached, almost tangible as he teethed her clitoris, pulled on her pubic hairs, bit his fingernails into her thighs. There was something else beneath the scent that he struggled to find just as he struggled to hold onto her clitoris between his teeth, pulling it as she yelped in pain and shuddered in the chair.

It couldn't be—it couldn't be what he had been looking for. It didn't feel right.

And yet her scent, that something other, it was *decay*. What he was looking for was falling apart, was dying, and if he didn't find it soon it would be gone forever, just so much mush and putrefaction like half-chewed hamburgers stuffed inside them where a foetus should be.

This had to be it, this tiny piece of her that bled a clear fluid into his throat, and so he bit down harder on it until she was jolting away beneath him, ankles and wrists yanking at the restraints and she was pleading him to stop somewhere amongst all those tears but that was what she came here for wasn't it? He bit harder still because he knew it was in there somewhere and it was dying so he had to take it now and so he did, he bit the thing right off amidst a spray of hot, crimson blood and he swallowed.

*

I don't know, doctor. I'm not sure what happened. I just went . . . a little crazy.

Looking at it now, I guess that temporary leave wasn't going to be so temporary after all was it? Poor woman. She was always so kind to me. I guess I might have loved her. I love them all, in a way.

Why?

Why not? You've got to love somebody.   ·

No. Not myself.

I don't even *like* myself.

Next?

To be honest, doctor, I'm not even that sure what happened next. I guess things had really started to go downhill by that point. I lived for that job.

It was too easy to go back to my old ways.

Come on, doctor, you've got my file right there. You know what I mean.

I'm pretty certain my own words won't be as eloquent as the ones you've got down there. I know but . . .

Fine. Okay.

I went back to the streets. The same ones we used to do when we first arrived here.

You know who 'we' is doctor. Don't make me say her name. Please.

(sighs)

Yes. Natalie.

I don't know. I guess some places just become your home whether you like it or not. But it made me feel better to be back there again. I didn't even go to pick someone up. I think I just needed to be there again.

I watched them from the bench we sometimes sat on. They were so young.

Yeah I know. I was sixteen. Natalie was fifteen.

Fifteen. God.

(whispers) *What did I do to her?*

Sometimes, when I think about it all, I find myself blaming her. I actually blame *her*. I tell myself it was her fault for not protesting enough when I took her away from that bastard, for going along with everything I said. The way she acted—she worshipped me.

I never got the chance to tell her I worshipped her.

But what else were we to do? We needed money.

I don't know, doctor. About seven months or so I think? The file should say how long. We got a place pretty soon and began to settle in. But I could see how unhappy she was.

Street hustling is okay to get by on—but no way to live.

It was actually one of hers that suggested she go to Trixie's. I think she tied him up with his seat belt in the back of his truck or something and he said she had a talent.

So we went along, had a trial period. Four weeks.

She never reached week three, doctor.

The sick bastard that suggested she go there in the first place was waiting for her one night. I think he'd been watching her for a while. I was late finishing.

(silence)

Most of it. In a . . . in a cardboard box nearby. 'Folded up like a used rag' was the policeman's delightful phrase, I believe.

I don't want to talk about this any more. This has nothing to do with what happened the other night.

I know, but you asked me . . .

Fine. Fine. Well now I *don't* want to talk about it.

(silence)

Can I have some more water?

*

It felt like he was easing back into a set of well-worn clothes as he began walking the old pitch. He was carefully aware of the territorialism that often erupted into violence, into death, amongst the hustlers so waited until the girl who had previously been walking the street was picked up in a Jeep and taken some place quieter.

Hands firmly in his pockets, he closed his eyes as he headed towards the corner at which he had, at one time, done most of his business, and could almost feel her beside him once more. Her tiny arms wrapped around his waist as she shivered in the cold. She always looked like she would break so easily but she was so *strong*.

Not strong enough, though.

He heard the low rumble of an expensive car sliding up behind him and before he knew what he was doing he had climbed in. It just felt so natural, so easy, like semen sliding down your throat, as he eased himself into the car.

She asked him if he knew somewhere they could go and so he told her about the old steel works nearby. As they turned the corner the panicked thought that the building might not be there any more crossed his mind—how much had changed around him as well as within him?—but it was still standing, a great concrete behemoth with ten-tonne shadows and steel girders for bones where the brickwork had crumbled or been knocked in. In places you could see the machinery that was the inner workings of what had once been a massive industrial heartbeat in the district, now rusted and rotten.

The car engine came to a smooth halt beside the rear entrance to the laundry that had serviced the workers.

155

When the woman told him what she wanted he knew that this was the right place to be, that fate had guided him here. He hadn't made a mistake.

The woman pressed a button on the car's mock-wooden dashboard and the front seats began to fall back into the rear ones. She climbed across the now-level seats and began taking off her shoes and stockings.

He watched her undress her lower half, easily reading that this was not something she did often. He glimpsed the rock on her finger and wondered what it was that made wedding rings repel oral sex.

She wore a spidery tattoo up one leg, from her calf to mid-thigh, shuffled nervously on the makeshift bed until he gave her a reassuring smile and placed one hand on each of her knees. She seemed reluctant to open them at first but in his short time on the streets he had become a master of his own face, of his own power and innocence and of the power of his innocence.

She gripped the head-supports of the rear seats as she watched his head bury itself in her lap.

She was dry with nervousness so he let his saliva lubricate her labia majora, as finely shaped as any he had ever seen. She had prepared herself beforehand—he could smell the vague traces of soap masking her musky scent. Slowly the folds opened for him, shivering minutely, beckoning his tongue.

Her whines came fast, her breathing quickly becoming rapid. He could now see the vague remnants of bruises on her inner thighs that were hidden by the tattoo and wondered how long it had been for her since someone had teased her clitoris as gently as he now did.

He remembered how he had torn the tiny bud of flesh from the woman weeks earlier and thought of how it still felt lodged in his throat even though he had cleaned himself out with bleach and his index finger.

He sucked the woman into his mouth, felt her hands slam into his back, fake fingernails splintering as she pressed him into her.

She was flowing with lubricant now, widening with each lick he gave her, filling his mouth with a honey-like substance that clogged his throat until he spat it back into her. Her lips had peeled back completely, the hole they revealed crying out for him, crying his *name*, something that moved around in there.

Pulling his head away slightly, he gripped either side of her opening with three fingers and pulled at it because he knew that this time, this time, he had found it.

sweet vagina

The woman groaned with momentary pain and bewilderment at what he was doing, then arched her back when he pushed his fingers inside her. His fingers, up to the knuckles. Beyond the knuckles.

Her vaginal lips seemed huge, slopping his hands as they vanished into her, searching, hunting inside her like a fleshy spider.

Tears were streaming before him now because the rotting smell had returned and he wondered if perhaps it was coming from him and not her as he caressed her lining—and then brushed against something soft and wet.

The woman began to protest as the pain became worse, his exploration no longer pleasurable, feeling like he was tearing her open down there. She gasped for him to stop but he wouldn't and before she could do anything it felt as if an acid bomb had exploded inside her, all fire and spikes of razor-pain, dripping out onto the car seats and he was pulling something out of her and smiling, crying, crying that he had found it, he had found it.

*

(silence)

Will it be considered murder, doctor? They haven't told me that yet.

They said it was only a couple of months, maybe two. What's the legal limit for abortion anyway? If it was that young then technically . . .

I know. I know.

How's the woman? If you do, will you let me know? I didn't mean to hurt her. I didn't mean to . . . do what I did.

Will you tell her I'm sorry?

Of course I mean it. I wouldn't have said it if I didn't.

What's going to happen now, doctor?

Evaluation?

Okay.

I don't think it really matters any more, anyway. I think I found what it was I was looking for.

It wasn't her fault, you know. Natalie. Sometimes I blame her, like I said. But I know it wasn't her fault.

None of it was.

She'd only told me a few days before . . . we were so happy.

That was one of the pieces they didn't find, doctor.

Oh. Yes, of course.

I'll look forward to seeing you again.

Just—just tell her I'm sorry. I know it won't . . .

Thank you, doctor.
No, I'll be fine. I'm okay now.
Of course.
Goodbye. (silence)

Open Wound
by
E.C. McMullen, Jr.

Between awake and asleep is the twilight of the mind. The dusk and dawn of the soul resides between two worlds: one fact, the other fantasy; but in that place, that in-between state, both worlds are just as real.

In that place Ruth remembered shards of edged memory. She remembered the woman who was brought in to the emergency room, having been run through from the back and out her belly by the drunk driver of a forklift. Her body's reaction had been to develop traumatic arthritis.

Ruth remembered the man who survived being struck by lightening. Within a few months, his hereditary male pattern baldness went Chia pet on him.

She remembered the little girl who accidentally cut the tip of her finger off down to the first knuckle. The doctor cleaned it, treated it but refused to sew it. Instead, he left the bandaged wound open and sternly told the dubious parents to change the bandages daily but not to seal the wound. Eight months later the girl's finger was completely healed—new bone, muscle, flesh, and nail. Everything she'd lost was back.

This is what her sleeping mind told her.

On the other hand . . .

This is what her waking mind told her.

Ruth smelled the scent of sweat, decay and stale air. The temperature was warm and her body was wet. There was the sound of others sleeping in the room. There were male sounds and, in addition to these, there were those same shards of edged memory.

Same shards, different memories; same coin different side.

Ruth remembered the men from the hospital: the paid research subjects.

She had argued with one of the doctors because this particular group of men was known for getting busted for drug use. When one project was over they would volunteer for the next.

"It's bad science," Ruth told Dr. Alan Retson. "These test subjects haven't waited for the long-term effects to wear off before they're back in here for the next project."

"It would be nice to have such a stable of clean, health conscious applicants to choose from," Dr. Retson said. "Unfortunately, few such people are willing to undergo chemical and drug testing at any price. We have to take what we can get."

Ruth argued from the point of bad science, but she mainly just didn't like them hanging around the hospital. They always looked mean and stupid, a look they enhanced with coarse language and belligerent attitudes. She suspected them of stealing prescription drugs as the pharmacy's stocks were dwindling unexpectedly.

This was the path her waking mind was walking, and Ruth was hesitant to follow. This was why she remained in that "in between" state.

Remembering her talk with Dr. Retson also led her to the part where she left his office to find the five men hanging around outside his door. They had heard what she'd said and from the looks they gave her, did not approve. Ruth was threatening their income from the research, and who knew what else that they were stealing from the hospital.

That was on a Monday. Tuesday she didn't see them at all. Wednesday they had returned and were as quiet as lead around her. The last thing she remembered about Wednesday was walking toward the hospital exit on her way to her car. She remembered nothing else about Wednesday after that.

Early Thursday Morning? Jesus Christ, she remembered that.

She remembered being held down on a damp floor. She remembered their cocks being pushed into her body and their needles into her veins. She knew she was being drugged so that she couldn't fight back but was still fully aware.

She remembered.

What was today? Today with the stale smells and the sound of snoring and slumber; mumbles through drowsy dreams. What day was this?

Ruth slowly woke from a dream of revenge, of fighting back, and into this twilight mindset. Remembering everything, past and present, Ruth opted for escape and brought herself fully awake; to whatever her world would be.

Her clothes were cold and damp and she was lying on a dirty bare mattress. She had to take a piss, God did she ever, and lifted herself up from the bed—careful so as not to wake the others.

She looked down at her clothes. They had dressed her in filthy men's clothes, wet with blood, her blood no doubt. Her hands were large; swollen with possible beatings and perhaps broken bones. Ruth wasn't sure because she felt no pain. Her body might be in shock or still under the effects of any one of the many drugs they shot into her. She felt strong though, strong enough to break out of here.

Quietly she opened the bathroom door. The bathroom was closer than the front door and there weren't four full-grown men between her and escape. Ruth hoped that with luck she could exit through the bathroom window. Her heart sank when she quickly discovered that this house had no window in the bathroom. Such wonderful, wonderful privacy!

It did have a mirror though, which she specifically avoided. There were any number of things they may have done to her last night and she wasn't up to seeing them. Right now she had to be strong and keep her spirits up. Her body didn't feel right—perhaps the drugs were wearing off—and she just needed to pee.

She didn't notice when she pulled her pants down. She was aware that something wasn't right when she sat on the filthy toilet seat. It was when she let go and a stream of orange urine shot out between her legs, missing the bowl completely, and splattered on the wall in front of her.

"What the hell?" she hissed. Now she was awake. Now she felt the lump between her thighs. And when she jumped up to see what had happened, she found herself looking at a man's penis between her legs.

Those sick bastards left a damn dildo inside of me! was her first thought.

Right on the heels of that was the second thought: *It's real!*

And then came the dizzying third thought: *It's mine?*

With her brain swimming through high tension adrenaline squirts, she inspected the alien artifact between her legs. All the inane possibilities leapt before her mind: *they grafted a man's penis on me while I was out; I'm still dreaming;* and the explanations became even more impossible and ridiculous until Ruth was finally confronted with the fact that there were no stitches, she was clearly awake, and she had a man's penis instead of a vagina. She inspected the deflating organ from every angle. She pulled on it, yanked on it in the hopes of revealing the trick. The skin of her body stretched with it . . . the new discovery! So focused was she on the shock of having a penis that it took her a while to realize that the skin that stretched with the penis—that had no stitches (no stitches whatsoever!)—was also covered in hair.

Ruth pulled off the T-shirt that covered her. Hair, hair everywhere on her body and . . .

Now she had to look in the mirror and did so before she could prepare herself for the shock.

A man's face, totally awestruck, looked back at her. The obscene abuse of the night before fled in the face of this utterly confusing reality.

Ruth's father, a caring, gentle man, was not given to casual profanity. But a phrase he used in the most unusual of circumstances (unusual for him, that is; Ruth believed herself a bit more worldly) leapt to her own lips at this moment.

"What in the living hell?"

"Oh shit!" shouted someone outside the door.

Self preservation overrode Ruth's confused sexuality. There was no window in the bathroom and the men were waking up. They were waking up fast by the sound of it.

"Tommy! Wake up, man! Stan! This is an emergency! The broad is gone!"

Voices in the next room went from drowsy to alert.

"She escaped?

"How the hell did that happen?"

"Where's Doug?"

"Who's in the bathroom?"

A sudden pounding on the door

"Doug! Doug! You in there? You got the girl in there with you?"

Someone spoke in a tone of hopeful relief, "Whew! That's all it is: Doug's got the bitch in the bathroom."

There was a pause in the pounding.

"Doug, you in there? Answer me, God damn it."

Ruth could hear them gathering outside the door. She backed up, but where would she go? How would she defend herself? In the manner of weapons there was the shower rod, but it was long and clumsy. There was the toilet scrubber, but you can't defend yourself with a bunch of bristles around a hole. Fast running out of options, Ruth could only look at herself again. Was she Doug?

She had to be Doug.

She had always been Doug.

Why did he ever think he was a woman named Ruth?

Whispering outside the door.

"Doug probably left to get some smokes, man. The bitch is in there."

There was a whole change in attitude outside the door.

"Okay, babe," one of them said, calm returning to his voice. "Your cover is blown, now come out of there."

Another voice spoke with a new worry.

"Hey guys, did you notice all the blood in the room?"

"Blood?"

"Shit! Carl ain't lying! Look at this mess!"

"Did we do that?"

Open Wound

Frantic pounding on the door again.

"Open up this God Damn door, you cunt!"

A very timid, worried voice spoke, "Maybe she crawled in there to die?"

A more heated voice, the voice of the one who had been knocking and shouting at the door, yelled. "She better not die in my fucking house, man! Bitch! Open this door! Don't you fucking die in my house!"

With a violent crash, the door suddenly jerked in its frame. Doug backed up, trying to think of his options. He was trapped, there was nowhere to go. Unlike last night, the terror of what was happening to her was not dulled by drugs.

The door burst open and the hulking form of the shouter bulldozed his way into the small space. With violent fury he lay eyes on Doug. His face went from mean and vicious to confused, and from there to fearful. His hulking stance changed to a terror of his own. Doug, still feeling like Ruth, was also terrified. He tripped over the rim of the tub and fell backwards into the empty bath.

"Doug?" the shouter asked.

The other men tried to squeeze in behind the shouter.

"What is it, Jim, what . . ?"

One by one, the men all looked at Doug.

"Doug, what happened to you?"

It took a while to get Doug out of the bathroom. There were too many things going on at once for the men to fully comprehend it all but the facts seemed to be this:

1- The doctor who tried to fuck them over—the one they drugged, beat, and gang-raped the night before—was gone.

2- The cops would soon be on their way, more than likely.

3- But the absolute worst was that Doug, who was covered in blood, had . . . *somehow* . . . shrunk.

Jim sat in a cushioned comfy chair while the three other men threw out fantastic explanations, ideas, and epithets. Lots of epithets, lots of profanity, nobody knew what was going on.

"We got to get out of here, Jim!" the one called Tommy said. "We're gonna get our asses busted."

"We're leaving," Jim said. "Stan!" One of the men turned his attention to Jim.

"Stan, go take a shower, get shaved, and get some clean clothes on. Do it now."

"What's the plan?" Stan asked.

"The plan," said Jim, "is we get the hell out of here. Look at this place! The carpet is soaked with blood! This house is a bad loss: Bad, bad! This is run for the border kind of bad."

While Stan took his shower, the rest of the guys—per Jim's instructions—washed their hands up to their elbows. When Stan was through, the rest handed him his cleanest clothes. When he was dressed they hoisted him into the air and carried him out the door. This way there was no blood on his shoes or any other part of him. Stan got the car and drove it around to the alley behind the house. The men ran out and jumped into the car, taking care to avoid touching Stan.

They pulled into a gas station a few blocks up the street. Stan kept the attendant busy with purchase and banter while the men, Doug included, went to the men's room located in the back of the building, separate from the store. They took turns running water over their blood-caked shoes and cleaning the soles with their toothbrushes. Like the others, Doug cleaned himself completely from the sink, drying off with paper towels. Then they took their clean clothes out of the plastic grocery bags they'd brought and got dressed.

"There," Jim said. "Fresh and clean. Let's go."

They drove a few blocks and then Stan traded places with Jim.

Doug sat in the back with Tommy and Mike.

From time to time, Jim took his eyes off the road to look at Doug from the rear view mirror.

"How do you feel, Doug?" he asked.

It seemed there was suspicion in the voice but Doug didn't know how or why. Perhaps Jim wasn't sure himself.

Taking a risk on their possible addictions, Doug said, "I could really use a shot of something."

Jim eyed him from the mirror.

"A shot of what?" he asked.

Not knowing a thing about Doug or his preferences, he said, "Anything would be good right now."

The other men chuckled and Jim smiled grimly. Doug felt like a sheep in wolf's clothing.

On the freeway, they drove past the hospital where Ruth worked and they'd submitted.

Jim kept watching Doug's eyelids flitter and blink. Finally he pulled the car into the right hand exit lane.

"What's going on, man?" Tommy asked.

"We're going to the hospital," was Jim's graven reply.

A flurry of profanity erupted in the car.

164

Open Wound

"Are you out of your fucking mind?" shouted Mike.

"We'll get busted!" Stan moaned.

Jim shouted them all down. "Then we get fucking busted!"

"We'll go to trial and if we don't like the way it goes we'll have that bitch killed before it's over! But Doug used to be over six feet and now he's only about five five! I wanna know why, God damn it! That ain't natural!"

"It's just one of those weird things, Jim!" Stan protested.

"Nothing is that weird!" Jim hollered. "We've been letting them pump us up with all kinds of shit over the past year. Plus we've been doing a bunch of junk to ourselves. Shit man! Look at Doug! I never thought that it would make us fucking shrink! And where did all that fucking blood come from? No way was it from the cunt! She couldn't have lost that much blood and lived!"

"Damn, Jim," Mike said. "Women bleed all the fucking time. It's natural."

The car came to a squealing halt, fishtailing as it did. Jim turned around in his seat.

"Any of you motherfuckers want to get out, get out now. I can deal with prison, but I'm not going to shrink to nothing! What's happening to Doug could happen to all of us and it ain't gonna happen to me. Who the fuck wants out?"

Put that way, and with Jim's roaring testosterone, nobody wanted to leave, although Tommy, sitting right next to Doug, pushed away and into Mike. Doug was anathema.

The men walked, nearly as a military unit, into the just cleaned emergency room of the hospital. Jim in front, Doug bringing up the rear.

I think I'm Ruth, Doug thought. *But I can't be Ruth. I'm a man. I've always been a man named Doug. I'm a rapist and a criminal. I live like an animal with four other men. I abuse drugs and make my living as a research subject for human experiments.*

Doug tried very hard but couldn't remember a single day as a man.

Perhaps I wasn't always a rapist, he thought. *Maybe what I did last night was so shocking that my mind became unbalanced. Perhaps I'm experiencing a transference of guilt: assuming that I'm the victim instead of the attacker. Is that right? Is that how it works?*

Jim was talking to the nurse on duty, demanding to see Dr. Retson. He reached out and grabbed Doug.

"Look at this. Yesterday Doug stood as tall as me, six foot three! Now he's only five foot six or so."

The nurse, dressed in roomy hospital smock and within her booth of Formica and glass was at home in her station. She listened to Jim's bizarre announcement and stated plainly, "That's impossible."

"It's fucking real!" Jim shouted. In his panic he didn't keep his voice down. The nurse physically reacted to Jim's words the way she would to a slap across her face. Jim's noise attracted the attention of several patrolmen a few doors down.

The Duty nurse had seen this group of men before and she vaguely remembered Doug. She bent over her station to look at Doug's feet, as if they were perhaps trying to trick her by cutting Doug off at the knees.

There was definitely something wrong with this man, the nurse decided. He was too petit for this crowd. Yet her mind wouldn't accept someone just shrinking—certainly not within a twenty-four hour period.

"Dr. Retson is busy right now," she said. Routine procedure kicked in and banished her confused thoughts. "I'll call him. Please sit over there."

Jim was too frightened to comply. He reached into her territory, grabbed the phone, and punched the intercom button.

"Dr. Retson!" Jim shouted. "Come to the emergency room stat!"

The policemen, who had been attracted to Jim's loud voice, now converged on his group.

They came up, quick and orderly: all dark uniforms and sidearms. Jim looked wild and frantic. Only now did he comprehend his behavior and question the rashness.

"What's the problem, Jim?" the first officer, a Barry Morris, asked. Jim and his little group of troublemakers were well known to the police in this precinct. "You want to step away from the nurse's station?"

"We're the lab rats here. We're employees!" Jim said, trying to tone down his voice and avoid trouble. The damn bitch was around here somewhere. She had to be. They should have gone to another hospital. But other hospitals didn't have Dr. Retson.

The other five cops surrounded the group and began pulling them away from Jim.

"I know what you do here, Jim," Officer Morris spoke even and firm. "Please step over here."

When Jim was isolated from the group Officer Morris made sure that all of Jim's attention was focused on him. "Now what's the problem?"

"We're fucking shrinking, man!"

"Mind your language, Jim," Morris said. Jim didn't know there was a second cop standing behind him. He heard a third cop calling for backup. Things were getting worse.

Open Wound

"This is a pubic place," Morris said matter-of-factly. "Now calm down and explain the problem to me."

"We're shrinking! Look at Doug!"

The police officer looked at Doug.

"That's not Doug, Jim. Doug is your height."

"He fucking shrunk, God damn it!"

Doug saw the officer behind Jim ready himself to bring the big man down.

"I told you about your language once, Jim. Now we either talk to each other like human beings or I'll have to arrest you and take you downtown until . . ."

"Will you look at Doug?" Jim gasped.

The officer looked over at Doug.

"What's your name, sir?"

"Doug," Doug answered.

"Doug what?"

"Doug . . ." Doug didn't know what to say. He didn't remember his last name. "I don't know," he said after a moment.

"Right," Morris said wearily. Then he turned to Jim. "What are you on right now, Jim?"

"I'm straight!" Jim said. "One hundred percent!"

"Sure you are," the officer said laconically. "And if we went over to your place and searched your house we wouldn't find anything unusual?"

Jim couldn't speak. There were illegal drugs to be sure. As well as the legal ones they stole from this hospital. But worst of all was the blood everywhere. What could he say? He had to really think and that was never his strong point.

What could he say to keep them from searching his house? What? He should have just jumped town. But they were shrinking! What could he do?

Jim pretended a look of defeat and turned to Doug. "I'm sorry, Doug. But I gotta tell them."

Tommy was the first to understand the roll over and shouted, "Jim, you fucking narc!"

*

In the last eight hours Doug had been arrested, fingerprinted, blood tested, given a urine sample, put in the city jail, then removed from there and put in the far-more-secure county jail.

His friends, in other cells, were there too. The cops had gotten a search warrant and found the blood, but that hadn't been the worst thing. Hidden behind one of the couches was a bloody skeleton, poorly flensed of meat.

Jim said that Doug had forced them all to rape the woman doctor who worked at the hospital. Ruth somebody . . . He was confused and genuinely surprised about the skeleton.

The others said Jim was the one who led the group. They were confused and equally surprised about the skeleton.

Doug didn't have an alibi and had been looking confused and surprised all day.

They all thought Ruth had escaped. No one could explain the skeleton of the man behind the couch or where the rest of him was. It was a mind bender to criminal and cop alike.

Instead of bars, the higher security county lockup had cinderblock walls and solid metal doors with tempered glass set at head height—head height for most people anyway.

At lights out, Doug's new roommate—a man who stood at least six-five—came to life.

"How are you doing there, Doug?" the man called from his top bunk. "My name's Rick."

Truthfully, Doug wasn't feeling too good. He hurt all over as if he felt the oncoming sickness of poisoning. "Not so good, Rick."

"Well, why don't you talk about it?"

"No thanks."

His cellmate was suddenly on the floor next to his bunk, his bad breath pushing right up Doug's nose.

"Doug," he said. "Let me tell you something. Now there's assholes in prison who are just fucked. They'll make you stick your tongue up their ass—not because they like it—but just to humiliate you. That's all they are about. Me, I'm not that way at all, but you had better be prepared for the worst."

Rick grabbed Doug's arm and shook it.

"You're a little guy, see? And little guys are bitches in the house. It's unfair, but that's the way it is."

"I've been in jail before," Doug said, though he couldn't remember a day of it.

Rick, in one swift action, pulled him out of his bunk.

"Then you know where I'm coming from, Doug." Rick stood towering over the smaller man. There were no zippers on the prison uniform so Rick just shucked the pants down.

Open Wound

"I want you to know that I'm not doing this to humiliate you, Doug. I just want sex."

The big man set his hands on Doug's shoulders, forcing him to bend down.

Through the dizzying swim of Doug's nausea, he knew he'd done this before.

Last night when the guys were raping him

But wait? Did they rape him or did they rape Ruth? Was that it? Perhaps there was no Ruth! Maybe he was blocking thoughts of his own rape and was using some mythic Ruth as a proxy.

But then why was he even in here? That doctor named Ruth was missing and . . .

And there was a cock, bobbing and hard, inches from his mouth.

His cellmate was making a pretense at being kind, but Doug was well aware of the mercurial flash tempers of such people when they didn't get their way.

"Put it in your mouth, Doug," Rick ordered. "There's no shame here." Rick's big hands pushed Doug's reluctant face closer to his cock. "Just put it in your mouth and suck. I'll do the rest."

Rick's cock was now pressed to Doug's lips and Doug knew he'd have to give in. Otherwise he would be beaten to a pulp, get his teeth knocked out, and Rick would probably fuck him first and then force a weaker, bleeding Doug to suck him off, fecal matter and all.

Doug took the hard flesh into his mouth and Rick moaned with approval.

"I'll do the rest, Doug," Rick said and used his hands to bob Doug's head on his cock like he was dribbling a basketball.

Doug was already feeling ill and this wasn't making things any better. He could smell his own stink and wondered why Rick didn't notice. Maybe the big man did smell the stench and opted for a simple blow job instead of a full ass fuck.

"You'll get better at this, Doug," Rick said. "By the time I'm through with you, you'll be a fine bitch. No one will want to hurt you in prison. You'll belong to the king of the house."

The pain was crawling all over Doug's body from the inside out now. It struck down past his human brain, past his animal brain, the pain and the instinct to survive grabbing him deep in his most primitive lizard brain, awakening instincts he never knew he had. Like humans instinctively curl into a fetal position when critically wounded, so something came alive in Doug's deepest id. Only it didn't belong to Doug.

Rick was close to orgasm and arched his back, urging his sperm forward and out. He took his hands away from Doug's head to hold his own while the intense euphoria trembled through him.

Ruth's head pushed itself out of Doug's face, Rick's cock still sliding within her lips. Rick came in Ruth's mouth while Doug's head stretched and tore, falling back to allow Ruth's shoulders to emerge.

Rick spurted a second shot, then a third, totally lost in his orgasm, and Ruth took it in. Ruth was doped up the first time, but now she was fully aware of what was happening. She was being raped again and there were no drugs to confuse her senses. Aware but unable to stop herself, her body was now ruled by her most primal, unknown instincts.

Doug's flesh was collapsing around her naked body and Ruth had no doubt what Rick would do when he found himself locked and alone in a cell with a woman. He would be stunned, but he would also attack her.

While Rick's head was still thrown back and strained with his pleasure, Ruth quickly removed her mouth from his penis. Without looking, Rick's hands slowly lowered to push Doug's head back onto his throbber to catch all of his come.

Instead, Ruth violently grabbed Rick's naked ass and bit into his abdomen, tearing flesh and drawing blood.

Rick's hands froze in mid air. His orgasm slowly ebbed, and he didn't know what to make of this new sensation. It hurt, but was it a good thing?

With her mouth wide, Ruth quickly bit again—as much as she could get—tearing flesh, muscle, and organ tissue.

Rick gasped a lungful of air to scream out in pain, but Ruth, a trained doctor, was aware of the position of the diaphragm and the intercostals. The meat between the ribs she could do nothing about but she rammed her small hands into the wound she made and forced Rick's organs out onto the floor. Then she pushed her face up, biting and searching for the diaphragm. She pushed against it, forcing the air back out of Rick before he had a chance to form a shout. Stunned, Rick didn't yell but looked at his own damage in utter amazement. His thoughts were shouting sirens through his mind.

A naked woman was now kneeling in front of him.

What the hell? he thought.

And the skin of a man was lying at her feet like old clothes.

What the fuck?

His insides were pouring out onto the floor.

Holy shit!

The woman's head disappeared into his belly.

Open Wound

Rick inhaled again, expanding his lungs to really yell for help this time. He tried to grab at Ruth's body and pull her out of him, but her naked flesh was wet and slick with his own blood, making her too slippery to hold. Ruth felt his diaphragm push against her nose and with her teeth and one hand grabbed it and tore it out of Rick's body.

Rick could no longer control his lungs to belt out a shout and the air wheezed out of his mouth as a whisper. His legs buckled, collapsed and he fell back, dragging Ruth on top of him. Ruth felt around and grabbed his rib cage and vertebrae. She wrapped her hands tight around these two sets of bones, her nails severing muscle tissue, and yanked as hard as she could. Then she tore and yanked again. Rick, stunned, though fully conscious, could only feel himself being killed. His arms no longer worked as his body's massive blood loss caused circulatory collapse and he went into shock.

In some strange distant way, almost as an observer, Ruth witnessed herself tearing a man apart. She was forcing his skeleton to come loose, and even reaching up to his face to hold it in place while she tore the skull out from within it.

With one more yank, Rick's skeleton—from the head down to the pelvis—was hanging outside of his body. Blood was everywhere.

The brain can live about four minutes without oxygen.

Rick's eyes, largely moored by muscle tissue to their sockets, could only stare unblinking at his own destruction. Ruth was vicious in her tearing of Rick from the inside out. Rick's brain, protected within his skull, and his nervous system, protected within its vertebrae, were paralyzed but conscious. He had gasped a lot of oxygen before Ruth tore out his diaphragm and lungs. It hadn't even been a minute yet. His glistening skull tapped lightly and painlessly on the hard floor as the strange woman tried to disengage more of his muscle from his bone.

He was awake!

He was aware!

He saw the folded dead flesh of the man he thought was Doug. He saw the naked body of Ruth ravenously burrow into him like a rabid animal. His entire upper skeleton collapsed onto the floor as, in Ruth's violent madness she accidentally tore his thigh bones from the tendons and ligaments that held them to his pelvis.

Rick lay there discarded, wanting to breathe, needing to breathe, but without the ability to do so. He was suffocating even while his head lay on the remains of his destroyed lungs. Minutes passed until the lack of oxygen brought Rick hallucinations. The hallucinations brought out dancing demons and long-suppressed fears. Second by second, Rick slowly faded into death and nightmarish visions of pain and torture.

*

Officer Ted Sellers had been a fingerprint analyst long enough to recognize a simple but stupid mistake when he saw one. He scanned the fingerprints into the computer anyway, just in case he needed to justify his decision.

Standing in Captain Rollings' office, Ted produced the information card and announced, "This isn't Doug Mays."

Ted had tried to keep it under wraps. He went to Julie, who had taken Doug's fingerprints and mug shot and filled out the card. Showing Julie her mistakes never yielded positive results. Julie was under the assumption, despite repeat evidence to the contrary, that she was perfect. Julie *always* shot herself in the foot by *always* denying her own responsibility until her nose was shoved into the proof. Many of her minor mistakes could have been corrected if Julie had only done them when she was told. But she was so ultra sensitive to even the mildest of criticism.

"I fingerprinted him myself, ma'am!" Julie defended.

Captain Ann Rollings looked at both of them. Ted was a professional who had a sterling record. Julie, on the other hand, had a reputation for sloppiness and blaming everyone but herself.

Ted spoke again, "I pulled the file on Doug Mays." He flourished a folder. Ted had clashed with Julie enough in the past to know he should cover his ass entirely.

"According to his file, Doug Mays is six-foot-three. Julie wrote five-foot-five on this guy's card." Ted pointed out the details. "Also, look at the mug shot. Sure this guy resembles Doug, but his bone structure is more delicate. Look at this old photo of Doug. He's a monster."

"He looked like his driver's license," Julie protested. "Brown hair, blue eyes, Caucasian . . ."

Ted brought out Doug's personal belongings.

"Who gave you that?" the captain said.

"I thought I might need it," Ted answered. He turned the packet upside down and Doug's license dropped out. Ted started to pick it up but Rollings grabbed it first. She looked at the license, at the mug shots, at the license again, and then scowled at Julie.

"Julie," she said. "What does this card say?"

Julie looked and said nothing.

Open Wound

"It says six-foot-three," the captain growled. "You could have solved this simple mistake yourself and I wouldn't have even been involved. Why do you go out of your way to get in trouble?"

"But he really is short, ma'am," Julie protested. "He's shorter than me!"

"Then you're telling me that the man you processed had a phony or stolen driver's license and you didn't catch it?"

Julie thought a moment. She had run out of excuses. If the rest of her story was to be believed then, "Yes, ma'am," Julie sulked.

"So," Rollings said. "Who is in cell D6?"

*

Ruth wondered if they monitored water use at the jail. She used the bed sheets to mop up the blood on the floor, squeeze them out in the toilet, flush and repeat. When she felt it was done she did her best to wash the sheet in the toilet water, again, flushing repeatedly. Finally she made Doug's bed with the blood-stained sheet. She put the coarse blanket over it. Then she took her bed sheet and went over the floor again. Then the rinse in the toilet, then the flushing and squeezing, then she did the floor again. Ruth wanted to make the blood disappear entirely. Not an easy thing to do in a dark cell.

Rick's body sucked up to her and fit perfectly though it sagged a bit around the waist. *Human flesh is so pliable*, her medical mind thought.

During her rage or whatever it was, she ate her fill of Rick before her normal mindset took over. Oddly enough, she didn't throw up. Ruth perfunctorily stuffed the leftover Rick into Doug's empty skin. Rick's skeleton, already inside Doug, held his old organs nicely in the small Doug suit. Doug's skin, grown around a smaller man, stretched a bit. He lost a few lines around the eyes but looked younger at any rate. The smell was obvious though. Doug had been dead for twenty-four hours. He was ripe.

After Ruth did the best she could to clean the cell she started to work on herself. There was very little water pressure coming out of the sink/toilet combo and there was no soap. Finally though, Rick's body was clean.

She wondered what to do next when the lights came on.

The door abruptly opened and two guards stood outside.

"Doug, or whatever your name is, come on out of there."

These were the night shift guards. They hadn't seen Doug before. They only knew that there was a tall man in the cell and a short man and that "Doug" was supposed to be the small guy.

Ruth, in her new Rick suit, moved forward.

One of the guards, eyeing the well-made empty bed, stopped her.

173

"Didn't you even sleep?"

"I . . . couldn't get to sleep," Ruth/Rick answered.

"So you made your bed instead," he said in an odd voice. "How very neat of you."

The guard looked at the body, covered in sheet and blanket, on the top bunk.

He watched.

Something wasn't right.

"Hey you," he said. "Move or something."

The man on the top bunk did nothing.

The guard stepped inside and stopped. He looked at the room. There were swirling smears of light and distinct reddish browns all over the lower wall and floor.

"What a dump," the guard said. "Doesn't anybody bother to clean these rooms?" He stepped over to the bunk, withdrew his night stick, stepped back in case the man woke up in a violent mood, and poked at the body.

"What's this guy's name again?" the first guard asked.

"Rick Annolie," the second guard said.

"Hey Rick," the first guard called out. "Mr. Annolie."

The guard looked at Ruth/Rick.

"You stand outside the cell," the first guard said. "And don't get cute because you're locked in here and there's nowhere to go."

The first guard nodded to his partner who withdrew his gun and trained it on the Doug/Rick body.

Carefully, the first guard grabbed a part of the blanket covering Doug/Rick and yanked it away.

The smell of human decay and blood filled the room.

The first guard made a face and nearly retched.

*

The entire county jail was in stage two lockdown. No prisoner transport, only personnel and sanctioned guests were allowed to enter or leave.

Doctor Retson had been called from the hospital only because Jim, Tommy, Stan, and Carl were going mad begging for him.

Captain Rollings sat at her desk while several of her guards and a few police officers stood or sat in her office. Dr. Retson sat patiently, wondering how the trouble stirred up by his test subjects could involve him.

"Its simple," the first guard said. "We have two guys in that cell. One is supposed to be Doug Mays, who is six-foot-three. The other is Rick Annolie, who is six-foot-six."

"The guy in there who is six-six is dead and he doesn't look like Rick. The guy who kinda looks like Rick is alive but only five-five. And now you're telling me that the guy who is supposed to be Doug Mays *isn't* Doug Mays and that we lost somebody . . ."

The captain interrupted him. "You need to calm down, officer."

"Did Julie fuck up the paperwork again? Is that . . ?"

"I said—" Rollings spoke sternly. "—Calm down!"

The captain looked at a monitor where Ruth/Rick sat alone in a room next to a desk. "First, we interred someone who looked like Doug Mays but wasn't tall enough to be Doug Mays. Now we wind up with someone who looks like Rick Annolie but isn't tall enough to be Rick Annolie."

"Maybe the tall man came and crushed them down," Dr. Retson quietly mused. Rollings glared at the doctor sternly, but everyone else ignored the comment.

"And," the first guard added, "we have the body of someone who looks like Doug Mays but is too tall to be Doug Mays."

Officer Barry Morris, who had gone off duty and was now back on his shift, spoke up. "I arrested the group of men that were with Doug at the hospital. They were trying to see you, Doctor."

"Yes," Doctor Retson said. "They're research subjects of mine."

Officer Morris continued. "The group's leader—Jim—said that Doug had shrunk overnight. They were concerned that they would all shrink."

"Ridiculous!" Dr. Retson huffed.

"Shrunk overnight?" the captain asked.

"They've been subjected to experimental drugs," Morris said. "They were worried that the drug was going to shrink them all. They got so frantic that we had to arrest them. That and the confession."

"What confession?" Dr. Retson asked.

"Jim said Doug killed a staff member of your hospital: one Doctor Ruth Campion. Has she made an appearance at your hospital yet?"

Dr. Retson was utterly surprised. "Ruth is dead?"

The police investigation was quite young and there was nothing solid enough to warrant official announcement. No trace of Ruth had been found, so Jim's confession was questionable. No one at the hospital had been told of the possible homicide and the questions to Ruth's whereabouts had been made quietly.

"We don't know for a fact that she is dead," Morris said. "She hasn't shown up at your hospital? There have been no calls?"

"None that I'm aware of," Dr. Retson said.

"Not aware?" Captain Rollings asked. "Isn't Dr. Campion one of your personal research staff?"

"Not as such," Dr. Retson said. He began a lie before he even knew where he was going with it. His first knee-jerk response was to protect his valued research from possible threat. "She assisted us in our . . ."

"She assisted," the captain interrupted, fast smelling a hoax. "But she had nothing to do with your research staff?"

"Well she worked there, with us, in a capacity . . ."

Captain Rollins interrupted again, knifing her way through Retson's words. She could spot a lengthy run-around when she heard one and chose to nip this in the bud. All she wanted were "yes's and no's".

"Was she part of your team, doctor—yes or no?"

"She was part of my team, yes." Retson floundered. All these police around him, staring at him! "But why am I being questioned like this? I have nothing to do with this!"

"It seems this all began," the captain said, "when five of your research subjects were apprehended at your hospital—all looking for you. Then we get a confession to a murder of one of the doctors on your research team. Then we go and search the house. The living room was covered in blood, but do you know what else we found?"

Doctor Retson shook his head no. Even Barry, who was off-duty then and not part of the search team, was unaware of what was found.

"We found," the captain continued, "a fresh male skeleton."

This kind of publicity could seriously damage the research. The company funding Retson's research had a potential big money winner on their hands and, in addition to the research grant; Retson had been offered stock options.

"What do you mean?" Retson asked weakly. "Fresh?"

"I mean," said the captain, "that there was still blood and muscle attached to it. Its spine was fresh; its brain was still inside the skull."

None of the officers or guards had been present during the search, but now they made faces of disgust as they vividly imagined the scene.

"Now we are having this major dilemma at my job," Rollins continued, almost cordially. "At first I thought it was the mistake of one of my own, but I have four men who are willing to go on record as saying that their friend shrunk during the night. Is there anything in your experimental drugs that could make someone shrink overnight?"

"It's ridiculous I tell you!" Dr. Retson shouted. "We're just testing an oral drug. It's a diet thing to relieve hunger pain. Besides, it's physically impossible to shrink a living human body. Especially overnight!"

"Perhaps they didn't notice at first," the captain said. "Could Doug have shrunk over the course of two days?"

"No!"

"Then it wasn't my fault?" Julie asked.

"Quiet, Julie," spat the captain. Someone was leading her around in circles and she didn't like it. "You still screwed up on the fingerprints," she added.

Ted spoke up. "Not on the fingerprints, Captain, on the description. The fingerprints do belong to Doug Mays, I checked them thoroughly. But the photo that is supposed to belong to Doug . . . and his height . . . it's all wrong."

"Same exact set of prints," the captain said, thinking. "Doug's friends say he shrunk—and if he did shrink, then that man in the cell is Doug."

"Was Doug," Ted offered. "Unless Doug suddenly grew over a foot and died."

The captain eyed Dr. Retson. "So it all comes back to you."

"It comes back to me?" Dr. Retson said through gritted teeth. "Doug shrunk, then grew tall, then died? That's impossible, Captain. This is just a stupid filing error on your part."

Captain Rollins was silent for a moment. She felt certain that all her bases were covered. She hoped to hell that she hadn't been taken in by another of Julie's boondoggles. There was way too much weirdness in this case. Most cases have one oddball thing a detective has to get around to understand the whole picture. But as Rollins' husband would say, this situation was screwed, blued, and tattooed.

One God damn thing after another, her mother would say. They were both right. In this scenario, one unbelievable thing led to an impossible thing and then an outrageous thing. It was crazy just to think about it. There was nothing solid to hold onto. Julie may have made a slight error, but this was way beyond Julie.

In the long uncomfortable silence of Captain Rollins' thoughts, Ted offered hope for something tangible, "Maybe it's just a filing error. We could re-check the dead guy and this new person's fingerprints?"

Rollins felt she was in over her head, out of her depth and sinking fast. Ted's suggestion brought her to the surface for a moment. Breaking from her fugue, she slowly picked up the phone to call the morgue, blinked at one of the guards and said, "Bring our mystery guest in here."

*

Ruth/Rick sat quietly at the table, alone in the room. Her sickness had passed as soon as she was within Rick's body. It was stomach-turning nausea to be inside the decaying Doug flesh. She knew that now. Yet outside the skin the very air burned and ate at her. As though her own nerves had rose to the surface of the epidermal layer and her flesh no longer offered protection from the outside. The mad pain drove her on, to burrow into Rick.

But now, for the moment at any rate, Ruth felt comfortable and strong inside Rick's body. Moreover, she felt safe in Rick. Rick was her in-between: Between her and the pain of the outside world. In fact, the union was so complete she couldn't tell where Rick ended and she began.

She flexed Rick's arms, his hands cuffed behind her back. Doug was big but had more fat than muscle. Rick was sculpted solid muscle and that strength was now Ruth's to use.

But why use it? Why not just break free from this body and be herself again? Sure it was painful; her stay in Doug had changed her somehow. But perhaps if she sloughed off Rick's skin then she would have to deal with the pain for a just a bit, only until her body re-adjusted to the outside again. It was some bizarre but natural physical phenomenon that had always existed but one she had never been aware of. No one ever had. It excited her professional curiosity and she mused over possible medical applications for this knowledge until she drew herself short. Her attempt to find logic in all of this died.

I must be going mad, she thought. *What I've done; what's happening to me is insane!*

The lock clicked and the door swung open and a female guard came in. The woman was hefty but only slightly taller than Ruth/Rick. There was nothing soft about the guard, though. She looked like she could handle ten Ruth/Ricks, despite the smaller man's big arms.

"Come with me, sir," she said.

Ruth/Rick looked at her name badge. "Officer Donna Layton?"

"Yes, sir. Get up and come with me now, sir."

Ruth/Rick got up uncomfortably, his cuffed hands almost useless in this position.

"Will someone take these cuffs off soon?" Ruth/Rick asked.

"I can't say, sir." Layton answered. So professional, so by the book: adhere to the strict rules and you'll be safe.

Ruth/Rick walked out into the hall. There were no cameras here, like there were in the room. This small area, with a wink and a nod, was where the lawyers came to talk. This was where the guards or officers could speak in private. Ahead and behind, at the juncture to other hallways, the cameras were everywhere. Ruth experimented with twisting her real hand inside Rick's hand. Rick's flesh wanted to hold onto hers—the

Open Wound

body was still fresh. Decay had not set in yet and Rick's flesh wanted to live. But Ruth's flesh wanted life even more, and its master had not abandoned it. Ever so slightly, Ruth found she could twist her own arm within Rick's. The handcuffs had been set to accommodate Rick's arm size and muscle. It was tight, but within Rick's there was also a certain amount of bloody slipperiness.

Layton closed the door and directed her prisoner up the hall.

Toward the cameras

Toward a meeting with the captain

In between start and destination, anything could happen.

*

The county prison had never known such uproar. The jail was in stage four lockdown. All cells were being searched. All guards had been called to duty. No one was allowed out, only in. There were inspectors and detectives and experts of every stripe arriving every minute. The captain moved carefully among so many bigwigs, knowing full well that since all had happened on her watch, her head was on the plate. She could defray some of the blame toward Officer Julie Disso, but while that might protect her job, it wouldn't protect her career.

When the mystery prisoner didn't show up and officer Layton didn't answer her radio, they did a search. In their one place—their unofficial, off the record private place in the whole county jail—they found their mystery prisoner's dead body, disemboweled and lying in a pool of blood.

It's one God damn thing after another, Captain Rollins thought. She could feel her synapses misfire, lost in total confusion. Thoughts rushed through her head, one chasing the other:

Why would Officer Donna Layton do such a thing? Was she the one behind all of this? Could it be possible that every freaky bizarre thing that had happened in this case was because of her? Could she really have been the one?

Already reports were coming back from the morgue. The forensic doctors had nothing but crazed news. The skeleton inside the dead body found in the cell didn't belong to Doug, though it was Doug's body, sans bones. It had been dead for at least twenty-four hours. The skeleton found in the gang's home had teeth that matched the dental records of one Doug Mays. But Doug had been seen walking around for at least twelve hours after the skeleton had been brought to the morgue. The finger prints of the mystery prisoner belonged to Rick, but the skeleton inside his body was that of a woman. The blood in the carpet of the house also belonged to

179

Doug. How could he have lost so much blood and still lived? And since that wasn't Dr. Ruth's blood, then what became of Dr. Ruth?

Even more pressing: what became of Officer Layton?

*

Officer Ruth/Donna drove down the highway in her stolen police car. She knew she couldn't keep it for long. And she couldn't wander around town in a county jail guard's uniform either.

The pain was like fire on her flesh when she left Rick's body. Her breath had grown short. Whatever living inside a human body had done to her, she would not be able to live without it. The pain of living outside the body wasn't something that she could adjust to. It was the pain of on-coming death.

The bodies she inhabited, once killed, would rot and be unlivable within twenty-four hours. In that time, every time, she'd have to find another "donor".

Ruth felt bad about killing Donna Layton. Doug and Rick had had it coming, but Donna had been a good woman. Ruth's primal animal survival was stronger than her social humane morals it seemed. Still, Ruth made herself a promise: that she would never kill another innocent. That's why she drove into the city and its massive population instead of away from it.

How many bad people live there? she wondered.

The Love in Her Regard
by
By Gerard Houarner

Blood carved channels through the sheen of sweat shimmering across the curve of Veronica's back. Minute muscle spasms launched quakes through the flesh surrounding the fresh, bleeding lips cut into her pale skin, traveling all the way around to breasts veiled in quivering shadow. Her breath came and left in short heaves, as if she was pacing herself for a marathon.

Fisher raised his hand. Sweat stung his eyes. His arm and shoulder were numb. His legs trembled as much from effort as from horror at what he had done to her body. He wanted to lick the blood and sweat from her, seal her wounds with kisses, turn the whip on himself, as he had already done accidentally several times, unintentionally punishing himself for his incompetence at fulfilling her need.

His only solace was her naked body bent before him, the smell of her sex pungent in the dusty basement air, signaling her readiness, if not willingness, for him.

"Now," she said, from a great, cold distance.

Veronica shuddered as Fisher brought the whip down and leather cracked against skin. She took the blow. He wept.

"Bring it down like a machete," she said, the crackle in her words threatening violence. "Let your shoulder drop, lead with your elbow, and snap your wrist down just before contact."

She turned her head to look back and up at him. Legs spread wide, leaning over and forward on steady, outstretched arms braced against the cement brick wall, she was the icon of vulnerability. But her gaze, hard beneath a furrowed brow, sharp enough to cut through the curling strands of auburn hair clinging to her face, fixed on him with the fury and force of a hurricane. He caught his breath, anticipating for a moment the rebellion he desired, the reversal of roles he craved. His cock stiffened as he stared at the open promise of her labia, imagining his tongue probing the cavity between them and tasting the moist morsel of clit meat within.

But her body remained submissive, even as she controlled him with her voice, her eyes, her presence. She was not ready to grant his desire.

He performed as instructed, and again, and another time, and more, and still she would not scream. She turned away, let her head hang down between her arms, as if she had already vomited everything inside her and had nothing left to hold her head up or keep her fragile stance steady against even the breeze from his blows. Her breathing never changed, though blood dribbled down her legs and ribs, dripped to the floor, splashing into a puddle of water. She never cried out, or whimpered, or even sighed.

Fisher reached deep into himself, past his repugnance for the act he was committing, the injury and pain he was causing, the wrongness of his position in relation to her. This was not what he ever wanted to do. Hurting others was, in fact, what he was most afraid of doing. His potential for committing such acts was the deepest source of his self-loathing. He knew he was not his father, of course, or his mother, or brothers and sisters, or cousins, or any of the bullies and thugs who had tortured him during his life. Nor was he their victim, anymore. He was just another man searching for the love of a woman. Veronica had promised him that love. Not in words, or in acts. The covenant was in her scent, her glance, the flow of her body and the sound of her voice. In her demands.

In what Veroncia was making him do was the cost of her love. He knew it. Felt it. He had only to dig further into himself, past easy torments he anticipated and enjoyed, beyond the degradations he offered to seal his bond with another. All that was needed to bask in the love of her regard- was surrender. Sacrifice not only the things he was used to giving, but the acts and feelings that were so hard for him to touch or express in himself.

He tried. The whip handle jumped and slipped in his sweaty hand with each blow landed. The broken fields of her flesh stung his eyes. But he fought to keep hitting her, to reach her by offering the act she desired, to connect with her by submitting to her will. He did what she wanted him to do, and did not demand that she be what he imagined she should be.

Her body was there. Her mind, her feelings, her spirit, all were laid out before him. But they were pieces of a puzzle he could not put together. Her absence from him, from his assault and her own pain, became a black hole of suppressed reaction, warping his own expectations and desires, sucking him into a compelling darkness that stretched him across an infinite moment, an infinite nothingness.

He screamed with each blow, when she would not. And then his scream filled the spaces between the blows, and spilled like a leak from an acid vat until his throat was raw and his strength was gone and the whip flew from his hand and he fell to the ground and lay broken on the filthy floor where he thought he belonged to be trampled when she left him.

"Make me feel," she said as she turned to him, each word an icicle piercing his flesh, chilling him from within. She looked down and through him, waiting.

Feel me, he begged, in his mind, knowing better than to speak as he crawled to where her belongings were piled. He cleaned and dressed her wounds with the supplies she had brought, dressed her, and followed her back upstairs, grateful she still bothered to look at him at all.

*

Through the telescope, Fisher watched Veronica slip out of a robe while listening for her instructions coming through on the cell phone's earpiece. Wind drove a cold rain into his face, and he adjusted the flaps of the plastic hood he wore over his head, making sure the microphone remained dry. The pebbles digging into the soft parts of his body were a distant song reminding him he was laid out on a roof several streets away from Veronica's apartment. The rooftop's grit, like the numbness spreading from his hips, thighs and elbows, and the cold seeping through clothes and fat and muscle to gnaw at the marrow of his bones, was a faint and futile distraction from his task.

Veronica knew. She was testing him. To be with her in his weakness, he had to be strong. To capitulate to her satisfaction, he had to have discipline. She was waiting for him to break under the exposure to the elements and the insanity of her demands. But she also gave him strength by parading through her apartment, flaunting her body in a series of provocative shifts and robes and gowns, letting him imagine how much pain that body might inflict on him, and dream about what might come after the pain: the taste her thighs and breasts, the feel her hair brushing across his skin, the smell of her neck, and the deep, throaty moan of pleasure his tongue might inspire.

It was by this secret encouragement that he knew she wanted him. The men and women who entered the apartment to fuck her while he watched didn't matter. The sounds they made over the open line, the things Veronica cried out in her passion, the promises she whispered to strangers and to those who knew her, were all empty. He had watched her face. None came as close to reaching Veronica as he did by simply suffering.

"Keep your hands away, you fuck," she said, not bothering to look out the window as she stretched and shook her head to loosen her hair from the confines of the towel she unwound from around her head. Water from her shower still glistened in the hollow between her breasts.

He never touched himself, never cheated. He lived with the ache for her, cherished the memory of her presence even as she seemed to push him further away. It was all a test. They both knew he was worthy. All he had to do was demonstrate his devotion.

He didn't even bother denying her implicit accusation.

"Now tell me what to do," she said, leaning against the living room window, pressing her nipples against the pane.

"Go to the kitchen."

She did.

"Take the third knife from the left end, first row."

"Yes."

"Come to the window."

She did.

"Lay a line down on the inside of your left arm."

She did. Slowly.

"Not so deep. Only a line, not a cut."

The bleeding ebbed as she responded to his command.

"Cut across the top, and the bottom."

She made them with delicate precision.

"Now slice, left to right."

She did, raising a thin layer of skin from her arm. Her cutting hand was steady. Neither arm wavered. Fisher watched without flinching.

"Clean off the blood. Let me see what's underneath.

She did, with a paper towel.

"Keep slicing."

When a swatch of bloody meat lay open between flaps of loose skin, she said, "Ask me."

Without hesitation, though he knew the question signaled an ending rather than a beginning, he said, "How does it feel?"

"So hot," Veronica whispered. "Your eyes, they're burning me. The knife, it's hard and strong, like your cock burrowing between my legs. The edge, that's your touch, opening me up. I can hear you breathing. All night, I've heard you. I was listening all along. I always knew you were there. Like now. Watching. A part of me."

But she was lying. Taunting him with words he wanted to hear. Testing his belief in the illusion of his control, probing the extent of his taking voyeuristic pleasures.

The Love in Her Regard

Her lie was a rape. She was tearing through him in a brutal mind fuck to take pieces of his self whether or not he wanted to give them, taking her pleasures while not allowing him any.

Take me, he wanted to say. Take all of me. But he knew she did not want to hear anything he had to say, and kept silent. He focused instead on her face, searching for the expression of a love for him as she stared out the window into the nothing between them.

*

The image on the computer screen was poor, barely above security camera quality. The sounds coming through the speakers hissed and crackled like signals from a probe diving into the storms of Jupiter. Voices rode over the background noise, but they spoke no words. Grunting, panting, crying out, squealing, laughing, moaning, the sounds filled his studio apartment, insinuating themselves into the kitchen cupboards, echoing in the bathroom, snuggling among folds of the sheets twisted on the fold-out couch bed with its single indentation of a sleeping form.

Fisher stared at the image of Veronica from the electronic perch of the screen looking down on her, naked, probably sweating body over the stripped muscular body of a young man. She moved in a rhythm he envied, sometimes fast, other times slow, punctuated by frantic onslaughts on the man's flesh.

Fisher shuddered. The device in him vibrated, reverberating to the reciprocal motion of the device Veronica was wearing, part of it stuck into the man's lubricated ass like the conquering end of a flagpole, the other half a golden horn swallowed by her sex. Like her device, Fisher's was secured to his body by leather straps, and had wires trailing off to power outputs and computers. The feedback broadcast was one way, from her to him. A small window at the bottom of the screen offered him limited control over the dual device she shared with her latest lover: the speed of its vibration and the temperature of its metal. The control broadcast was one way, from him to her.

He felt what she did, as well as the repercussions of what he did to her, along with a trickle of electronic feedback from the shaft in the man underneath her. The circuit of her pleasure ran through Fisher, but he was further away from her, in body, spirit, feeling, than he had ever been. He was more distant from her than when he did not know her at all.

"Watch me," she said, looking up into the camera.

"I am."

"How would you do it? Faster? Slower? Tell me?"

185

Decadence 2

The other man whimpered as she changed her rhythm, thrust harder, deeper. The stranger's convulsions shuddered through the double-ended device Veronica pounded into him. Fisher calibrated the instrument, ashamed of his pathetic contribution to the act. Veronica's slick flesh consumed the other end of smooth metal instrument, which absorbed and transmitted her physical actions and reactions to the dildo shoved up Fisher's ass. He choked on the sob he wanted to release.

Instead, he told her what to do next. She did as he said. Tears stung his eyes, but would not fall.

What did he have to do to please her? To make her love him? To feel like he belonged to her?

Over the slapping of flesh and leather, the animal echoes, the hint of trickling blood on the screen image, he asked, "What do I have to do to earn your love?"

"What do you have to lose?" she answered.

*

She called him, but he refused to answer, to even listen to the messages she left. She sent him email, letters, left notes on his door and at his job. She left him panties and bras she had worn, redolent with her scent. He burned them, along with the pictures and videos and audio tapes she planted everywhere, even in his apartment. He sprayed deodorizer to mask the perfume she wore during her forays into his small studio, and had the locks changed. When the her seeding continued, he installed an alarm system.

"Are you worthy?" she'd scream at him from across the street, or a window, or a passing cab, or from behind and down the block he walked on. Whenever he turned to look, she was gone.

She never let him see her in the flesh. Never let him taste and feel and smell her true presence, in the moment. He starved for her, grew thin and emaciated in spirit from the lack of her. But he had been dying, anyway, he reasoned, pounding on walls that only grew thicker and taller the harder he tried to breach them. Maybe it was better to die from loneliness than from the frustration of not being strong enough to take what she had to give.

He tried to remember his life before he met her, to see if he should return to it. But everything outside of the existence they had shared was blank.

*

186

The Love in Her Regard

Fisher had forgotten how terrible life without her had been. He tried to fill the emptiness with family and friends, but they only accentuated what was missing, reminding him with their casual brutality of the reasons he had pursued Veronica in the first place. Work was a barren valley he dreaded crossing, knowing that what lay on the other side of each day was just as bad as what he'd left behind that morning, and finding nothing to keep him in the shelter of his job's tasks and duties.

She stopped coming after him. That was worse than her intrusions. He felt as if he had been cast in and out of hell without the chance of ever finding heaven. At least when she called him, he could believe he had finally provoked a reaction from her. He could hope he might have come to mean something to her. The last vestige of a relationship fell away when she forgot him.

He considered suicide, but the terror of eternal emptiness paralyzed him.

He called her. Left messages, emailed her, sent letters. She did not answer. He went to her apartment building, watched her come and go. What would she do if she knew he had dared to cross the boundary between them by his secret observation? What more could she do?

Nothing, he decided.

"I have to see you," he said, stepping in front of her as she rounded the corner to her block one day. She took him in with a glance. The stun gun was at his neck before he knew what she was doing. She left him on the sidewalk, gagging on his words, trembling from the fire racing through his body in circles, as if searching for an exit.

He broke into her apartment and waited for her to come home. He had never been in it, though he knew all its intimate details, from the telescope and the cameras, which he tore loose from their mounts scattered throughout the rooms. He took his clothes off, slashed them, stuffed them into a garbage bin, soaked with alcohol and ready to burn. But not yet. Afterwards. After their meeting, no matter what happened between them, there would be nothing left.

Naked, nestled in the intimacy of her home, he savored everything she was, she could have been, to him.

She wasn't shocked when she came home and saw him sitting, legs spread, cock stiff, on a chair. He stood, disappointed. Even this violation couldn't penetrate the armor of her indifference to him.

She attacked him with calculated efficiency, feinting with the bags she carried, then aiming a kick to his balls. He blocked her leg with the chair, and immediately regretted the move, thinking she was coming around and last giving him what he wanted. But she avoided meeting his gaze and hid behind a stoic, almost alien demeanor, as if possessed by a spirit repulsed by having the slightest connection to him.

She closed with him, attempting a throw, but he pushed her off balance and knocked her to the ground, punched her once, twice in the head. She rolled on the ground, stunned, vulnerable. He wanted to beat her, with the chair, with a club, with his fists. But that would make him someone he was not, could not be.

He had to act. Something still had to be done. He ripped her clothes off, spread her legs on the floor. Kneeled between her thighs. Kissed her belly, her nipples, smelled her. She tried to push him off, and he punched her again.

His erection wouldn't come. What he was doing was wrong. What he had done to Veronica did not belong to him. He was not responsible. Everything was out of sync, disconnected, shattered.

He screamed. Backed off. Stumbled to the kitchen. Found the knives. An idea gave him focus: make her skin herself in front of him, this time? He went back to the living room. She was gone. No. A flurry of movement out of the corner of his eye told him no, but too late. She was on him, silent, lips shut tight, eyes dead. As he turned and blocked, the knives in his hands caught in her body. She struggled like a prisoner snagged on barb wire, managing only to get the blades deeper into her body. He was startled by the realization that this was her intent.

She sagged in his arms. He let her down, gently. "No," he whispered, drawing out the blades. But the bleeding wouldn't stop. It came and it came over them both.

"Make me feel," she said, turning away, looking to the door.

Fisher collapsed. Her blood flowed to him, warmed his foot, his leg. His cock grew hard. The hospital—but no, it was too late. She had felt him, the worst of him. He couldn't see her breathing, anymore, and the blood flow had slowed, as if it had all drained out of her already. Dread opened inside him like a poisoned blossom, revealing what he had done: kill the thing he wanted.

He sobbed, quietly, in tiny heaves. Looking to the corner of the room where he had thrown the knives, he thought it was time to cut out the root of what was wrong with him. He got to his knees, smelled the alcohol, considered an alternative. Finding matches in the kitchen, he lit his clothes up. Fire took hold, setting off smoke alarms, melting the plastic trash can, catching on the sofa.

He lay down next to Veronica, waiting for the smoke to grow so thick he could die. He put an arm over her, buried his face in her hair.

The Love in Her Regard

He was still alive when the firemen arrived. They put the fire out quickly, but he fought off his rescuers, and four men had to grab him by the arms and legs to remove him. Still fighting though he could hardly breath, he caught a glimpse of Veronica's face as the firemen took him out. Her eyes were open as she stared through the doorway. Smoke obscured her expression for a moment, but the movement of men roiled the clouds and through a part, a smile was revealed.

Forcing words through his coughing, Fisher begged the firemen to let him stay so he could kiss her lips and follow her where she'd gone. She had invited him, he wanted to say. At last, the mask had fallen away, revealing the joy she'd felt in her final moment. He had reached her, satisfied her, and in that last moment she had given him the benediction of having pleased her, the reward of her loving regard.

But they took him away, so he shut his eyes, and kept them shut, so the memory of that love might never fade.

Printed in the United States
5827